T R O L L   F E L L

KATHERINE LANGRISH

TROLL FELL

HARPERCOLLINS*PUBLISHERS*

Library of Congress Cataloging-in-Publication Data
Langrish, Katherine.
Troll Fell / Katherine Langrish.—1st ed.
p. cm.
Summary: Forced to live with his evil identical-twin uncles after his
father's death, twelve-year-old Peer tries to find a way to stop their plan to
sell the neighbor's children to the trolls.
ISBN 0-06-058304-5 — ISBN 0-06-058305-3 (lib. bdg.)
[1. Orphans—Fiction. 2. Trolls—Fiction. 3. Uncles—Fiction. 4. Twins—
Fiction. 5. Vikings—Fiction.] I. Title.
PZ7.L2697Tr 2004
[Fic]—dc22
                                                        2003017480

Typography by Nicole de las Heras
1 2 3 4 5 6 7 8 9 10
❖
First Edition
First published in hardcover in Great Britain by Collins, an imprint of
HarperCollins*Publishers* Ltd, in 2004.

This book is for my mother and father

Among the many people I have to thank:
Alan Stoyel and Critchell Britten, for patiently and kindly
answering dozens of questions about watermills;
Susan Price, for the tail-wagging troll;
Lyndsay Stringfellow, for letting me talk trolls on innumerable walks;
Liz Kessler of Cornerstones, for warmth, enthusiasm,
spot-on criticism, and friendship;
Catherine Clarke, agent extraordinaire;
Zoë Clarke, Robin Stamm, and all at HarperCollins;
and Dave, Alice, and Isobel—first and best of readers

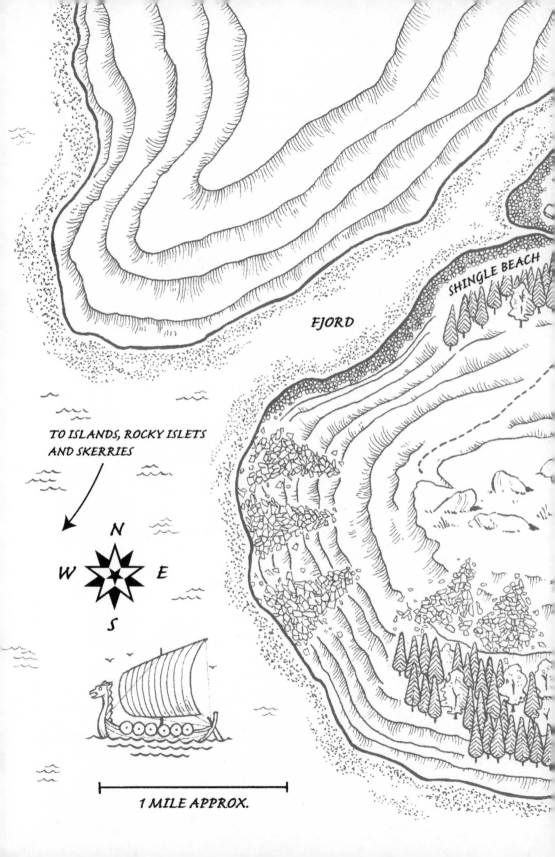

SHINGLE BEACH

FJORD

TO ISLANDS, ROCKY ISLETS
AND SKERRIES

N

W *E

S

1 MILE APPROX.

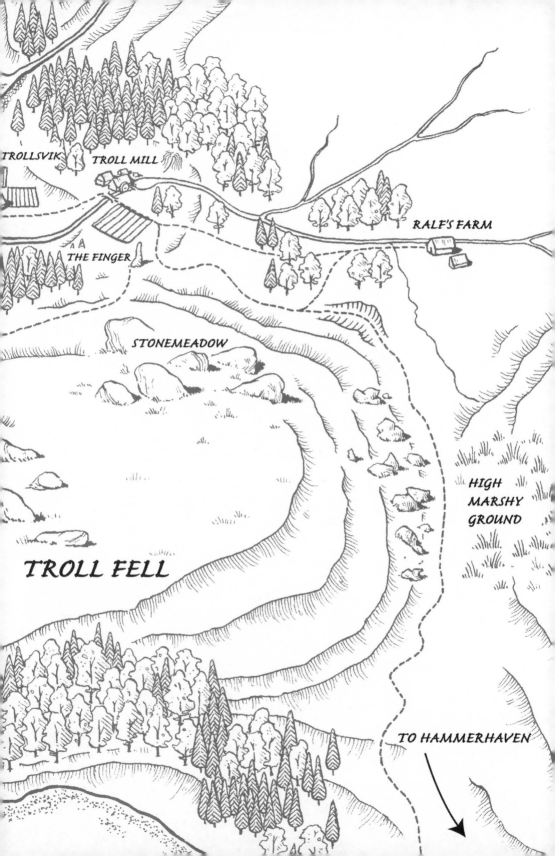

CHAPTER 1
The Coming of Uncle Baldur

Peer Ulfsson stood miserably at his father's funeral pyre, watching the sparks whirl up like millions of shining spirits streaking away into the dark.

Dizzily he followed their bright career, unwilling to lower his eyes. The fire gobbled everything like a starving monster, crackling and crunching on bone-dry branches, hissing and spitting on green timber, licking up dribbles of resin from bleeding chunks of pinewood.

The heat struck his face and scorched his clothes. Tears baked on his cheeks. But his back was freezing, and a raw wind fingered the nape of his neck.

Father! thought Peer desperately. *Where have you gone?*

Suddenly he was sure the whole thing must be a bad dream. If he turned round, his father would be standing close, ready to give him a comforting squeeze. *Behind me—just behind me!* thought Peer. He turned slowly, stiffly, wanting to see his father's thin, tanned face carved with deep lines of laughter and life. The black wind cut tears from his eyes. The sloping shingle beach ran steep and empty into the sea.

A small body bumped Peer's legs. He reached down. His dog, Loki, leaned against him, a rough-haired, flea-bitten brown mongrel—all the family Peer had left. Friends and neighbors crowded in a ring around the pyre, patiently watching and waiting. Their faces were curves of light and hollows of darkness: the flames lit up their steaming breath like dragon smoke; they blew on their fingers and turned up their collars against the piercing wind.

The pyre flung violent shadows up and down the beach. Stones bigger than a man's head blackened and cracked around it. Hidden in its white depths, his father's body lay folded in flames.

Over the fire the night air wobbled and shook, magnifying the shapes of the people opposite. It was like looking through a magic glass into a world of ghosts and monsters, perhaps the world to which his father's spirit was passing, beginning the long journey to the land of the dead. Peer gazed, awed, into the hot shimmer. *What if he comes to me? What if I see him?* Smoke unraveled in the air like half-finished gestures. Was that a pale face turning toward him? A dim arm waving? Peer's breath stuck. A shadow lurched into life, beyond the fire. *It can't be!* He glanced round in panic. *Can anyone else see it?* The shadow tramped forward, man-shaped, looming up behind the people, who hadn't noticed—who still hadn't noticed—

Peer gave a strangled shout. "What's that?"

A huge man lumbered into the circle of firelight, a sort of black haystack with thick, groping arms. His scowling face shone red in the firelight as he elbowed rudely through the crowd. People turned, scattering. A mutter of alarm ran around the gathering.

Shoving forward, the stranger tramped right up to the pyre and turned, his boots carelessly planted among the glowing ashes. Now he was a black giant against the flames. Everyone stared in uneasy silence. What did he want?

He spoke in a high, cracked voice, shrill as a whistle. "I've come for the boy. Which is Ulf's son?"

Nobody answered. A shiver ran across the crowd. The men closest to Peer shuffled quietly nearer, drawing close around him. Catching the movement, the giant turned slowly, watching them. He lifted his head like a wolf smelling out its prey. Peer forgot to breathe. Their eyes met, and he winced. Sharp as little black glittering drills, those eyes seemed to bore through to the back of his head.

The stranger gave a satisfied grunt and bore down on him like a landslide. Enormous fingers crunched on his arm, hauling him out of the crowd. High over his head the reedy voice piped tonelessly, "I'm your uncle Baldur Grimsson. From now on, you'll be living with me!"

"But I haven't got an uncle!" Peer gasped.

The huge stranger paid no attention. He dragged Peer's arm up, twisting it. Peer yelped in pain, and Loki began to growl.

"I don't like saying things twice!" the man menaced. "I'm your Uncle Baldur, the miller of Trollsvik. Come on!" He challenged the crowd. "You all know it's true. Tell him so, before I twist his arm off!"

"Why—" Brand the shipbuilder stepped forward uncertainly, rubbing his hands. Peer stared at him in disbelief. Brand spread his arms helplessly. "This—that is to say, Peer, your father did tell me once—"

His wife, Ingrid, pushed in front of him, glaring. "Let go of the boy, you brute! How dare you show your face here? We all know that poor Ulf never had anything to do with you!"

"*Is* this my uncle?" Peer whispered. He twisted his head and looked up at Uncle Baldur. It was like looking up at a dark cliff. First came a powerful chest, then a thick neck, gleaming like naked rock. There was a black beard like a rook's nest. Then a face of stony slabs with bristling black eyebrows for ledges. At the top came a tangled bush of black hair.

Loki's body tensed against Peer's legs, quivering with growls. In another moment he would bite. Uncle Baldur knew it too, and Peer read the death penalty in his face. "Loki!" he cried sharply, afraid. "Quiet!"

Loki subsided. Uncle Baldur let Peer go and bent his shaggy head to look at the dog.

"What d'you call *that*?" he taunted.

"He's my dog, Loki," said Peer defiantly, rubbing his bruised arm.

"*That,* a dog? Wait till *my* dog meets him. He'll eat 'im!" Uncle Baldur tipped back his head and yelped with laughter. Peer glared at him. Brand put a protective arm around his shoulder.

"You can't take the boy away," he began. "We're looking after him!"

"You? Who are you?" spat Uncle Baldur.

"He's the master shipbuilder of Hammerhaven, that's who he is!" declared Ingrid angrily, folding her arms. "Peer's poor father was his best carpenter!"

"Best of a bad lot, eh?" sneered Uncle Baldur. "Could he make a barrel that didn't leak?"

Brand glared at Baldur. "Ulf did a wonderful job on the new ship. Never made a mistake!"

"No? But he sliced himself with a chisel and died when it turned bad!" scoffed Uncle Baldur. "Some carpenter!"

Peer's heart rapped like a hammer, hurting his chest. He leaped forward. "Don't talk about my father like that! You want to know what he could do? *That's* what he could do! *That's* what he made! See!" He pointed defiantly past Uncle Baldur.

High over the heads of the crowd reared the fierce dragon neck and head of the new longship. People stepped back, opening a path to where it lay chocked upright on the shelving beach. And the dragon head glared straight at Uncle Baldur, ogling him threateningly, as if it commanded the sea behind it, whose dark armies of marching waves rushed snarling up the shingle.

Uncle Baldur rocked back, off balance. He lowered his head and clenched his fists. Then he shrugged. "A dragon ship! A pretty toy!" he jeered, turning his back on it. The crowd muttered angrily, but Uncle Baldur ignored them. He seized Peer's arm again. "You'll come now. I'm a busy man. I've a mill to run, and no time to waste!"

With a bang, a piece of wood exploded in the heart of the pyre. People dodged as the fire spat glowing fragments at their feet. The whole burning structure slipped and settled. Brand stepped in front of Uncle Baldur, barring his way.

"You won't drag the boy away from his father's funeral!" he exclaimed. "Why—it's not even over!"

"A funeral? And I thought it was a pig roast!" Uncle Baldur crowed with laughter. Sickened, Peer jerked his arm free, as the crowd surged angrily forward, some crying, "Shame!" They surrounded Uncle Baldur, who shifted uneasily, looking around. "Can't you take a joke?" he complained.

"Show some respect!" said Brand curtly.

Uncle Baldur grunted. Summing up the crowd with his sharp black eyes, he said at last, "Very well. I'll stay a day or two. There'll be stuff to sell off, I suppose?" Jerking his head toward Brand, he asked Peer shrilly, "Has he paid up your dad's last wages—eh?"

"Yes! Of course he has," Peer stammered angrily. "He's been very kind to me—he's arranged everything."

"Nothing owing?" Uncle Baldur scowled, disappointed. "I'll soon see. Your father may have been a halfwit; but nobody cheats *me*."

Behind him, the funeral pyre collapsed into a pile of glowing ash and sighed out a last stream of sparks, which sped away forever.

With the eagerness of a pig digging for truffles, Uncle Baldur set about selling off Peer's home. Stools, pots, blankets, Ulf's cherished mallets and bright chisels—Uncle Baldur squeezed the last penny out of every deal. At first the neighbors paid generously for Peer's goods. Then they realized where the money was going.

Brand dared to complain. Uncle Baldur stared at him coldly and jingled the silver and copper in his pocket. "It's mine," he said flatly. "Ulf owed me money."

"That's not true!" Peer flashed.

"Prove it!" jeered his uncle. "And what's that ring you've got? Silver, eh? Boys don't wear rings. Give it here!"

"No! It was my father's!" Peer backed away, hands behind his back. Uncle Baldur grabbed him, forcing his fingers open. He wrenched the ring off and tried pushing it over his own hairy knuckles, but it was too tight. He bit it. "Silver," he nodded, and stuffed it in his pocket.

Fat, comfortable Ingrid took Peer in and tried to mother

him. "Cheer up, my pet," she crooned, pushing a honey cake into his hand. Peer let his hand fall. The honey cake disappeared into the eager jaws of Loki, who was lurking under the table.

"Ingrid," Peer said in desperation, "how can that fat beast be my uncle?"

Ingrid's plump face cramped into worried folds. She sat down heavily and reached across the table to pat his hand. "It's a sad story, Peer. Your father never wanted to tell you. He was just a boy when his own father died, and his mother married the miller at Trollsvik, the other side of Troll Fell. Poor soul, she lived to regret it. The old miller was a cruel, hard man."

Peer flushed and his fists clenched. "He beat my father?"

"Well," said Ingrid cautiously, "what your father could not stand was to see his mother knocked about. So he ran away, you see, and never saw her again. And in the meantime she had two more boys, and this Baldur is one of them. They're your father's own half-brothers, but as far as I know, he never laid eyes on them."

She got up and bustled about, lifting her wooden bread bowl from the hearth and pouring a yeasty froth into the warm flour.

"Still, the old miller's dead now, and his wife, too. Perhaps things will all come right at last! Maybe it's meant to happen. If your uncles don't marry, the mill could come to you one day! I know your uncle Baldur is very rough spoken, and not a bit like your father, but blood is thicker than water. After all, he did come to find you! Surely he'll look after you, you poor, poor boy."

"I don't want to live with him!" Peer shivered. "Or at his mill. What will I do there, way up over Troll Fell? I won't have any friends."

"Perhaps you'll like it," said Ingrid hopefully. "Though Troll Fell itself is a bleak, unchancy place," she added, frowning. "I've heard many an odd tale— But there! Your uncles are the millers, so I'm sure you'll live in style. Millers are always well-to-do."

Peer was silent.

"Ingrid?" He cleared his throat. "Couldn't I—couldn't I stay here with you?"

"Oh, my dearie," cried Ingrid, "don't think we haven't thought about it. But we can't. He's your uncle, you see. He's got a right to you, and we haven't."

"No," said Peer bitterly. "Of course not. I understand."

Ingrid flushed deeply. She tried to put an arm round him, but Peer hunched his shoulder at her. "We only want the best for you," she pleaded. "And don't forget," she went on, thumping the dough, "he's not your only uncle. There's another brother up at the mill, isn't there? Don't you think your father would have wanted you to try?"

"Maybe. Yes," said Peer. He shut his eyes on a sudden glimpse of his father, turning over a piece of oak and saying as he often did, "You've got to make the best of the wood you're given, Peer. And that's true in life, too!" He could almost smell the sweet sawdust clinging to his father's clothes.

"I'm worried. About Loki," he muttered presently, twiddling a piece of dough between his fingers. He pulled little bits off, rolled them into balls, and flicked them away. "Uncle Baldur said his dog would eat him. I don't even know if I'm going to be allowed to keep him!" His voice shook.

"Now that's silly!" said Ingrid briskly. "Loki will make friends with your uncle's dog, you'll see! You'll be all right, won't you, boy?" she said to Loki, who thumped his tail.

An ox cart drove up outside. Loki sprang to his feet barking. The door thudded open and the room darkened as Uncle Baldur bent his head and shoulders to come through.

"Boy!" Uncle Baldur squealed. "Are those chickens in the yard yours? I thought so. I'm taking them. Catch them and put them in the cart. We're leaving. *Run!*"

Peer fled outside, Loki at his heels. A fine row blew up indoors as his uncle accused Ingrid of trying to steal the chickens. Peer began stalking a fat speckled hen, but she squawked in fright and ran. Peer chased her. Loki joined in. He dashed at the hens, barking excitedly. Feathers flew as the hens scattered, cackling wildly. "Bad dog! Stop it, Loki!" Peer cried, but Loki had lost his head and was hurtling around the yard with a mouthful of brown tailfeathers.

The house door slammed open, bouncing off the wall. Uncle Baldur burst through, bent down, heaved up the heavy doorstop and hurled it at Loki. There were two shrieks, one from Peer and the other from Loki, who lay down suddenly and licked his flank, whimpering.

"You could have killed him!" Peer yelled. His uncle turned on him.

"If he ever chases my chickens again, I *will*," he wheezed savagely. "Now catch them, and tie them up with this." He threw Peer a hank of twine. "Be quick!"

The exhausted hens crowded together in a frilly huddle. Peer captured them and tied their feet together. "Sorry!" he mumbled to them as he carried them in pairs to the ox cart. There they lay on the splintery boards, gargling faintly. As Peer finished, Uncle Baldur came up dragging a reluctant Loki along by a string around his neck.

"Fasten 'im to the tail of the cart," his uncle ordered. "He can run along behind." He grinned, sneering. "It's a long way. Think he'll make it?"

Loki limped pathetically. "Can't he ride?" Peer faltered. "Look, he's lame. . . ."

His voice died under Uncle Baldur's unwinking stare, and miserably he did as he was told. Then he clambered up into the cart himself. It was time to go.

Ingrid came out to see him off, wiping first her hands and then her eyes on her apron.

"You poor lamb!" she wailed. "Dragged off at a moment's notice! And Brand's down at the shipyard and can't even say good-bye. What he'll say when he hears, I don't dare to think! Come back soon, Peer, and see us!"

"I will if I can," he promised glumly. The cart tipped, creaking, as Uncle Baldur hauled himself up. He took a new piece of twine from his pocket and tied one end around the rail of the cart. Then he tied the other end, in a businesslike manner, around Peer's right wrist. Peer's mouth fell open. He tried to jerk away, and got his ears slapped.

"What*ever* are you doing?" shrieked Ingrid, bustling forward. "Untie the boy, you brute!"

Uncle Baldur looked around at her, mildly surprised. "Got to fasten up the livestock," he explained. "Chickens *or* boys— can't have 'em escaping, running around loose." Ingrid opened her mouth—and shut it. She looked at Peer. Peer looked back. *See?* he told her silently.

"Gee! Hoick!" screamed Uncle Baldur, climbing on to the driving seat and cracking his whip over the oxen. The cart lurched. Peer stared resolutely forward. He didn't wave good-bye to Ingrid.

Soon the town of Hammerhaven was out of sight. The steep, rough road twisted up into stony and boggy moorland, looping round white rocks and black pools of peat water. Low woods of birch and spruce grew on both sides of the road, and rough clumps of heather and bilberry. If the oxen tried to snatch a mouthful as they passed, Uncle Baldur's whip snapped out.

"Garn! Grr! Hoick, hoick!" The cart tilted like the deck of a ship as one wheel rose over a huge boulder, then dropped with a crash that nearly drove Peer's spine right through his skull. The oxen snorted, straining to drag not only the cart but big fat Uncle Baldur up the steep slope.

"Uncle," Peer hinted. "Shall I get out and walk?"

But his uncle ignored him. Peer muttered a bad word under his breath and sat down uncomfortably on a heap of sacks. His arm was stretched awkwardly up, still tied with twine to the rail of the cart. The pile of chickens slid about, flapping as the cart jolted. He counted them. They were all there: the little black one with the red comb, the three speckled sisters, the five big brown ones. They rolled red-rimmed eyes at him and squawked.

"It's not my fault," he told them sadly.

Over the end of the cart he could see Loki, trotting along with his head and tail low. Peer called. Loki glanced up briefly. He looked miserable, but the limp had gone—he'd been faking it, Peer decided.

They came around a bend in the road. Peer turned his head, then pulled himself up on to his knees and gazed.

In front, dwarfing Uncle Baldur's bulky shoulders, the land swooped upward. In heaves and hollows and scallops, crag above crag, upland beyond upland: in murky shouldering ridges, clotted with trees, tumbling with rockfalls, the flanks of Troll Fell rose before him. The narrow, rutted track scrambled breathlessly toward the skyline and vanished.

Tipping his head back, Peer stared upward at the summit,

where he thought he could discern a savage crown of rocks. But as he watched, the clouds came lower. The top of Troll Fell wrapped itself in mist.

The light was fading. Fine cold rain began to soak into Peer's clothes. He dragged out a sack and draped it over his shoulders. Uncle Baldur pulled up the hood of his thick cloak.

Great shadowy boulders loomed up out of the drizzle on both sides of the track. They seemed to stare at Peer as he huddled uneasily in the bottom of the cart. One looked like a giant's head with shallow scooped-out eyes and sneering mouth. One had a blind muzzle poking at the sky. Something bolted out from under it as the cart passed, kicking itself up the hillside with powerful leaps. Peer sat up, startled, as it swerved out of sight. What was that? Too big for a hare—and he thought he'd seen *elbows....*

From the hidden crest of Troll Fell rolled a sinister chuckle of thunder. A wind sprang up, hissing through the rocks. Mud sprayed from the great wooden cartwheels. Peer clutched the sodden sack under his chin and sat jolting and shivering.

At last he realized from the angle of the cart that they were over the saddle of the hill, beginning to descend toward Trollsvik. Leaning forward, he looked down into a great shadowy basin. A few faint lights freckled the dim valley. That must be the village. Frozen and soaked, he thought longingly of dry clothes, a fire, hot drinks, and food. He had hardly spoken to his uncle all the way, but now he called out as politely as he could, "Uncle? How far is the mill?"

Uncle Baldur jerked his head to the left and pointed. "Down there, among the trees yonder. A matter of half a mile. Beside the brook." He sounded quite civil for once, and Peer was encouraged. Perhaps his uncle could be normal after all.

To his surprise, Uncle Baldur spoke over his shoulder again. "Home!" he cried in his shrill toad's croak. "Lived there all me life, and me father before me, and *his* father before *him*! Millers all."

"That's nice," Peer agreed, between chattering teeth.

"Needs new machinery," complained his uncle. "And a new wheel, and the dam repaired," he added. "If I had the money—if I had my rights—"

Well, you've got my money now, thought Peer bitterly.

"A pity your father was dirt poor," his uncle went on. "I'm proud of that place. I'd do a lot for that place. I'm the miller. The miller is an important man. I *deserve* to be rich. I *will* be rich. Hark!"

He leaned back hard, forcing the oxen to stop. The track here plunged between steep banks, and the cart slewed, blocking the road. Loki yelped as the string yanked him off his feet. Peer cried out in distress, but Uncle Baldur twisted around, straining his thick neck and raising one hand.

"Quiet!" he muttered. "Hear that? Someone coming. Catching us up."

Peer stared uneasily into the night, listening. It was too dark to see properly. What had Uncle Baldur heard? Why would he stop on this wild, lonely road? He held his breath.

15

Was that a bird shrieking—that long, burbling cry drifting on the wind?

"Who is it? Who is it?" Uncle Baldur hissed eagerly. "Could be friends of mine, boy—I've got some funny friends. People you'd be surprised to meet!" He giggled, and Peer's skin crawled. The darkness, the whole wild hillside, suddenly anywhere seemed safer than staying with Uncle Baldur in this cart. He tugged the twine that held his wrist, testing it. It felt tight and strong. He couldn't jump out and run.

Stones clattered on the track close behind. Loki scuttled under the tail of the cart, and Peer heard him growling. He braced himself. What was coming?

There was a loud, disapproving snort. Out of the rain emerged the dim shape of a small, wet pony picking its way downhill, carrying a rider and a packsaddle. On seeing the cart, it flung up its head and shied. There was no room to pass. The rider shouted, "Hello there! Can you move that cart? I can't get through."

Uncle Baldur sat motionless for a second, taking deep breaths of fury. To Peer's amazement he then flung down the reins and surged to his feet, teetering on the cart's narrow step. His shock of black hair and tangled beard mingled with the thunderclouds: he looked like a mighty headless pillar.

"Ralf Eiriksson!" he screamed. "I know you, you cheating piece of stinking offal! How dare you creep around up here, you—you crawling worm!"

"Baldur Grimsson!" groaned the rider wearily. "Just my

luck! Shift your cart, you fat fool. I'm trying to get home."

"Liar!" Uncle Baldur swayed dangerously, shaking his fist. "Thief! You watch out. If the trolls don't get you, I will! You'll steal no more. That's finished! If the Gaffer—"

Troll Fell cracked out a blinding whip of lightning and a heart-stopping jolt of thunder. The rain began falling twice as hard. Beaten by the downpour, Uncle Baldur threw himself back onto his seat and grabbed for the reins. The oxen slowly plodded forward. Without another word, the rider trotted briskly past, and soon struck off along an even rougher track that led away to the right.

Gritting his teeth, Peer clung to the side of the cart as it crashed and slithered down the slope.

Well, that's it, he said to himself. *Uncle Baldur is mad. Completely crazy.*

Sick, cold, and miserable, he tried to picture his father, as if the memory could blot out Uncle Baldur. He thought of his father's bright, kind eyes, his thin shoulders hunched from bending over his chisel and plane. What would he say now, if only he knew?

I can guess, he told himself sternly. *He'd say, "Keep your heart up, Peer!" Like Ingrid said, I've got another uncle at the mill, and he can't be as bad as this. There can be only one Uncle Baldur. Maybe Uncle Grim will take after my side of the family. Maybe—just maybe—he might even be a little bit like Father!*

The cart rattled down one last slope and trundled over a shaky wooden bridge. Peer looked down apprehensively at the black glancing water hurtling underneath. "Gee!" howled Uncle Baldur, cracking his whip. The sound was lost in the roar of the stream. On the other side of the bridge, Peer saw the mill.

It crouched dismally on the bank, squinting into the stream, a long black building that looked as if it had been cold for ages and didn't know how to get warm again. Wild trees pressed around it, tossing despairing arms in the wind. Uncle Baldur drove the cart around the end of the building, into a pinched little yard on the other side. As the sky lit up again with lightning, Peer saw to his right the stained frontage of the mill, with dripping thatch hanging low over sly little black windows. To his left lurked a dark barn, with a gaping entrance like an open mouth. Ahead stretched a line of mean-looking sheds. The weary oxen splashed to a halt, and a wolflike baying broke out from some unseen dog. Uncle Baldur dropped the reins, stretching his arms till the joints cracked.

"Home!" he proclaimed, jumping down. He strode across to the door of the mill and kicked it open. Weak firelight leaked into the yard. "Grim!" he called triumphantly. "I'm back. And I've *got him*!" The door banged shut behind him. Peer sat out in the rain, shivering with hope and fear.

"Uncle Grim *will* be different," he muttered aloud desperately. "I know he will. There can't be another Uncle Baldur. Even his own brother couldn't—"

The latch lifted with a noisy click, and he heard a new, deep voice saying loudly, "Let's take a look at him, then!"

The mill door swung slowly open, shuddering. Peer held his breath. Out strode the burly shape of Uncle Baldur. At his heels trod someone else—someone unbelievably familiar. Flabbergasted, Peer squinted through the rain, telling himself it couldn't be true. But it was. There was nothing left to hope for. He shook his head in horrified despair.

CHAPTER 2

The Departure of Ralf

In a small, damp farmhouse higher up the valley, Hilde
scowled down at her knitting needles. Her head ached
from the strain of peering at the stitches in the firelight. She
dropped one, and muttered angrily as a ladder ran down the
rough gray sock she was making. It was impossible to con-
centrate. She felt too worried. And she knew her mother did
too, although she was calmly patching a pair of trousers.
Hilde took a deep breath.

"Ma? He's so late. Do you think he's all right?"

Before Gudrun could answer, the wind pounced on the
house like a wolf on a sheep, snarling and worrying it, as if
trying to tear it loose from the hillside. Eerie voices wailed
and chattered outside as the rain struck the closed wooden
shutters. It was a night for wolves, trolls, bears. Hilde imag-

ined her father out there, riding home over the shaggy black shoulder of Troll Fell, lashed by rain. Even if he was hurt or in trouble, she and her mother could only wait, anxiously listening, while her old grandfather dozed fitfully by the fire. But just then she heard a muffled shout, and the clop and clatter of the pony's feet trotting into the yard.

"At last!" said Gudrun, smiling in relief. As Hilde ran joyfully out into the wild, wet night, the wind snatched the heavy farmhouse door from her hands and slammed it violently behind her.

"I'm back!" said her father, throwing her the reins. "Rub him down well, but hurry! I've got news." Ralf's long blond hair was plastered to his head, and his boots and leggings were covered in mud.

"You're soaking! Go in and get dry," said Hilde, leading the steaming pony into the stable. Ralf followed her to unbuckle the packs. "How was the trip?"

"Fine! I got everything your mother wanted from the market. It's been a long day, though. And I overtook that madman Baldur Grimsson coming back over Troll Fell."

"What happened?" asked Hilde sharply.

"Nothing to worry about! He yelled a few insults, as usual. That's not my news! Hilde, you'll never guess—" Ralf stopped and gave her a strange look, excited and apprehensive.

"What? What is it?" Hilde stopped grooming the pony.

"There's a new ship in the harbor, Hilde!" His blue eyes flashed with excitement. "A new longship, ready to sail! And

I—well, no, I'd better tell your mother first. Now hurry, hurry up and you'll soon hear all about it!" He tugged her long hair and left her.

Hilde bit her lip thoughtfully. She rubbed the pony dry and threw down fresh straw, feeling uncomfortable and alarmed—trying not to think what he might be up to.

She wanted to be inside with the family. It was creepy out here with the wind howling. The small lantern cast huge shadows. She whistled to keep up her courage, but the whistle faded.

Kari, the little barn cat who kept down the rats and mice, came strolling along the edge of the manger. She ducked her head, purring loudly as Hilde tickled her. But she suddenly froze. Her ears flattened, her eyes glared, and she spat furiously. Hilde turned and saw with horror a thin black arm coming through the loophole in the door. It felt around for the latch. She screamed and hit it with the broom. Immediately, the hand vanished.

"Trolls!" Hilde hissed. "Not *again!*" Dropping the broom, she grabbed the pitchfork and waited breathlessly, but nothing more happened. After a moment she let out her breath, tiptoed to the door, and peered out. Falling rain glittered in the doorway. At her feet a black shadow shifted. Squatting there in the mud, all arms and legs, with its knees up past its large black ears, was a thing about the size of a large dog. It made her think of a spider, a fat, paunchy body slung between long legs. She saw damp, bald skin twitching in the rain.

Glowing yellow eyes blinked from a black pug face. For one fascinated second they stared at each other, troll and girl; then Hilde was splattered with mud as the troll sprang away in a couple of long liquid jumps.

Hilde flew across the yard and wrenched open the farmhouse door to tell everyone about it. She tumbled straight into a colossal row.

Her father and mother were shouting so loudly that Hilde put both hands over her ears. The door slammed again with a deafening bang. And so she forgot the troll, and didn't see it leap as suddenly as a frog onto the low eaves of their thick turf roof and go scrambling up to the ridge.

"I never heard such a ridiculous idea in my WHOLE LIFE!" Hilde's mother was yelling at Ralf. "You're a FARMER, not some sort of VIKING!"

"Why should it be ridiculous?" Ralf bellowed back. "That's what half those fellows ARE—farmers *and* Vikings!"

His wife made a spitting sound of contempt, and Ralf, scarlet in the face, leaned back against the wall in an effort to look careless and cool. It failed badly. He folded his arms and put on a defiant smile, and Gudrun went for him. Plaits flying, she grabbed him by the arms and shook him.

"It's not FUNNY!" she shouted up at his face.

"Mother—Father! Stop it," cried Hilde. "What's happening? Stop it—you'll wake up the little ones!"

In fact the twins were already awake—and bawling.

The house shivered as the wind managed an extra-strong

blast. All the birch trees growing up the sides of Troll Fell reeled and danced. The troll clinging to the roof whimpered, and one of its large black ears blew inside out like a dog's. It shook itself crossly and squirmed along the ridge to where a hole had been cut to let smoke escape. It peered over. Below was the fierce red eye of the fire. The troll got a lungful of heat and smoke and pulled back, coughing and chattering to itself: *"Hutututu!"* But the sound was lost in a rattle of icy rain. Grains of sleet fell hissing into the fire.

"Very well," said Gudrun, suddenly deadly quiet, letting Ralf go. "Let's hear what your *father* thinks about this! You, his only son, to go off and leave him? To go sailing off into storms and whirlpools and goodness knows what else, on a *longship*? How can you think of it? It will break his heart!"

"Why don't you let him speak for himself?" Ralf roared. "And why don't you give us both some supper? Starving us while you nag at me!"

Hilde glanced at her grandfather, Eirik, who was sitting in his favorite place near the fire, and saw his eye brighten at the suggestion of supper. Gudrun saw it, too. She fetched them both a jug of ale and a bowl of groute, warm barley porridge, served as Eirik liked it with a big lump of butter.

"Now, Eirik, tell Ralf what you think of this mad idea," she demanded, twisting her hands in her apron while Eirik carefully stirred in the butter. "Going off on a Viking ship? Imagine! You must forbid it. He'll listen to you."

But Eirik's eyes lit up. "Aha, if only I were a young fellow again! A brand-new ship that rides like a swan. Like a dragon! *Long Serpent*, they're calling her? Oh, to follow the whales' road, seeking adventure!" He tasted his groute and his eye fell on Hilde. " 'The whales' road'; d'you know what that means, my girl?"

"Yes, Grandfather," said Hilde kindly. "It's the sea."

Eirik was off. Leaning back in his chair, he broke into a chant from some long saga he was making about Harald the Seafarer, waving his spoon to the beat. Gudrun rolled her eyes crossly, but Hilde clapped softly in time to the rhythm. Ralf tiptoed over to the twins, little Sigurd and Sigrid. He sat down between them, an arm round each, and whispered. Suddenly they came jumping out of bed.

"Pa's going to be a Viking!" they shrieked.

"He's going to bring us presents!"

"An amber necklace!"

"A real dagger!"

Gudrun whirled round, her eyes flashing. "Ralf!" she cried. "Stop bribing those children!"

Eirik's poem reached its climax, all dead heroes and burning ships. He sat back happily. Ralf cheered. Gudrun glared at him.

"Oh, that's a *fine* way to end up, isn't it, floating face down in the water? And very likely, too. And who do you think is going to look after the farm while you're away?"

"Gudrun," Ralf argued. "It's only for the summer. Just a few weeks. I've sown the wheat and the oats already, and I'll be back before you know I've gone."

"And what about the sheep?" demanded Gudrun. "Somebody's stealing them; three lambs gone already. It's the trolls, or else those Grimsson brothers down at the mill. And that's another thing. I can't send our corn to the mill any longer, it comes back short—and dirty. Hilde and I do all the grinding. *I* don't have time to run the farm!"

Up on the roof the troll remembered the flavor of roast lamb. It licked its lips with a thin black tongue.

"Speaking of the millers," Ralf began, obviously hoping to change the subject, "did I tell you? I met Baldur Grimsson tonight as I came home!"

"Was there any trouble?" asked Gudrun quickly.

"No, no," Ralf soothed her. "The man's a fool. He sat in his cart in the pouring rain, shouting at me!"

"May he catch his death!" sniffed Gudrun.

"Why did he shout at you, Pa?" asked Sigrid, wide-eyed.

"Because he doesn't like me!" Ralf grinned.

"Why not?"

"It's all because of Pa's golden cup," said Hilde wisely. "Isn't it?"

"That's right, Hilde. He'd love to get his hands on that," said Ralf with relish. "My troll treasure, my lucky cup!"

"*Unlucky* cup, more like," sniffed Gudrun. But Sigurd and Sigrid jumped up and down, begging, "Tell us the story again, Pa!"

"All right!" began Ralf, scooping the twins up on to his

knees. "It was a wild night just like this, maybe ten years ago. Like tonight, I was riding home from the market at Hammerhaven. I was halfway over Troll Fell, tired and wet and weary, when I saw a bright light glowing from the top of the crag and heard snatches of music gusting on the wind."

"Curiosity killed the cat," Gudrun muttered.

"I turned the pony off the road and kicked him into a trot up the hillside. I was in one of our own fields, the high one called the Stonemeadow. At the top of the slope I could hardly believe my eyes. The whole rocky summit of the hill had been lifted up, like a great stone lid! It was resting on four stout red pillars. The space underneath was shining with golden light, and there were scores, maybe hundreds, of trolls, all shapes and sizes, skipping and dancing, and the noise they were making!—louder than a sheep fair, what with bleating and baaing, mewing and caterwauling, horns wailing, drums pounding, and squeaking of one-string fiddles!"

"How *could* they lift the whole top of Troll Fell, Pa?" asked Sigurd.

"As easily as you take off the top of your egg," joked Ralf. He sobered. "Who knows what powers they have, my son? I only tell you what I saw, saw with my own eyes. They were feasting in the great space under the hill: all sorts of food spread out on gold and silver dishes, and little troll serving-men jumping about between the dancers, balancing great loaded trays and never spilling a drop, clever as jugglers! It made me laugh out loud!

"But the pony shied. I'd been so busy staring, I hadn't noticed this troll girl creeping up on me till she popped up right by the pony's shoulder. She held out a beautiful golden cup filled to the brim with something steaming hot—spiced ale I thought, and I took it from her gratefully, cold and wet as I was!"

"Madness!" muttered Gudrun.

Ralf looked at the children. "Just before I gulped it down," he said slowly, "I noticed the look on her face. There was a gleam in her slanting eyes, a wicked sparkle! And her ears, her *hairy, pointed* ears—twitched forward. I saw she was *up to no good!*"

"Go on!" said the children breathlessly.

Ralf leaned forward. "So, I lifted the cup, pretending to sip. Then I jerked the whole drink out over my shoulder. It splashed out smoking, some onto the ground and some onto the pony's tail, where it singed off half his hair! There's an awful yell from the troll girl, and the next thing the pony and I are off down the hill, galloping for our lives. I've still got the golden cup in one hand—and half the trolls of Troll Fell are tearing after us!"

Soot showered into the fire. Alf, the old sheepdog, pricked his ears uneasily. Up on the roof the troll lay flat, with one large ear unfurled over the smoke hole. Its tail lashed about like a cat's, and it was growling. But none of the humans noticed. They were too wrapped up in the story. Ralf wiped his face, his hand trembling with remembered excitement, and laughed.

"I didn't dare go home," he continued. "The trolls would have torn your mother and Hilde to pieces!"

"What about us?" shouted Sigrid.

"You weren't born, brats," said Hilde cheerfully. "Go on, Pa!"

"I had one chance," said Ralf. "At the tall stone called the Finger, I turned off the road on to the big plowed field above the mill. The pony could go quicker over the soft ground, you see, but the trolls found it heavy going across the furrows, and I guess the clay clogged their feet. I got to the millstream ahead of them, jumped off, and dragged the pony through the water. There was no bridge then. I was safe! The trolls couldn't follow me over the brook."

"Were they angry?" asked Sigurd, shivering.

"Spitting like cats and hissing like kettles!" said Ralf. "They threw stones and clods at me, but it was nearly daybreak and off they scuttled up the hillside. The pony and I were spent. I staggered over to the mill and banged on the door. They were all asleep inside, and as I banged again and waited, I heard— no, I *felt*, through the soles of my feet, a sort of far-off grating shudder as the top of Troll Fell sank into its place again."

He stopped thoughtfully.

"And then?" prompted Hilde.

"The old miller, Grim, threw the door open swearing.

What was I doing there so early, and so on—and then he saw the golden cup. His eyes nearly came out on stalks. A minute later he couldn't do enough for me. He kicked his sons out of bed, made room for me by the fire, sent his wife running for ale and bread, and it was 'Toast your feet, Ralf, and tell us what happened!'"

"And you did!" said Gudrun grimly.

"Yes," sighed Ralf, "of course I did. I told them everything." He turned to Hilde. "Fetch down the cup, Hilde. Let's look at it again."

Up on the roof the troll got very excited. It skirmished round and round the smoke hole, like a dog trying to see down a burrow. It dug its nails deep into the sods and leaned over dangerously, trying to get an upside-down glimpse of the golden goblet, which Hilde lifted from the shelf and carried over to her father.

"Lovely!" Ralf whispered, tilting it. The bowl was wide. Two handles like serpents looped from the rim to the foot. The gold shone so richly in the firelight, it looked as if it could melt over his fingers like butter. Ralf stroked it gently, but Gudrun tightened her lips and looked away.

"Why don't we ever use it?" asked Sigrid admiringly.

"Use that?" cried Gudrun in horror. "Never! It's real bad luck, you mark my words. Many a time I've asked your father to take it back up the hill and leave it. But he's too stubborn."

"It's so pretty," said Sigrid. She stretched out to touch it, but Gudrun smacked her hand away.

"Gudrun!" Ralf grumbled. "Always worrying! Who'd believe my story without this cup? My prize, won fair and square! Bad luck goes to people with bad hearts. We have nothing to fear."

"Did the old miller like it?" asked Sigurd.

"Oh yes," said Ralf seriously. "'Troll treasure!' said old Grim. 'We could do with a bit of that, couldn't we, boys?' I began to feel uncomfortable. After all, nobody knew where I was. I got up to go—and there were the two boys in front of me, blocking the door, and old Grim behind me, picking up a log from the woodpile!"

Hilde whistled.

"There I was," said Ralf, "and there was Grim and his boys, big lads even then! I do believe there would have been murder done—if it hadn't been for Bjorn and Arnë Egilsson, who came to the door at that moment with some barley to grind. Yes, I might have been knocked on the head for that cup."

"And that's why the millers hate us?" asked Hilde. Beginning to feel sleepy, she stretched and yawned, glad that her parents were no longer quarreling. "Because you've got the cup and they haven't?"

"There's more to it than that," said Gudrun. "Old Grim was crazy to have that cup, or something just like it. He came round pestering your father to show him the exact spot on the fell where he saw all this. Wanted to dig his way into the hill."

"Old fool!" Ralf growled. "Dig his way into a nest of trolls?"

"We said no, and wished him good riddance," said

Gudrun. "But next day he was back. Wanted to buy the Stone-meadow from your father and dig it up!"

"I turned him down flat," said Ralf. "'If there's any treasure up there,' I told him, 'it belongs to the trolls and they'll be guarding it. I won't sell!'"

"Now that was sense!" said Gudrun. "But what happened? Next day, old Grim's telling everyone who'll listen that Ralf's cheated him—taken the money and kept the land!"

"A dirty lie!" said Ralf, reddening.

"But old Grim's dead now, isn't he?" asked Hilde.

"Oh yes," said Ralf, "he died last winter. But you know why, don't you? He hung about on that hill in all weathers, search-ing for the way in, and he got caught in a snowstorm. His two sons went searching for him."

"I've heard they found him lying under the crag, clawing at the rocks," added Gudrun. "Weeping that he'd found the gate and could hear the gatekeeper laughing at him from inside the hill! They carried him back to the mill, but he was too far gone. They blame your father for his death, of course."

"That's not fair!" said Hilde.

"It's not fair," said Gudrun, "but it's the way things are. Which makes it madness for your father to be thinking of taking off on a foolhardy voyage and leaving me to cope with it all."

Hilde groaned inwardly. Now the quarrel would begin all over again!

"Ralf," Gudrun begged. "You know these trips are a gamble.

Ten to one you'll make no profit!"

Ralf scratched his head uncomfortably. "It's not just for profit," he tried to explain. "I want—I want some adventure, Gudrun. All my life I've lived here, in this little valley. I want"—he took a deep breath—"new skies, new seas, new places!" He looked at her pleadingly. "Can't you see?"

"All I can see," Gudrun flashed, "is that you're throwing good money after bad, for the sake of a selfish pleasure trip!"

Ralf went scarlet. "If the money worries you, sell this!" he roared, seizing the golden cup and brandishing it at her. "It's gold, it will fetch a fine price, and I know you've always hated it! There's security for you! But I'm sailing on that longship!"

"You'll drown!" sobbed Gudrun. "And all the time I'm waiting and waiting for you, you'll be riding over Hel's bridge with the rest of the dead!"

There was an awful silence. The little ones stared with big, solemn eyes. Hilde bit her lip. Eirik coughed nervously and took a cautious spoonful of his cooling groute. Ralf put the cup quietly down and took Gudrun by the shoulders. He gave her a little shake and said gently, "You're a wonderful woman, Gudrun. I married a grand woman, sure enough. But I've got to take this chance of going a-Viking!"

A gust of wind buffeted the house. Draughts crept and moaned through cracks and crannies. Gudrun drew a deep, shaky breath.

"When do you go?" she asked unsteadily. Ralf looked down at the floor.

"Tomorrow morning," he admitted in a low voice. "I'm sorry, Gudrun. The ship sails tomorrow."

"*Tomorrow?*" Gudrun's lips whitened. She turned her face against Ralf's shoulder and shuddered. "Ralf, Ralf!" she murmured. "It's no weather for sailors!"

"This will be the last of the spring gales," Ralf consoled her.

Up on the roof the troll lost interest in the conversation. It sat riding the ridge, waving its arms in the wind, and calling loudly, "Hoooo! Hutututututu!"

"How the wind shrieks!" said Gudrun, and she took the poker and stirred up the fire. A stream of sparks shot up through the smoke hole. The startled troll threw itself into a backward somersault and rolled down off the roof, landing on its feet in the muddy yard. It prowled inquisitively around the buildings, leaving odd little eight-toed footprints in the mud. The farmhouse door had a horseshoe nailed over it. The troll tutted and muttered, and made a detour around it. Then it went on, prying into every corner of the farmyard, leaving smears of bad luck, like snail tracks, on everything it touched.

CHAPTER 3

Talking to the Nis

There can't be another Uncle Baldur! After the first stunned
moment, Peer began to laugh, tight, hiccuping laughter
that hurt his chest. Unable to stop, he bent over the rail of the
cart, gasping in agony.

Uncle Grim and Uncle Baldur were identical twins.

Side by side they strutted up to the cart. He looked wildly
from one to the other. Same barrel chests and muscular,
knotted arms, same thick necks, same mean little eyes peering from masses of black tangled beard and hair. One of them
was still wrapped up in a wet cloak, however, while the other
seemed to have been eating supper, for he was holding a knife
with a piece of meat skewered to the point.

"Shut up," said this one to Peer. "And get down." Only the
voice was different—deep and rough.

"Now let me guess!" said Peer with mad recklessness. "Who can you be? Oooh—tricky one! But wait, I've got it! You're my uncle Grim! Yes? You *are* alike, aren't you! Like peas in a pod. Do you ever get muddled up? I'm your—"

"Get down," growled Uncle Grim, in exactly the same way as before.

"—nephew, Peer!" Peer finished impudently. He held up his wrist, still firmly tethered to the side of the cart, and waggled his fingers.

Uncle Grim snapped the twine with a contemptuous jerk. Then he frowned, lifted his knife, and squinted at the point. He sucked the piece of meat off, licked the blade, and sliced through the string holding Loki. He stared hard at Peer.

"*Now* get down," he ordered, through his food. He turned to his brother as Peer jumped stiffly down. "He's not much, is he?"

"But he'll do," grunted Uncle Baldur. "He can start now. Here, you!" He thrust the lantern at Peer. "Take this! Put the oxen in the stalls. Put the hens in the barn. Feed them. Move!" He threw an arm over his brother's shoulders, and as the two of them slouched away toward the mill, Peer heard Baldur saying, "What's in the pot? Stew? I'll have some of that!"

The door shut. Peer stood in the mud, the rain drumming on his head, the lantern shaking in his hand. All desire to laugh left him. Loki picked himself up out of the puddle and shook himself wearily. He whined. Peer drew a deep breath. "All right, Loki. Let's get on with it, boy!"

Struggling with the wet harness, he unhitched the oxen and led them into their stalls. He tried to rub them dry with wisps of straw. He unloaded the hens and set them loose on the barn floor, where an arrogant black cockerel and a couple of scrawny females came strutting to inspect them. He found some corn and scattered it. By now the stiffness had worn off, but he was damp, cold, and exhausted. The hens found places to roost, clucking suspiciously. Loki curled up in the straw and fell fast asleep. Peer decided to leave him there. He hadn't forgotten what Uncle Baldur had said about his dog eating Loki, and he certainly had heard a big dog barking inside the mill. He took up the lantern and set off across the yard, picking his way through the mud. The storm was passing, and tatters of cloud blew wildly overhead. It had stopped raining.

The mill looked black and forbidding. Not a glimmer of light escaped from the tightly closed shutters. Peer hoped he hadn't been locked out. His stomach growled. There was stew inside, waiting for him! But he stopped at the door, afraid to go in. Did they expect him to knock? Voices mumbled inside. Were they talking about him?

He put his head to the door and listened.

"Not worth much!" Baldur was saying.

There was a sort of thump and clink. "Count it anyway," said Grim's deep voice, and Peer realized that Uncle Baldur had thrown a bag of money down. Next came a muffled, rhythmical chanting. His uncles were counting the money together. They kept stopping and cursing and getting it wrong.

"Thirty, thirty-one," Baldur finished at last. "Lock it up!" His voice grew fainter as he moved farther from the door. "We don't want the boy getting his hands on it."

Peer clenched his fists. "That's my money, you thieves!" he whispered furiously. A lid creaked open and crashed shut. They had hidden his money in some chest, and if he walked in now, he might see where it was.

"About the lad," came Baldur's voice. Peer stopped. He glued his ear to the wet wood. Unfortunately Baldur seemed to be walking about, for he could hear feet clumping to and fro, and the words came in snatches.

"—time to take him to the Gaffer?" Peer heard, and something like, "—no point in taking him too soon."

The Gaffer? He said that before, up on the hill, thought Peer with an uneasy shiver. *What does it mean?* He strained his ears again. Rumble, whistle, rumble, went the two voices. He thought he heard something about "trolls," followed quite clearly by "Plenty of time before the wedding." A succession of thuds sounded like both of his uncles taking their boots off and kicking them across the room. Finally he heard one of them, Grim it must be, say loudly, "At least we'll get some work out of him first."

That seemed to conclude the discussion. Peer straightened up and scratched his head. A chilly wind blew around his ears and a fresh rain shower rattled out of the sky. Inside the mill one of the brothers was saying, "Hasn't that pesky lad finished *yet*?" Hastily Peer knocked and lifted the latch.

With a bloodcurdling bellow, the most enormous dog Peer had ever seen launched itself from its place by the fireside directly at his throat. Huge rows of yellow, dripping teeth were closing in his face when Uncle Grim put out a casual arm and yanked the monster backward off its feet, roaring, "Down, Grendel!"

The huge dog cringed. "Come in and shut the door," Grim growled roughly to Peer. "Don't stand there like a fool. Let him smell you. Then he'll know you."

Nervously Peer held out his hand, expecting the animal to take it off at the wrist. Grendel stood taller than a wolf. His coat was brindled, brown and black, and a thick ruff of coarse fur grew over his shoulders and down his spine. Hackles up, he lowered his massive head and smelled Peer's hand as if it were garbage, rumbling distrustfully. Uncle Grim gave Grendel an affectionate slap and rubbed him round the jaws. "Who's a good doggie? Who's a good boy, then?" he cooed. Peer wiped a slobbery hand on his trousers. He thought that Grendel looked a real killer—just the sort of dog the Grimsson brothers *would* have.

"This dog's a killer," boasted Uncle Grim, as if he could read Peer's mind. "Best dog in the valley. Wins every fight. Not a scratch on him. That's what I call a proper dog!"

Thank goodness I didn't bring Loki in! Peer shuddered. Uncle Grim fussed over Grendel, tugging his ears and calling him a good fellow. Grateful to be ignored, Peer looked around at his new home.

A sullen fire smoldered in the middle of the room. Uncle Baldur sat beside it on a stool, guzzling stew from a bowl in his lap and toasting his bare feet. His wet socks steamed on the black hearthstones. He twiddled his vast, hairy toes over the embers. His long, curved toenails looked like dirty claws.

The narrow, smoke-stained room was a jumble of rickety furniture, bins, barrels, and old tools. A table, crumbling with wood worm, leaned against the wall on tottering legs. Two bunk beds trailed tangles of untidy blankets onto the floor.

At the far end of the room a short ladder led up to a kind of loft with a raised platform for the millstones. Though it was very dark up there, Peer could make out various looming shapes of mill machinery: hoists and hoppers, chains and hooks. A huge pair of iron scales hung from the roof. Swags of rope looped from beam to beam.

Uncle Baldur belched loudly and put his dish on the floor for Grendel. Suddenly the room spun around Peer. Sick and dizzy, he put his hand against the wall for support and snatched it quickly away, his palm covered in gray dust and sticky black cobwebs. Cobwebs clung everywhere to the walls, loaded with old flour. Underfoot, the dirt floor felt spongy and damp from a thick deposit of ancient bran. A sweetish smell of rotten grain and moldy flour blended with the stink of Uncle Baldur's cheesy socks. There was also a lingering odor of stew.

Peer swallowed queasily. He said faintly, "I did what you said, Uncle Baldur. I fed the animals and put them away. Is there—is there any stew?"

"Over there," his uncle grunted, jerking his head toward a black iron pot sitting in the embers. Peer took a look. It was nearly empty.

"But it's all gone," he said in dismay.

"*All gone?*" Uncle Baldur's face blackened. "*All gone?* This boy's been spoiled, Grim. I can see that. The boy's been spoiled!"

"There's plenty there," growled Grim. "Wipe out the pot with bread and be thankful. Waste not, want not."

Silently Peer knelt down. He found a dry heel of bread and scraped it around inside the pot. There was no meat left, barely a spoonful of gravy and a few fragments of onion, but the warm iron pot was comforting to hold, and he chewed the bread hungrily, saving a crust for Loki. When he had finished, he looked up and found Uncle Baldur staring at him broodingly. His uncle's dark little eyes glittered meanly, and he buried his thick fingers in his beard and scratched, rasping slowly up and down.

Peer stared back warily. His uncle convulsed. He doubled up, choking, and slapped his knees violently. He jerked to and fro, snorting for breath. "Ha, ha, ha!" he gasped. His face turned purple. "Hee, hee! Oh, dear. Oh, dear me!" He pointed at Peer. "Look at him, Grim! Look at him! Some might call him a bad bargain, but to me—to me, he's worth his weight in gold!"

The two brothers howled with laughter. "That's funny!" Grim roared, punching his brother's shoulder. "Worth his weight in—oh, very good!"

Peer looked at them. Whatever the joke was, it was clearly not a nice one. But what was the good of protesting? It would only make them laugh louder. He gave a deliberate yawn. "I'm tired, Uncle Baldur. Where do I sleep?"

"Eh?" Uncle Baldur turned to him, tears of laughter glistening on his hairy face. He wiped them away and snorted. "The pipsqueak's *tired*, Grim. He wants to *sleep*. Where shall we put him?"

"On the floor with the dog?" Peer suggested sarcastically. The two wide bunks belonged to his uncles, so he fully expected to be told something of the kind. But Uncle Grim lumbered to his feet.

"Under the millstones," he grunted. He tramped down the room toward the loft ladder, but instead of climbing it, he burrowed into a corner, kicked aside a couple of dusty baskets and a broken crate, and revealed a small wooden door not more than three feet high. Peer followed him warily. Uncle Grim opened the little door. It was not a cupboard. Behind it was blackness, a strong damp smell, and a sound of trickling water.

Before he could protest, Uncle Grim grabbed Peer by the arm, forced him to his knees, and shoved him through into the dark space beyond. Peer pitched forward on to his face. With a flump, a pile of moldy sacks landed on his legs. "You can sleep on those!" his uncle shouted. Peer jerked and kicked to free his legs. He stopped breathing. His throat closed up. He scrambled to his feet and hit his head a stunning blow.

Stars spangled the darkness. He felt above him madly. His hands fumbled along a huge rounded beam of wood and found the cold blunt teeth of an enormous cogwheel. He turned in desperation. A thin line of light indicated the closed door. His chest heaved. Air gushed into his lungs.

"*Uncle Baldur!*" Peer screamed. He threw himself at the door, hammering on it. "Let me *out*! Let me *out*!"

He pounded the door, shrieking, and the rotten catch gave way. The door swung wide, a magical glimpse of firelight and safety. Sobbing in relief, Peer crawled out and leaped to his feet. Uncle Baldur advanced upon him.

"No!" Peer cried. He ducked under Uncle Baldur's arm and backed up the room, shaking. "Uncle Baldur, no, don't make me sleep in there. Please! I'll sleep in the barn with Loki, I'd rather, really!"

"You'll sleep where I tell you to sleep!" Uncle Baldur reached out for him.

"I'll shout and yell all night!" Peer glared at him wildly. "You won't sleep a wink!"

Uncle Baldur stopped. He frowned at Peer. "What's wrong with you?" he sneered. "Bedding down near all that fine machinery—I'd have loved it when I was a lad!"

"On nice soft sacks!" Grim offered.

"It's too small—I can't breathe. Cramped—dark!" panted Peer, shamefaced, his heart still pounding.

His uncles stared at him, their mouths slack in disbelief. Slowly Baldur began to grin. "Cramped! Dark!" he mimicked.

His grin developed into a chuckle. "D'you hear that, Grim? He's afraid of the dark! The boy's *afraid of the dark*!"

For the second time that night, the two brothers roared with laughter, while Peer glowered at the floor. They pounded one another on the back, they coughed and choked and staggered about. At last Uncle Baldur recovered. The old, bad-tempered scowl settled back on his face.

"So go and sleep in the barn!" he snarled at Peer, who nodded speechlessly, his cheeks flaming.

"It's late, you know!" yawned Grim.

"Bedtime," nodded his brother. They sat down heavily on their bunks, wrestled with the blankets, wrapped themselves up, and turned over.

Peer tiptoed past. On his way to the door he had to step over Grendel, who opened one glinting red eye and wrinkled his lips in a silent snarl. Quickly and quietly Peer got through the door and crossed the yard.

The barn was dark, but it felt high and sweet and airy. Peer pulled crackling straw up over his knees and woke Loki, who gobbled the crust Peer had saved for him.

"There's no more," said Peer. He pushed aside Loki's hopeful nose and lay down, exhausted.

It was not completely dark in the barn. Outside, the sky had cleared and the moon had risen. A few bright stripes of moonlight lay across the floor and wooden stalls. Peer lay on his back, too tired to sleep, his mind working restlessly.

There's something funny going on.

What does Uncle Baldur want me for?

He tossed and turned, pulling more straw over him. Gradually he fell into uneasy dreams. Beside him Loki slept, whimpering and twitching.

A strange sound crept into Peer's sleep. He dreamed of a hoarse little voice, panting and muttering to itself, "Up we go. Here we are!" There was a scrabbling like rats in the rafters, and a smell of porridge. Peer rolled over.

"Up we go," muttered the hoarse little voice again, and then more loudly, "Move over, you great fat hen. Budge, I say!" This was followed by a squawk. One of the hens fell off the rafter and minced indignantly away to find another perch. Peer screwed up his eyes and tried to focus. He could see nothing but black shapes and shadows.

"Aaah!" A long sigh from overhead set his hair on end. The smell of porridge was quite strong. There came a sound of lapping or slurping. This went on for a few minutes. Peer listened, fascinated.

"No butter!" the little voice said discontentedly. "No butter in me groute!" It mumbled to itself in disappointment. "The cheapskates, the skinflints, the hard-hearted misers! But wait! Maybe the butter's at the bottom. Let's find out." The slurping began again. Next came a sucking sound, as if the person—or whatever it was—had scraped the bowl with its fingers and was licking them off. There was a silence.

"No butter," sulked the voice in deep displeasure. A wooden bowl dropped out of the rafters straight onto Peer's head.

"Ow!" said Peer.

There was a gasp and a scuffle. The next time the voice spoke it was from a corner on the other side of the barn.

"Who's there?" it quavered.

"I'm Peer Ulfsson," said Peer. "Who are you?"

"Nobody," said the voice quickly. "Nobody at all."

Loki had woken up when the bowl fell, but Peer stroked him gently to reassure him. He didn't want any barking.

"I think you're a Nis," he said to the voice. A Nis was a sort of house spirit. Peer had heard about them but never expected to meet one. "Are you a Nis?" he persisted.

There was a bit of a silence. "What if I am?" the voice asked huffily.

Peer wanted to be friends with *someone* in this place, and now he thought he knew a way. "Didn't they give you any butter?" he asked sympathetically.

This set the creature off. "Plain groute," it exclaimed bitterly. "Nary a bit of butter for poor Nithing, but plain barley porridge! Me that does half the work around here, me that sweeps and dusts and cleans, me that polishes away cobwebs!" Remembering the dust and dirt he had seen earlier, Peer doubted that it did any of these things well, but he did not say so. Probably the Nis would work better if it was fed well.

"And they has mountains of butter," the Nis went on, working itself up, "in the dairy. In a wooden barrel," it added darkly, "to keep off cats and mice and the likes of me. Plain groute they gives me, in a bowl by the fire, and I sees it and I fetches it away, and I tastes it—and no butter."

"I know how you feel," said Peer. "They didn't give me any stew, either."

The idea that somebody else might be hard done by seemed to take the Nis by surprise. Peer still could not see it, but he heard it jumping lightly closer among the rafters. "Close your eyes and hold out your hand," it chanted in its scratchy little voice. Peer did so. Something warm and smooth was slipped into his palm.

"Have an egg," said the voice with a squeak of laughter. Peer closed his fingers over the egg. He did not really want to eat it raw and saw no way of cooking it. He decided to give it to Loki for his breakfast. He thanked the Nis. It skipped about above.

"No butter." It was still brooding over its wrongs. "I has a cousin, Peer Ulfsson—I has lots of cousins—but I has a cousin over in Jutland who wrung the neckses of the very best beasts in the stable because they forgot his butter. I could do that."

Peer thought the Nis was probably boasting, but to please it, he begged it not to. "After all, it's not the *animals'* fault," he pointed out. "It's the Grimssons'."

"Could you get me butter?"

"I shouldn't think so," said Peer gloomily. "If they caught me stealing butter, I should think they'd half kill me. I don't think I'm going to get much to eat here either. I'm sorry," he added.

"Hmm!" said the Nis. And it spoke no more that night. In the morning when Peer woke up, he wondered if it had been a dream.

Then he looked at the straw beside him. Loki looked eagerly as well, his brown ears pricked. He knew what an egg was. Peer broke it for him and he lapped it up noisily. "You sound like the Nis," said Peer, stretching stiff arms and brushing pieces of hay off his clothes. The oxen moved restlessly in their stalls, waiting to be fed. Peer opened the barn door and let out the hens to forage for themselves. He forked some hay down for the oxen. It was still very early morning and there was no sign of his uncles. Peer didn't fancy waking them up.

"Let's go and explore, Loki!" he said to the dog. "Come on!" He pushed open the barn door, and Loki bounded cheerfully out.

CHAPTER 4

Meeting Hilde

Although the sky was fresh and clear, the yard still lay in chilly shadow. Peer splashed through the puddles, keeping a wary eye on the silent mill, its blind shutters and tattered thatch. The reed thatching had once been twisted into fancy horns at each end of the roof, now so damaged they looked like crooked ears. A dismal thread of smoke wavered from the smoke hole and trickled into the yard, as if it were too tired to rise. There was no sign of anyone awake.

Peer walked out of the yard and around the end of the building to the bridge. He leaned on the rail, looking upstream at the big wooden waterwheel. It towered higher than his head, a motionless monster, its dark teeth dripping. The central shaft, thick as a man's thigh, ran through an aperture into the side of the mill. Peer recognized it, wincing. No wonder his head felt bruised!

He stared up the narrow channel of the mill race and shivered. A cold breath came off the water, which flowed listlessly under the wheel in inky creases, since the sluice gate was shut. Beside the wheel, the overspill from the millpond plunged into white fury over a little weir and went boiling down under the bridge. Hesitant swirls of foam detached themselves and went venturing up the mill race on back eddies before losing heart and hurrying off downstream again. Peer watched the changing patterns until he felt dizzy. Then he crossed over and turned left up the bank to take a look at the millpond.

It was a gloomy place, even on this sunny morning. Twisted willows frowned into the water, as if they were studying their own reflections and disliked what they saw. Patches of green slime rotated slowly on the dark brown water, which seemed hardly to move except at the very edge of the weir, where it developed glassy streaks and furrows and tumbled smoothly over into the ferment below. Peer sniffed. There was a damp, cold reek about the place.

He walked farther along the bank, till his way was blocked by a narrow, deep-cut channel, fed by an open sluice in the side of the millpond. The water sprayed in a glittering arc over a sill slotted between wooden posts, and dashed noisily away to join the tailrace below the bridge. Peer threw a leaf onto the surface of the pond and watched it move imperceptibly toward the open sluice before suddenly flashing over and down.

He turned back. Loki had run off, nosing into the reeds with his tail high. He dashed back and jumped at Peer with muddy paws.

"Get down!" Peer pushed him off. "Phew! That mud stinks!" It was fine, thick, black mud, the sort that dries to a hard gray shell. Peer grabbed Loki and tried to wipe his paws with a handful of grass, and Loki tried to help by lavishly licking both his own paws and Peer's fingers. In the middle of this mess Peer heard a pony coming down the road toward the mill, and looked up.

A girl of about his own age was riding it, brightly clothed in a blue woolen dress with red stitching. On her head she wore a jaunty red-and-yellow cap, and her hair was done in two long plaits tied with pieces of red-and-blue wool. She sat sideways on the shaggy little pony, with a basket on her knee. Her eyes widened when she saw Peer, and she pulled the pony to a stop.

"Hello!" she called. "Who are you?"

She looked clean and colorful. Peer looked down at himself. His old clothes were drab and torn, and his hands were smeared with mud.

"My name's Peer Ulfsson," he mumbled.

"*Ulf's* son?" said the girl. "Now wait, I know everyone, don't tell me. I'll get it. Yes! There was an Ulf who was old Grim's stepson. Is that him?"

Peer nodded. "But he died last week," he told her.

"Oh, I'm sorry! I'm so sorry, Peer. Is that why you're here? Have you—?"

"I've come to live with my uncles," Peer agreed.

"That's terrible for you!" the girl cried. "Whoops!" She clapped a hand over her mouth, but her eyes gleamed. "Perhaps you like them?"

"No, not much," said Peer cautiously. "What's your name?"

"Hilde, Ralf's daughter. Welcome to the valley!" said Hilde with a flourish. "Come and visit us if you like. Ours is the highest farm in the valley, we own most of the north side of Troll Fell. You won't meet my father, Ralf, though, because he went away this morning. My mother's really upset. He's gone off to Hammerhaven to join some wretched new longship they've been building, and he's going to be away all summer. What's the matter?"

"Nothing!" Peer growled. "It's the ship my father helped to build, that's all!"

"Oh!" Hilde went red. She said awkwardly, "Then you and I ought to be friends. Pa says the ship is wonderful—he's so proud to be sailing on her. Hey!" She pointed at Loki. "Look at your dog!"

They both laughed in relief. Loki and the pony had stretched out their necks as far as they could and were sniffing each other, nose to nose. The pony snorted loudly and Loki nearly fell over backward in fright.

"Don't let him go near that millpond," Hilde warned.

"Why not? He can swim."

"I know, but Granny Green-teeth lives in there. That's why there aren't any ducks or moorhens. She pulls them under and eats them. So people say."

"Really?" asked Peer with a shiver. He turned and looked at the sullen brown water with its oily reflections. It was easy to believe that Hilde could be right.

"What's she like?" he inquired.

"She has green teeth, of course," said Hilde. "Pointed. Some people say she has webbed feet. Green weedy hair. I don't know, I've never seen her, but a man in the village met an enormous eel one night, sliding along in the grass—and that was her too!"

"How did he know?" asked Peer reasonably.

"He just did! And that's not all," said Hilde darkly. "There are all sorts of spooky stories about this mill. I don't envy you, living here. Still, you probably won't have very much to do."

"Why not?"

"Well, for one thing I'm afraid your uncles are so unpopular that a lot of us went back to hand grinding at home." She pulled a face. "Mother makes me do it. I hate it. You see, the Grimssons are lazy. They think they're *so* important just because they're the millers, and yet the mill only runs once in a while. They're always cheating people and not giving fair measure. Our flour used to come back full of chaff and dirt, which they put in on purpose. We even found a dead mouse once."

"Why would they do that?" asked Peer in irritated disbelief. He began to think he didn't like this girl. Couldn't she say anything good about the place?

"We have a feud with them," said Hilde cheerfully. "They claim they own one of our fields. They don't, of course." She grinned at him. "I suppose that means we have a feud with you, too, if you're family."

"A feud!" Peer exclaimed, ignoring the last bit. "And your father's called Ralf?"

"Ralf Eiriksson."

"I saw him last night! Didn't he come over Troll Fell in all that rain? So *that's* why my uncle was yelling. I thought I'd seen your pony before!"

"You were there? Pa never said. What happened exactly?"

"It was so dark and wet, he probably didn't see me," Peer told her. "I was getting soaked in the bottom of the cart. He came up behind us where the road is narrow. I don't know who my uncle thought was coming, but as soon as he heard your father's voice, he went crazy. He stood up and began shrieking and yelling—"

"Yelling what?"

"He called him a crawling worm," said Peer. "And a thief."

"*Did he!*" Hilde flashed. She clenched her knuckles on the reins and prepared to ride on.

"Hey, you asked!" said Peer. "It's not my fault. And if you

hate them so much, why are you here this morning?"

Hilde gave a scornful laugh. "I'm not coming to your precious mill! I'm riding past, on my way down to the village." She patted her basket. "I'm going to see Bjorn the fisherman, and trade some cheese and butter. Mother wants fish and my grandfather Eirik fancies a roast crab for his tea."

Cheese! Butter! Roasted crabs! Peer swallowed. He suddenly realized how terribly hungry he felt. His downcast look must have touched Hilde, for she said in a more friendly way, "Well, I hope you'll like living here. Your uncles will give you an easy time at first, won't they? I know! I can bring our corn to you now, instead of to your uncles. If you don't tell them who it's from, maybe they'll grind it properly for us. That would be a joke!"

"I don't really think I could," began Peer stiffly, feeling sure that her jokes could get him into a lot of trouble.

"Oh, forget it!" said Hilde impatiently. "Of course I didn't mean it." She gave him a look, plainly wondering how anyone could be so boring and serious, and Peer flushed. Hilde waved. "I'll be seeing you!" she cried.

She rode across the wooden bridge and on down the hill. Peer blew out his cheeks.

"Who cares what *she* thinks?" he muttered. "Eh, Loki?"

Despondently he called Loki to heel and trailed back into the yard. The mill door was open, and he saw one of his uncles standing disheveled in the morning sunshine, scratching under his arms and staring darkly after Hilde's back as her pony picked its neat-footed way down the road to the village. He summoned Peer with a jerk of the head.

"Were you talking to that lass?" he demanded.

"Yes, Uncle Grim," said Peer meekly.

He received a slap that made his head ring and his eyes water. "That's for chattering and wasting time," growled his uncle. "Your time is my time now, see? And time is money. What did she say?"

"If you don't want me to talk to her, why do you want to know?" asked Peer angrily, rubbing his ear.

Uncle Grim lifted his hand again.

"Oh, well, let me see." Peer pretended to think. "She asked me who I was. I told her my name. Then she told me her name is Hilde, and she welcomed me to the valley, which she seems to think she owns. Isn't this interesting?"

Uncle Grim didn't seem to notice sarcasm. "What else?" he asked.

Peer wasn't going to repeat what Hilde had said about the mill. He racked his brains for something else. "Oh, yes!" he remembered. "She said her father went away this morning. He's going off a-Viking for the summer, on the new longship."

Uncle Grim's black beard split open in a very nasty smile, showing all his brown-and-yellow teeth.

"Well, well, well! Is he indeed?" he rumbled. He bent low and put his face close to Peer's. In a hot gust of bad breath he whispered, "Do you know, sonny, you may be surprisingly useful?" Straightening, he bellowed, "Baldur? Guess what? Our little nevvie has some interesting news! Ralf Eiriksson has gone a-Viking. Leaving his family *all alone.*" He clapped Peer hard on the back and sent him staggering. "Come inside, my boy, and have some breakfast!"

With a sinking heart Peer realized that he had said the wrong thing. He followed his uncle into the mill, not noticing Loki trotting along behind him. It was so dark inside after the morning sunshine that he failed to see Grendel lying stretched out by the fire. But Grendel saw Loki. He surged to his feet like a hairy earthquake and strutted forward, growling and bristling.

Peer whirled in alarm. Loki stood there, his tail wagging slower and slower as he lost confidence. Grendel crept forward, throbbing with cruelty, his eyes riveted on the intruder, long trails of saliva drooling from his jaws.

"Grendel! Bad dog! Down!" cried Peer.

"He'll not listen to *you*," said Uncle Baldur scornfully from his seat at the table. Loki's tail disappeared under his stomach. He raised his own short hackles in pitiful defiance.

"Please—quickly!" begged Peer, trying to bundle Loki backward out of the door. "Tell him Loki's a friend. Please! Can't we introduce them, or something?"

In no hurry, Uncle Baldur finished his mouthful. "Down, Grendel!" he ordered. The huge dog flicked a glance at his master and hesitated.

"Get down, sir!" screamed Uncle Baldur, slapping his hand

on the table. Slowly Grendel sat. He shook his head, spattering Peer with froth and saliva, and at last lowered himself to the floor, still glaring at Loki with unforgiving menace.

Peer opened the door, and Loki vanished into the yard.

"Come here, laddie," said Uncle Baldur to Peer, cutting himself some more cheese. He gulped his ale, spilling it down his front. Peer approached reluctantly, till he was standing between his uncle's outstretched legs. Crumbs of bread and cheese speckled his uncle's beard. His stained shirt gaped open at the throat, exposing another tangle of black hair. A flea jumped out. Uncle Baldur pinched it between two thick fingers. When it popped, he wiped his fingers on his shirt and reached for more bread.

"See here," he said to Peer, nodding at Grendel. "That dog only obeys me and Grim. Right? He hates other dogs. He's a born fighter."

"Killed half a dozen," agreed Grim in a sort of proud growl.

"So if you want to keep *your* dog in one piece, you watch your step and start making yourself very, very useful." Uncle Baldur stared Peer straight in the eye. "Otherwise we might organize a little dogfight. Understand?"

Peer understood. He compressed his lips and nodded, as slightly as he dared.

"Right!" Baldur broke wind noisily and began to pick his teeth with a dirty fingernail. "Now what's all this about Ralf Eiriksson?" he asked, exploring a back molar.

"I don't know," said Peer sullenly. "No!" he added, catching his breath. "I mean, I talked to his daughter Hilde and she says he's walked to Hammerhaven this morning. He's going a-Viking for the summer. That's all I know, I didn't ask anymore. I didn't know you'd be interested," he added feebly, hating himself for crawling.

His uncles winked at each other. Uncle Baldur removed the finger from his mouth and rubbed his hands together, chuckling gleefully. He kicked Peer on the ankle.

"Where did the girl go?"

"Down to the village. She was going to buy fish."

"I want to see her on the way back," said Uncle Baldur. He jabbed Peer in the chest. "You look out for her, and make sure you bring her to me. Right?"

He turned to the table, not waiting for Peer to reply, and tossed him a stale end of bread. "Eat that and get on with the chores," he said abruptly. "Grim'll show you what to do. And remember—fetch me that girl!"

CHAPTER 5

Trouble at the Mill

Hilde's shoes sank into the wet sand, and she rubbed her arms, willing the sun to climb higher. It was chilly here. The shadow of Troll Fell leaned over the beach and out across the water. The pebbles glistened from last night's rain and from the retreating tide. Cold gray waves splashed on the shore.

"Half a dozen herring and a couple of crabs? Done!" agreed Bjorn cheerfully. He shouted to his brother, who sat in the boat sorting the catch. "Find us a couple of good big crabs, Arnë!" He turned back to Hilde. "Any news?"

"I should say so!" said Hilde gloomily. "My father's leaving—going off for the whole summer on a longship they've built at Hammerhaven."

Bjorn whistled. "Hey, Arnë," he yelled. "Come and listen to this!"

Arnë clambered out of the boat with a live crab in each hand, and Hilde discovered that explaining it all to two interested young men cheered her up—especially when Arnë fixed his dreamy blue eyes on her face.

"Lucky Ralf," he exclaimed. "I wish I'd heard about it. What's the ship like?"

"Lovely," Hilde assured him. "She's got a dragon head, all carved and painted."

"Yes," Bjorn laughed, "but how long is she? How many oars?"

Hilde didn't know. "Ask the boy at the mill," she suggested waspishly. "He ought to know—his father built her."

"What boy?"

"The millers' nephew. I just met him this morning. They've taken him in because his father died."

Bjorn's eyebrows rose. "The millers have taken in an orphan? What's he like?"

"He's all right," said Hilde without much enthusiasm. "He seems a bit nervous."

"I'd be nervous in his shoes," said Bjorn darkly. He elbowed his brother in the ribs. "Arnë! Dreamer! Hand over those crabs!"

With her basket full of herring and the two live crabs wrapped firmly in a cloth, Hilde rode whistling back up the steep path out of the village. The world brightened as the sun nudged up over the edge of the mountain. She thought about Pa. What a lovely morning to go to sea! How proud and happy he must feel!

Her high spirits lasted until she came in sight of the mill, crouching dismally under the trees. Even the spring sunshine could not gild its battered timbers and slimy black thatch. The brook rushed away from it, tumbling over itself in a white cascade as it tried to escape. Nobody happy had ever lived there.

Hilde gathered up her reins in case the millers' huge dog ran out to frighten the pony. She felt sorry for the boy, Peer, but she didn't want to stop. She trotted forward, hoping to get quickly past. As she reached the bridge, Peer dashed out of the mill yard, waving. She drew rein.

He ran up, looking pale and miserable. "I'm sorry, Hilde. My uncles want to talk to you. Will you come?"

Hilde turned the pony into the yard. Both the Grimsson brothers were there, lounging on the doorstep. They lowered their heads threateningly—like a couple of prize bulls, Hilde thought. Peer lurked guiltily to one side, darting anxious glances at his uncles.

"What d'you want?" Hilde demanded.

"A little *bird* told us," Baldur sneered in his high voice, "that Daddy's gone away. The great Ralf Eiriksson, who thinks he's so important. Is that right? Eh?"

"Only for the summer," said Hilde icily. "He'll be back before winter with a bunch of his Viking friends, so don't give me any trouble, Baldur Grimsson."

"Vikings!" said Baldur. He spat lavishly. "I don't give *that* for Vikings. And going to sea is a risky business. There's storms and rocks and lee shores."

Grim nodded in agreement. "And sea serpents," he grunted. Hilde snorted rudely.

"Wait and see," went on Baldur, scowling at his twin brother. "He won't *ever* be coming home again!"

"He's as good as dead!" said Grim. Together they flung their heads back and shook with forced laughter.

"Is that all you want to say?" snapped Hilde. The brothers stopped laughing.

"You carry a message for me, girl," snarled Baldur. "Tell your *mother*—and your *grandfather*—" he emphasized the words with a stab of his thick forefinger "—to keep off that land on Troll Fell that belongs to *us*. Keep right off it, yes? Unless you want a lot of trouble."

"Deep trouble," echoed Grim.

"But you could buy it," Baldur suggested cunningly. "We might consider selling it to you—at the price of a certain golden cup!"

Hilde went white. "You haven't a shadow of a claim to that land!" she exploded. "How dare you threaten us?"

Baldur came up close and grabbed the pony by the bridle. "Ask your mother which she'd prefer," he whispered. Spit sprayed from his mouth, and Hilde leaned away. "That golden cup, or a quiet life? The land is ours. You'll learn to respect that! Those sheep you have up there have been eating at our expense! That makes them our sheep! You and your family keep out of the Stonemeadow."

He jerked hard on the bridle and stepped back, and as the

pony flung up its head in fright, he whistled loudly. With a bloodcurdling bark Grendel came hurtling out of the mill. "See 'em off, lad!" shouted Grim.

Hilde grabbed the mane. The pony whirled out of the yard and bolted over the bridge and up the hill. She was falling! Desperately hanging on to her bouncing basket, she hauled wildly on the reins. The terrified pony danced to a snorting halt, and she slithered off sideways. Her legs wobbled. She patted the shuddering pony. "It's all right! Don't be silly!" she soothed. "The dog's not after you now!"

The pony rolled a wild eye and kicked. A little brown dog burst out of the bushes. Hilde shook back her hair and stood up straight. "Hello!" she challenged. There were wincing and crackling sounds as someone tackled the steep and brambly shortcut up the side of the hill. Peer's pale and dirty face became visible as he parted some branches. "Are you all right?" he puffed.

"Yes! No thanks to you," Hilde snapped. She glared at him. "Was it you, by any chance, who told those—those *oafs*—that my father has gone away?"

"Yes, it was," Peer admitted. "I didn't mean to do any harm. I didn't know it was important. I'm sorry, Hilde."

"Oh, don't worry," said Hilde, suddenly recovering her temper. "Stop apologizing. You haven't done anything. They'd have heard soon enough. Everybody knows everything in a little place like this." She checked her basket. A spiny claw came poking out. "I've still got Grandpa's crabs, thank goodness. Did you *hear* what those awful men said to me?" She looked up. "Why are you hiding in the bushes, Peer? Are you scared of the millers? Or are you scared of me?"

Peer flushed. He didn't answer. Hilde gave him a sharp look. "Well," she said, "Mother's going to be horrified when she hears about this. I expect there will be trouble. I'm sorry, Peer, but I absolutely detest your uncles!"

"So do I!" Peer blurted savagely. "I don't know why they want me. They've stolen all my father's money, and there's some strange plan going on that I don't understand. Something about trolls, and a wedding! And they've threatened to set their dog on Loki if I don't do everything they say. He'll be killed!"

"That's terrible!" cried Hilde. She snapped her fingers at Loki, who ran up and sniffed her hand. She stroked him. Loki immediately collapsed onto his back to let her rub his tummy. He lay with his paws folded up under his chin, back legs outstretched, eyes shut in bliss. Hilde tickled his chest.

"Trolls, and a wedding?" she repeated, frowning. "I can't imagine. Of course, old Grim, their father, was always poking about the Stonemeadow looking for the trolls' treasure."

"*Was* he? Why?"

"Hmm. It's a long story. Have you got time? And anyway, whose side are you on?"

"I want to be on your side," said Peer, troubled. "But they're my uncles and I've got to live with them. I've got nowhere else to go."

"*Baldur and Grim! The terrible twins!*" sang Hilde cheekily. "I think they should be called Bristle and Gristle, myself."

Peer gave a snort of laughter. "They have a pig called Bristles! A boar, in fact. And now I think about it, it does look just like them—covered in black hair."

"Fat," added Hilde.

"Yes, and greedy and bad tempered! I had to feed it this morning and it knocked the bucket out of my hand and trod on my foot."

"Do your uncles eat out of buckets?" giggled Hilde.

"They ought to!" said Peer, grinning. He felt much better. It seemed a long time since he had joked with a friend.

"They're exactly alike, aren't they? Can you tell them apart?"

"Not until they talk," said Peer. He thought for a moment. "And even though his voice is funny, Baldur talks more. Grim hardly says anything. If one of them's ranting and raving at me, it'll be Baldur!"

Hilde patted the ground beside her. "Sit down and I'll tell you about the trolls. It's a good story and it's true. You see, many years ago my father was riding over Troll Fell late one night, when he stumbled on a troll banquet. They had the top of the hill lifted up on red pillars. . . ." She told Peer what had happened, and how Ralf had raced to the mill for shelter and old Grim had seen the golden goblet.

"Mother swears it's unlucky," she went on, "and it certainly was for Grim. He spent the rest of his days wandering around Troll Fell, looking for the gate into the hill."

"What gate? I thought you said the whole place was up on pillars?"

"I think they only do that for special occasions. But there must *be* a gateway into the hill. We have trolls the way other people have rats and mice, and they're all getting out somewhere. And wherever it is, Grim seems to have found it, only it was winter, and he collapsed up there and died later."

"So my uncles probably know where it is," said Peer thoughtfully.

"Yes, but what good is that? The trolls aren't going to come out and just give them presents," said Hilde. She was still scratching Loki's tummy. "Goodness, Loki, how much more of this do you want?"

"Oh, he'll go on forever," said Peer, laughing.

"Well," said Hilde seriously, "I hope your uncles haven't been making friends with the trolls. That could be a real problem for all of us. You keep an eye on them, Peer!"

"I'll try," he promised. But a distant bellow came floating up from the mill, and he went rather pale and jumped up. "I'd better go."

"Yes, you'd better," said Hilde, sorry for him. "What a shame. Watch out for yourself, Peer. We *are* friends now, aren't we?" She stood up and offered her hand, which Peer took shyly. "See you soon!" she called, jumping on the pony and urging it into a brisk trot up the hill.

Peer raced toward the mill, Loki bounding ahead. He reached the yard to find his uncles talking to a carter, a surly-looking man who had just unloaded some sacks of barley for grinding. The two brothers stood leaning together with their arms across each other's shoulders, and as Peer arrived, panting, they both twisted their heads to look at him, grotesque as a two-headed giant from a story. *The terrible twins!* Peer grinned. The mill was ugly enough for a giant's stronghold, and Grendel made an excellent monster. The huge dog lay in a patch of sunshine by the mill door, gnawing a large bone. He raised his head and snarled at Loki, who pottered past and cocked a leg on the corner of the barn.

"Grind it small," shouted the carter over the noise of the wheels as he drove his cart out into the lane. "We want fine meal. I'll collect tomorrow." So—the mill did sometimes have customers!

"You're a lucky boy," croaked Uncle Baldur, turning to Peer, who eyed him suspiciously. "You're going to learn something most sniveling little orphan boys would give their eyeteeth for. What d'you say to that?" Peer stared at his feet stubbornly.

"You're going to learn about the mill, boy," went on Uncle Baldur. "Grim's a farmer, but me—*I'm* the miller." He rapped his chest proudly. "I hope you're thankful."

"Thankful!" Something flamed up in Peer's chest. "Thankful!" He drew a quivering breath. "You stole my father's money, you treat me like a slave, you can't even remember my *name*! What have I got to be thankful for? And you don't own that girl's fields. You just want to steal them, too, now her father's away!"

Baldur raised one casual fist the size of a ham and clouted Peer. Peer found himself sitting on the ground, clutching his ringing head. His flame of independence shriveled to a black twist and went out.

With a scuffle of light feet, Loki streaked across the yard, teeth bared, aiming for Uncle Baldur's leg. Grendel rose silently from the doorstep and hurled himself at Loki.

"Loki!" Peer screamed. Loki glanced back, saw Grendel out of the corner of his eye, and veered away in a cloud of dust. Peer got up shakily. Grendel dropped his hackles and slouched back to his bone.

"Come inside," said Uncle Baldur as if nothing had happened. "I'll show you what to do. You pay attention to me, because you'll be doing a lot of this."

"You're not going to take me to the Gaffer, then?" said Peer without thinking.

Uncle Baldur swung around, fast for such a big man. "What?" he said in a menacing whisper.

Peer backed away. He thought fast. "Something Uncle Grim told me," he invented quickly. "He said, um, if I wasn't a good boy and worked hard, you'd give me to the Gaffer." And come to think of it, it sounded exactly the sort of thing Uncle Grim *would* say.

Uncle Baldur clearly believed it. He muttered something under his breath about Grim being a chattering fool and then grabbed Peer, dragged him off his feet, and pushed his thick bearded lips up to Peer's ear.

"The Gaffer," he whispered, "is the King of Troll Fell, see? And he lives up there under the crags, not far away. And naughty little boys, why, he likes to tear them in pieces! So watch your step, laddie."

Peer rubbed slime from his ear, wondering if this was true. But he had no time to think about it. Uncle Baldur led him in and climbed the creaking ladder to the loft where the millstones were. Peer followed, overhung by his uncle's bulky bottom, and found himself standing on a dark, dusty platform, badly lit by one drafty little louvered window high in the apex of the roof. Right in front of him in the middle of the floor sat the two millstones, one above the other, cartwheel-sized slabs of gritstone rimmed with iron.

"Power!" Baldur wheezed, slapping the upper millstone. "See how heavy that is? But finely balanced. What drives it? Water power. Ah, but who controls the water? Me, the miller!

"The stream *obeys* me, boy. I control it with my sluice gates. And when I let it flow, it has no choice but to turn my waterwheel and drive my millstones.

"It all comes down to power. The power of the water, the power of the stones, all harnessed by my machinery.

"And it makes me the most powerful man in the valley. Without this, believe it or not, I'd be just another farmer, like the rest of them. Like Grim." He shook his head as though this were indeed hard to believe, and gave the millstone another affectionate pat.

"Now then!" he went on, straightening up. "See that?" Peer

looked up, banging his head on the corner of a big wooden box with sloping sides that hung from the rafters, suspended over the millstones on four thick ropes. "The hopper," his uncle grunted. "You fill it with barley, which runs out through this hole in the bottom, see—and trickles along this little tray we call the shoe. That shakes it down through *this* hole in the upper millstone. Which is called the runnerstone. Because it's the one that turns. Understand?"

To his own surprise, Peer did. Hoping to please his uncle, he tried to show an interest in spite of his empty stomach, aching head, and wobbly legs. "Does everyone bring their corn here?" he asked. Perhaps Hilde had been exaggerating. Probably the mill was doing quite well after all.

But Uncle Baldur's black eyebrows drew together in a scowl. "They soon will," he growled, "now that blackguard Ralf Eiriksson has gone. Spreading tales about my flour . . . telling everyone I put chalk in it—or dirt . . ." He shook his fist. "I'll make this the best mill in the valley. I'll put in another wheel—another pair of stones! They'll come to me from miles away! But first—" He stopped, as if he had been going to say something he didn't want Peer to hear. "But first," he said in a different tone of voice, "get that hopper filled, boy, I haven't got all night!"

To lift the sack high enough to pour the barley into the hopper was quite beyond Peer. With a bad-tempered grunt, Uncle Baldur did it. His muscles bunched as he hefted the sack in his thick arms and let the glossy grain pour effortlessly into the hopper. Then he took Peer outside to open the sluice and start the wheel.

It was getting late. The sun had set, and it was cold by the stream. Peer looked anxiously about for Loki as he followed his uncle up to the milldam. The water looked more sinister than ever as evening fell. A little breeze shivered the surface and the trees sighed sadly. Were Hilde's scary stories true? He hoped with all his heart that Loki kept away from this dark water.

Uncle Baldur didn't seem bothered. He tramped roughly up the path to the sluice and showed Peer a wooden handle, which worked the sluice gate. He stood on a narrow plank bridge and simply tugged the gate up. It slid up and down between grooves in two big timber posts. He banged some wedges in to keep it stuck in place. A vigorous rush of water boiled from the bottom of the sluice, filling the air with thunder, and the great black waterwheel stirred into life! Peer stared in fascination as the giant paddles endlessly descended to strike the water.

"It *is* powerful!" he whispered.

Uncle Baldur brought him sharply back to life with a clip round his ear. "You'll do that job next time," he said. "And don't hang about here after dark, or Granny Green-teeth will get you."

Oh, he cares! Peer thought sarcastically. "Who *is* Granny Green-teeth?" he inquired aloud, rubbing his ear.

"She lives at the bottom of the pond," said Uncle Baldur grimly, "which is why there's no fish worth catching. She likes to come up at night, the old besom. So look out!"

Peer looked over his shoulder as they walked back to the mill. It was now almost quite dark. But what was that patch of weeds floating in the shadow of the trees? Could it be the spreading hair of Granny Green-teeth, rising from her slimy bed? He heard a quiet splash—was that a fish? He hurried after his uncle. The night breeze whispered in the bushes—only the breeze—but when he heard rustling steps and panting breath, he panicked. Granny Green-teeth was after him! Or who knew what else lurked about this awful place? Uncle Baldur's great strides carried him on ahead. Peer rushed after him. Something crashed through a nearby bramble bush and leaped onto the path. Peer's heart nearly stopped: then he saw it was Loki.

"Loki!" he gasped in relief. "You crazy dog!" Relieved to have found him, Loki gave his coat a good hard shake and lashed his tail. Peer hugged him. "Come on," he said, and they ran into the yard together.

Uncle Baldur had already gone into the house and fetched himself a light snack of bread and sausage. "Put that dog away," he commanded. "Then you can go and do the chores. Sweep the stalls. Feed the pigs. Go and see Grim, he'll tell you what to do."

"Uncle Baldur," Peer faltered. "I'm awfully hungry."

"And not a mouthful will you get till your work is done," said Uncle Baldur sternly. "We have no use for greed and laziness here." And so saying, he took a huge bite from the chunk of bread he was holding and stuffed the sausage in after it whole.

CHAPTER 6

Tales of the Dovrefell

A mile or so farther up the valley, Hilde was eating supper with her family. The savoury smell of roasting crabs filled the warm room. Through mouthfuls, she told her family all about the day's adventures. Eirik and Gudrun listened, frowning, while Sigrid and Sigurd played on the floor with the kittens.

Gudrun shook her head. "Your father never should have left!" she exclaimed. "I've said to him a thousand times, we'd have trouble with those Grimsson boys, but will he listen? He's too easygoing, that's his trouble."

"Well," said Hilde, reaching for more bread. "You could give them the golden cup, I suppose." She cocked an eyebrow at her mother, grinning faintly.

"Over my dead body!" said Gudrun promptly. "I've never

wanted the thing, but it's your father's pride and joy. They can't have it."

"I thought you'd say that. I'd better ride up to the Stonemeadow now and again, don't you think? To keep an eye on the sheep up there?"

"Oh, no you won't!" snapped Gudrun. "And risk running into those two and their savage dog? What could you do, anyhow?"

"Oh, well!" said Hilde. "I don't mean try to fight with them or anything, but at least I would know if any of our animals go missing. Besides, my new friend Peer says he thinks something odd is going on between the Grimssons and the trolls. He's heard them talking—"

"I feel really sorry for that boy," interrupted Gudrun. "Eirik, come and eat; your crabs are ready!"

Eirik sat down happily, rubbing his hands and sniffing the scented steam rising from his dish. "Ah, you're a good girl, Hilde, you picked a fine big crab for your old grandfather."

"Don't *you* think I ought to go up on Troll Fell, Grandpa?" persisted Hilde. She threw out her chest and tossed back her hair, rather fancying herself as the family's gallant guardian, bravely patroling the hills. "So if Baldur Grimsson steals our sheep we can at least complain?"

"Well," began Eirik, working at a meaty claw with the point of his knife.

"Hilde," said Gudrun firmly. "I command you, as your mother, to do no such thing. I'd be worried stiff! It can all be safely left to Ralf, when he comes home. Just stay away from the mill *and* the trolls and try to keep out of trouble!"

"Oh, all right," Hilde grumbled. "Just lead a dull, boring, ordinary life. Yes, I know! You're right. But there'd be no heroes or stories or sagas if everyone acted that way! I do wish something exciting could happen to me!"

"Well, the exciting thing that can happen to you right now," said Gudrun, wiping the bowls clean with a piece of stale bread, "is that you can go and milk the cow, which you ought to have done already."

Hilde got up slowly and went to do as she was told. She felt flat and grumpy, as if nothing would go right. But once outside she felt better. It was a perfect spring evening. Although the sun had set, the wide western sky still reflected light. Hilde loved living so high up the valley. It was very quiet, except for far-off sheep bleating, and the nearby munching sounds of the cow and the pony tearing up grass. Hilde climbed the steep pasture toward them, carrying her bucket and stool, her shoes soaking up dew. With surprise she suddenly heard a new sound, the unmistakable high-pitched rattle of milk squirting into a metal pan, accompanied by a weird gruff humming like a very large bee. Goose bumps rose on her skin. She broke into a run and saw a small hairy troll squatting beside Bonny the cow, milking her into a copper pail.

"Clear off!" shouted Hilde, swinging her bucket. The cow tossed her head up and wheeled away, while the troll snatched up its pail and scampered off up the hillside, where Hilde soon lost sight of it in the twilight. She stood panting, hands on hips. "The cheek of it! Hey, Bonny," she said to the cow, "don't you know better than to let trolls come stealing your milk?"

The cow snorted as though she didn't care. Hilde had to soothe and stroke her before she would stand still. But the troll had milked her nearly dry, and Hilde went back to the house with no more than a cupful at the bottom of her pail. As she came to the door, her mother called out, "Bring the broom in with you, Hilde."

"What broom?" Hilde asked.

"Isn't it there?" Gudrun came out. "But I'm sure I left it right by the door," she said, annoyed. "I can't lay my hands on anything. . . . Is that all the milk?" She was even more put out when she heard Hilde's tale.

"They probably stole the broom, too," said Hilde. "You see, Mother? It's not so easy to keep out of trouble."

"The little varmints!" said Eirik, peering into the milk bucket. "Worse than rats and mice. They wouldn't be so bold if my son was here: no, they wouldn't come robbing us then!"

"They're becoming a perfect plague," Gudrun worried.

"I'm just a useless old man," said Eirik gloomily. "When I was a young fellow, I could have thrown anyone who so much as stepped on my shadow clean over the barn! No pack of trolls would have bothered me then. Now I'm old and no use to anyone."

"Oh, Father-in-law!" Gudrun scolded him affectionately. "Don't talk like that. We need you very much indeed, for—for wisdom and advice."

"Advice! Women never listen to advice," scoffed Eirik, but he looked pleased.

"And we need Grandad for telling stories!" piped up Sigrid from the floor. Eirik reached down beside his chair and tugged her plait with his gnarled old hand. "And you want one now, do you, missy? What is it to be about?"

"Trolls!" said Sigrid.

"Now, let me think," Eirik began. "Let me see. Of course, there's plenty of stories about trolls around here. We live on the very doorstep of Troll Fell, don't we? But here's a story from another place, far to the north, the wild mountains of the Dovrefell, where there are even more trolls than we have here, yes, all kinds of trolls, and some of them giants, by what I've heard!"

Don't frighten them! Gudrun mouthed. Eirik winked reassuringly.

"Giants!" Sigurd and Sigrid pressed themselves close to Eirik's knees.

"Oh, yes." Eirik nodded wisely. "Our trolls around here seem little things, don't they, but they do come all sizes, and the one in this story was a giantess, a little bit taller than a man! She must have been pretty, I daresay—"

"A pretty troll!" interrupted Sigrid, laughing.

"Yes, she had long yellow hair and a nice long tail that she wagged when she was happy. And she got married to a young farmer, and wagged her tail at the wedding."

Gudrun and Hilde were both laughing now.

"Now I don't say this story is true!" said Eirik with a twinkle in his eye. "But the friends and neighbors of this young farmer thought he was out of his mind to go marrying a troll. They were disgusted. They wouldn't talk to his bride, or visit her, even though she kept the house as clean as a new pin. She sat there all day by herself and got very lonely."

"Poor troll!" said Sigrid.

"I don't think so," said Sigurd. "I think he was stupid to marry a troll."

"See what happened," said Eirik solemnly. "This went on for a while, and one day her old father came to pay her a visit. He was a grim old troll from underneath the Dovrefell, bigger than she was, and when he found his daughter sitting crying, he said, '*What's all this?*'" Eirik deepened his voice to a growl. "'Is it your husband? If he isn't kind to you, I'll tear off his arms and legs!'

"'Oh no,' said the troll bride, 'it isn't my husband, it's the neighbors. They won't have anything to do with me, and I'm so-o-o lonely!' and she began to cry again.

"'Come along with me,' said her father, rolling up his sleeves and dragging her out of the house with him. 'We're going to have a little ball game. Will you throw, or shall I?'

"'Oh, no, Father,' said the troll bride, who knew exactly what he meant to do. 'You throw, and I'll catch.'

"So the grim old troll went stamping around the village, chasing the people out of their houses, and when he got hold of them he threw them right over the Hall roof, and his daughter caught them on the other side, and stood them carefully back on their feet and dusted them down.

"When everyone in the village had been thrown over the roof, the old troll came around the Hall, just a little out of breath, and he looked at the terrified crowd, and he said, 'Now you'd better start being very very nice to my daughter. Because if not,' and he glared, 'if not—why, I'll come back for another ball game—only, this time, my daughter will throw, and *I* will catch!'"

Gudrun and Hilde chuckled. Sigrid looked puzzled. "I don't understand," she began.

"Well, do you think the old troll would really have caught them?" Hilde asked her.

"Oh!" Sigrid's face cleared. "He would have let them fall!"

"Or eaten them up," said Sigurd with relish.

"That's right!" Eirik nodded. "Well, after that, you'd never believe how polite the neighbors were to the troll bride. They called around to see her every day and gave her flowers and cakes and baskets of eggs. She was as happy as the day was long, and wagged her tail merrily. . . . And that's a story from the Dovrefell." He smiled and stopped.

"Bedtime," said Gudrun to the twins.

"I'm proud of you, Grandfather," said Hilde, hugging him. "You're a poet *and* a storyteller!"

"Dear me," said Gudrun, shaking her head. "Trolls and Grimssons, all in one day! Whatever are we coming to? Hilde, you'd better make sure and milk Bonny earlier from now on, before the trolls get at her. The children will have to drink water tonight."

I wonder where Pa is now, thought Hilde, as the worries of the day returned to her. *I hope we'll manage without him. But at least he's alive—not like Peer Ulfsson's father. Poor lad! He must hate living at the mill. And I wonder what he's doing now?*

Peer was by himself, eating his frugal supper. His uncles had given him an onion, a small piece of moldy cheese, some rather stale bread, and the end of a rancid sausage and then gone off somewhere, leaving him alone to mind the mill. Alone except for Loki, because they had taken Grendel with them. Peer was happy about that! The little dog lay sprawled out by the fire, his eyes blissfully shut. Peer sat on a stool next to him.

The mill was noisily alive; it was grinding busily. Everything vibrated. Old dust trickled and cobwebs shook on the walls. Up in the loft, finely ground meal was snowing from the rim of the millstones and piling up on the wooden platform. Peer's job was to climb up from time to time and sweep it into sacks. He did not like it: the dark shadows, where you could break your ankle on bits of broken machinery, worm-eaten cogwheels with half the teeth missing, a worn old millstone propped against the wall. And the noises were so spooky: the rhythmic thumping of the water wheel like a dark heart beating, the creaking machinery, the clatter of the shoe that shook down the grain, and the sibilant mutter of the rotating millstone.

Peer nibbled his sausage experimentally and decided to give it to Loki. He looked about. He was still hungry, but he could see nothing else to eat. The table was cluttered with dirty dishes, rinds, and crusts, which he was determined not to touch. There was a bowl of cold groute that his uncle had put on the floor by the fire, but it did not look very appetizing.

"I suppose that's for the Nis anyway," thought Peer. "Even Grendel seems to have left it alone. Though he's probably stuffed full, the greedy brute!"

That evening Grim, who did most of the cooking, had fried some thick rashers of bacon, which the two brothers gobbled greedily, wiping up the grease from the pan with big chunks of new bread. Grendel, drooling by Grim's knee, was rewarded with several crisp pieces, while Peer watched hungrily from his cold corner. He had plucked up his courage.

"Uncle Grim? Could I have some bacon?"

"Bacon is bad for boys," replied Uncle Grim unblinkingly.

"Keeps 'em awake at nights," agreed Uncle Baldur, licking his glistening fingers with a fat red tongue.

"Gives 'em bad dreams," said Grim.

"Bad blood!" said Baldur.

"Bacon is too rich for boys," they chanted together.

So Peer got none, though his mouth watered at the smell,

while Grendel licked his messy chops after the last brown rasher. "*Good* old Grendel," cooed Uncle Grim, rubbing his ears. "Faithful fellow! Good dog." Grendel's heavy jaws parted in a grin and he seemed to look sideways at Peer as if to say, *You see? I am the favorite here.*

Peer got up restlessly and prowled around the room. His uncles hadn't said how late they'd be. He suspected they had gone out drinking, though he didn't know where. It was a good time to try and find where they had hidden his father's money.

There were several wooden bins built on either side of the ladder to the loft. Peer tried the lids, cocking an anxious ear for his uncles' return. Most of the bins were empty except for a few dusty grains at the bottom. One held a tangle of old leather harness. And one would not open. The lid was securely fastened with a large padlock.

"This must be it!" muttered Peer. He rattled at the lid uselessly. Over by the fire, Loki half-lifted his head. "I'm sure it's here, Loki," Peer told him. But that did not help very much.

It was time to go up to the grinding loft and sweep the flour into sacks. Reluctantly he climbed the rickety ladder, wishing he could stay by the fire with Loki. Sure enough, a soft pile of mealy flour lay in a ring around the millstones. Peer took a small wooden shovel and scraped it into the sack. He stood on tiptoe and peeped into the hopper, which was getting low. Uncle Baldur had left some half-full sacks of barley, which he could just lift. He refilled the hopper, taking care not to touch the revolving runnerstone. Pleased with himself, he was about to climb back down when a tremendous commotion broke out from below, a volley of hysterical barks from Loki!

Peer stopped, alarmed. It couldn't be his uncles coming back. Loki was too sensible to bark at them. It might be thieves. It might be some perfectly innocent visitor to the mill. But it was very late, quite dark outside. He looked down over the edge of the loft. Loki had his hackles up, growling and wagging his tail excitedly. Suddenly he jumped and snapped at something above his head, then backed a few steps and barked some more, looking upward. He was watching something in the rafters. Relieved, Peer slid down the ladder.

"Loki, shut up!" he said sternly. "It'll only be a rat." Loki ignored him and went on growling. "All right," Peer told him, "I'll have your space by the fire, then!" and he sat down on the dirty rush mat and reached out his hands to the warmth. He yawned. He was supposed to stay awake till his uncles got back, but he suddenly felt terribly sleepy. His eyes closed and his head nodded forward, but Loki barked again and he woke with a jerk. "Stop it, Loki!" he mumbled in annoyance. Loki gave him an apologetic glance, but continued to stand at attention, staring upward eagerly.

Peer's head drooped again, but as his eyelids closed he heard a familiar little voice. "See my leg?" it giggled. There was another flurry of barks from Loki, who jumped about as if on springs.

Peer's eyes flew open. It was hard to see by the light of the dying fire, but something was sitting on one of the cross-beams. A spindly little leg covered in a worn gray stocking dangled from the beam and waved about temptingly, just over Loki's head. "See my little leg?" teased the voice again. Loki exploded in a frustrated fury of leaps and barks.

"Loki, stop it!" Peer got up and grabbed his pet. He closed his hand round Loki's muzzle to keep his mouth shut. Loki pawed at him and whined beseechingly.

"It's only the Nis, silly," said Peer. "Now be quiet!" He let Loki go and stared up into the beams. The leg had been withdrawn and he could just see a dim shape up there sitting with its arms wrapped round its knees.

"Hullo!" he said.

"You've spoiled the fun," the Nis sulked.

"I'm sorry. But it was very noisy," Peer pointed out.

The Nis shuffled around on the beam till it had turned its back on him.

"How was the groute this evening? Have they given you any butter?" asked Peer cunningly. The Nis came to life at once.

"I doesn't know, Peer Ulfsson. Has they? Let's see."

It ran briskly along the beam and down the wall like a big spider. Peer watched in delight as it scampered over the table and down to the bowl of groute. It was a little, gray, whiskery thing, with big hands and long knobbly fingers. Its ragged gray clothing seemed to be a part of it, but it wore a little red cap on its head. Loki backed away grumbling and went to lie down in the coldest part of the room, his back turned.

The Nis was lifting the bowl and supping the groute. "Cold!" it muttered bitterly. "Cold as their cruel hearts, and lumpy, too." It stirred the bowl with its fingers and scooped up the last of the groute in messy splodges, then sat distastefully licking its fingers.

"Was there any butter?" asked Peer. The Nis shook its head.

"Now for the housework!" it said suddenly. "I has to do the housework, Peer Ulfsson. As long as they feeds me, I has to do the work! But I doesn't have to do it well. See me!"

Fascinated, Peer watched as the little Nis seized a broom bigger than itself and went leaping about the room like a grasshopper, sweeping up great clouds of floury dust. Sneezing vigorously, it cleared the dishes from the table and hid the bones under Uncle Baldur's pillow. It polished the plates with one of Uncle Grim's shirts and shook the stale crusts and crumbs into his best deerskin boots. The pieces of bacon rind it dropped in front of Loki, who ate them suspiciously. It managed to crack the big earthenware bread crock. Finally it put three wooden spoons and the frying pan tidily away under Uncle Grim's straw mattress.

"Well done," said Peer. "The room looks quite neat!"

The Nis gave a squeaky laugh.

"Do you always tidy up like that?" asked Peer, who was fairly sure that the Nis had been showing off specially for him. "Won't they be furious?"

"What can they do?" asked the Nis. "I doesn't want much, Peer Ulfsson. Only a bit of butter in my groute, or a drop of honey to keep me sweet." Its attention wandered. Loki had gone off to sleep, and the Nis began sneaking up on him, obviously with the intention of pulling his tail.

"Don't do that!" said Peer hastily. "Where have my uncles gone, anyway? I'm sure you know everything about them," he flattered it.

"Gone to the Stonemeadow. Shh!" The Nis laid a long finger to its lips and tiptoed closer to Loki.

"Oh, please leave him alone! The Stonemeadow? I'm sure I've heard of that. Where is it?"

The Nis gave up crossly. "On Troll Fell," it snapped.

"Troll Fell? I thought they'd gone out drinking. What are they doing there, Nis? Are they talking to trolls?" Peer asked curiously.

The Nis looked at him out of the corners of its eyes.

"Please tell me," begged Peer. "I heard them talking about the trolls before, and something about taking me to the—to the Gaffer. Do you know him? The king of the Trolls? And something else about a wedding. Do you know anything about that?"

The Nis yawned, irritated by so many direct questions. It ran off into the corner where the big scales hung and jumped lightly into one pan, which hardly moved. It sat there bouncing gently and would not look around.

Peer saw he had gone about things the wrong way. But he

was tired and cross himself, as well as worried. *I wish I had some butter,* he thought grumblingly. *That would make the little wretch talk.* And suddenly he thought of Hilde. If only he'd had the sense to ask her for some!

"Nis!" he called quietly. "I think you're very clever."

The Nis sniffed.

"I have a friend who has lots of butter, and the next time I see her, I shall ask her to give me a big lump all for you."

The Nis twitched and the scales swayed.

"So please be my friend, Nis, and I'll be yours." Peer stopped as his voice shook. He so badly wanted friends, and it was hard to have to manage this difficult little creature.

The Nis relented and turned around. It sat in the pan with its legs dangling and leaned backward on the chains to make the scales swing. "What does you want to know, Peer Ulfsson?" it asked importantly.

"Well—" Peer didn't know where to start. "What's this wedding?"

"Oh!" The Nis got very excited. "A very big wedding indeed! At midwinter, the Gaffer, the Old Man of Troll Fell, will marry his son to—guess who?"

"I can't guess," said Peer.

"Guess! Guess!" the Nis insisted.

"I can't," Peer laughed. "Tell me!"

The Nis paused for effect, then said in a hushed voice, "To the King of the Dovrefell's daughter!" It sat back.

"Goodness!" said Peer. It meant something to him after all.

Even he had heard of the trolls of the Dovrefell, the wild mountain range to the north. "So—that's quite an important match?" he suggested.

The Nis nodded. "Everyone is going, Peer Ulfsson. Of course, this isn't the eldest daughter. The King of the Dovrefell has many children. But they say this one is the most beautiful, because the eldest daughter has two tails. There will be such a feast!" It wriggled with delight and cracked its knuckles.

"Are you going?" Peer inquired.

The Nis's face fell. "I doesn't know," it admitted. "Food and drink, as much as you can hold, music and dancing and the hill raised up on red pillars—but they hasn't invited poor Nithing yet."

"But there's plenty of time, if it's not till midwinter. It sounds very exciting, Nis, but what has it got to do with Uncle Baldur and Uncle Grim?"

The Nis sniggered, tapping its nose with a spindly forefinger.

"Well," said Peer, "what are they doing up on Troll Fell in the middle of the night? They must be visiting the trolls. Right?"

"Middle of the night is daytime for trolls," the Nis pointed out scornfully. "If Grimssons go knocking on the troll gate at noon, what will they hear? Snores."

"I see that. But what do they want with the trolls at all?"

The Nis was getting bored and fidgety. "Treasure," it said, yawning and showing a pink tongue and sharp little teeth like a cat's.

"Troll gold? Yes, but surely," said Peer, struggling to make sense of it all, "surely the trolls won't give them any? I don't understand."

There was a loud squeak as the scales tipped. Like a squirrel the Nis leaped out of sight into the rafters, and at the same moment heavy feet sounded outside the door, the latch lifted, and Loki sprang to his feet. In tramped Uncle Baldur and Uncle Grim, shedding clods from their muddy boots, cold night air pouring from them like water. They looked sour and displeased. Grendel loped close behind them. He snarled at Loki, who squeezed himself against the doorpost and nipped outside.

Startled, Peer scrambled up. Uncle Baldur took him by the ear, led him to the door, and booted him out, saying simply, "Make yourself useful, you idle young layabout. I want the wheel stopped now."

"But, Uncle, I don't know how," Peer called at the closing door.

Uncle Baldur paused with the door a couple of inches open. "Go round and lower the sluice gate, of course. And then get off to the barn. Don't come knocking and disturbing us—it's late!"

And the door slammed shut.

CHAPTER 7
Granny Green-teeth

The yard was cold. It was well past midnight. The Milky Way shimmered overhead and a star fell over the barn roof. Peer shivered and wrapped his arms across his chest. Loki waited beside him, looking anxiously up at his face.

"Now what's going on?" Peer muttered to Loki. "They didn't look too happy, did they? I guess their interview with the King of Troll Fell didn't go too well. No need to take it out on us, though. Lower the sluice gate! At this hour?"

His teeth chattered, and Loki whined softly. Peer didn't know which was scarier, to disobey Uncle Baldur or to go up near that dark millpond by himself.

"You can go in the barn, at least," he told Loki, dragging him there by the collar. He pushed him into the dark interior and told him to sit. Loki's eyes gleamed in the dark, and again he whined gently.

"Stay!" Peer ordered. "I'm not risking you!" Shutting the barn door on him, he turned and went out of the yard toward the wooden bridge. The mill clacked loudly as it worked on in the quiet night. The wheel churned ceaselessly, chopping the water with dripping blades that glinted in the starlight. Peer leaned on the rail to watch for a few seconds, trying to gather enough courage to go on.

In the corner of his eye a black shadow moved, and he whipped around, his heart beating wildly. Then he relaxed. It was only someone traveling home late, a woman dressed in dark clothes and a scarf over her head, plodding uphill toward the bridge. She was using a stick to help herself along. Peer was relieved to see someone.

As the woman put out her hand to grasp the rail of the bridge, she saw him and stopped. Realizing that she might be nervous herself, Peer called out softly, "It's all right. I'm— the miller's boy. Only the miller's boy . . ."

"The miller's boy!" repeated the woman as if surprised. "And what is the miller's boy doing out here so late?"

"I have to close the sluice gate," explained Peer.

"Ah!" The woman looked at him closely. It was too dark for Peer to see much of her face, but her eyes glittered brightly in the starlight. "So late at night, that's a job for the miller himself," she said reprovingly. "A big man like him shouldn't be sending a boy out. How old are you, son?"

"Twelve," said Peer, lifting his chin.

"And you're not afraid? They say Granny Green-teeth lives in the millstream."

"A bit," Peer confessed, "but if I don't go, my uncles will be angry."

"And you're more afraid of them." The woman nodded angrily. "Ah! Baldur Grimsson, Grim Grimsson, I'd make you sorry if I had my way!" She shook her finger at the dark mill before turning to Peer again.

"I'll come along with you, my son, if you like."

Peer hesitated. There was something about the old woman that made him shiver, but his father had taught him to be polite to old people, and he didn't know how to refuse. Besides, it was true her company would make him feel braver, though the rough path to the sluice seemed no place for an old lady to be hobbling along at night. He made her a stiff little bow and offered her his arm. She took it with a chuckle and a cough.

"Good boy, good boy! Quite the young lord, eh? You didn't learn your manners from the Grimssons. What's your name?"

"Peer Ulfsson—ma'am," said Peer, wincing a little as her cold claw dug into his arm. She was surprisingly smelly, too, now he was close to her—closer than he liked. Her clothes seemed to be damp, or moldy or something—there was an odd, dank smell hanging about them.

But he was grateful she was there. As they passed the millrace, he knew he would have been terrified by himself. The threshing wheel and rushing water made him dizzy; there was a cold draft, fanned by the wheel, he supposed; and the smell of weeds and wet stone and black slime got stronger and stronger. He tripped on a stone and the old woman steadied him, hugging his arm to her side. She felt strong, and cold.

They came up to the bank of the millpond, and the woman released his arm so that he could edge onto the narrow walkway above the sluice. The pond was so black, he could not see where the surface lay. He shuffled carefully out along the rough plank, wishing there was a guide rail, and grabbed the handle of the sluice gate. He remembered it acted like a simple shutter. He just had to pull out the wedges and push it down. He fumbled around and found them. Pulling them out was hard but he managed it, though one dropped into the water, and then he leaned all his weight on the handle, driving the sluice gate down against the pressure of the water. It felt like cutting through the neck of a great black water monster. Down it went and jolted to a halt. The wheel slowed, its great vanes dripping. The rattle and grumble of the mill faltered and ceased. Only the sound of the water filled his ears, splashing and tumbling over the weir.

"Well done," said the old woman. She stretched out her arm to help Peer off the bridge. He took hold of her hand and then let go with a cry. It was clammy—and wet—and webbed.

The late moon was rising. He could see more easily and his

eyes had grown used to the dark. She stood there quietly at the end of the plank, leaning on her stick. He saw now that her long skirt and cloak were not damp but wet—soaking wet. How had she got so wet? The hair rose on his neck as he began to suspect. She raised her arms, pulling her scarf away from her head in fronds of trailing weed. She smiled, and even in the starlight he could see her teeth were sharp points. Peer's knees actually knocked together and his hand shook on the sluice handle. How could he have been so foolish? He had come up here with Granny Green-teeth herself!

As if she could read his mind, the woman nodded. "Yes!" she said. "So brave of the miller and his fine brother, to send a boy instead of themselves! Unlucky for you! But one day I'll get my hands on them."

Peer tried to swallow. His mouth was very dry. The old woman still did not move, and he could not get past her. He was stuck on the narrow plank above the water.

"I—I didn't know you walked," he heard himself say hoarsely. "I thought you just lived in the millpond—and sometimes came up."

The woman chuckled, like the brook gurgling over stones at night. "Oh, no! I often take an evening stroll—in one shape or another. Sometimes I come knocking on the mill door! That always frightens them!" She stared at him. "Poor boy, you didn't know me. Shall I tell you how?" She leaned forward, and Peer leaned back.

"Always watch for the sign of the river," she whispered in a low voice. "A dripping hem or sleeve, wet footprints on the floor."

Peer nodded again, his eyes wide. Granny Green-teeth drew back, as if satisfied that she had scared him.

"I hate the miller, boy," she hissed. "Oh, I hate him, thinking he owns *my* water, boasting about his powerful mill! But now I will punish him. I will take you."

"No!" Peer stammered. His legs shook and he clung to the post of the sluice to hold himself up. The black water seemed very near. "No, please—besides, he doesn't care a thing about me. Neither of them do. The only thing they care about is their dog, Grendel. Please!"

"So?" Granny Green-teeth paused, as if thinking. Peer waited, shivering. At last she spoke again, showing sharp triangular teeth in a dark smile.

"Then I shall send that dog, Grendel, with an apple in his mouth, as a dish for my friend the Dovreking's daughter, at her midwinter wedding! But as for you! You're wrong, my son. The miller has plans for you."

"What plans?" Peer asked desperately.

Granny Green-teeth became garrulous—like the old woman he had supposed her to be. She leaned both hands on her stick.

"We'll have a little gossip, shall we?" she chuckled. "I hear it all, you know. Every stream on Troll Fell runs into *my* river!

"After the old miller died—and good riddance; I hate the lot of 'em—the two young ones knew where the troll gate was. And they wouldn't let it alone! Knocking and banging, day after day—hoping to get at the gold, you see. They even tried bribes. Imagine that! They left fine white loaves there, and trout stolen from *my* water. Ah! Yet they never gave *me* anything!" Granny Green-teeth worked her mouth as though chewing on something bitter, and she spat.

"And this went on and on, didn't it? Oh yes: and dropping water wears away stone, so at last the troll king got tired of all this constant hammering and shouting outside his gate. Not seemly, was it?

"So to get rid of them he thinks up something difficult. He sends word: *My eldest son will be married at midwinter. He wishes to present his bride-to-be with a slave boy, as a betrothal gift. Bring me a slave boy, and I will reward you with gold!*"

Granny Green-teeth nodded spitefully at Peer. "And that's where you come in, my son. Like it or not, your precious uncles—your flesh and blood—will sell you to the trolls for a basketful of golden trinkets!"

Peer gaped at Granny Green-teeth. His head was spinning.

"So now you'll put a stop to it, won't you?" Granny Green-teeth coaxed him. "You'll help old Granny. Baldur Grimsson wants that gold to build a bigger mill, to put another wheel in *my* water. I'd drown him, sooner! But he never puts a foot wrong: he knows I'm after him."

"Please," Peer croaked, "let me go!"

"Ah, but *where* will you go?" she cried. "You don't want to be a slave boy, do you? Of course you don't. So come with me,

Peer, come with me." She stretched out her arms to him, and her voice became a low, musical murmur, like the stream in summer. "I'll take you—I'll love you—I'll look after you. Who else will? I'll give you an everlasting bed. Come with me, down under the water, and rest. Rest your weary bones."

The rank, rotten, water smells grew stronger and stronger. White mist rose from the surface of the millpond, flowing in soft wreaths over the plank bridge and swirling gently around his knees. His teeth chattered and his head swam. He could no longer see the bridge or the water. How easy it would be to let go, to fall into the soft mist. All for the best, maybe.

"All for the bessst," Granny Green-teeth agreed, in a soft hiss.

Far away a dog barked. Loki? Peer blinked, suddenly wide awake. He looked at the old woman. "No!" he said slowly. "Loki needs me. No! I won't!"

There was a whisper of wind. The mist blew away into the willows.

Granny Green-teeth nodded to him. "You're stronger than you look, Peer Ulfsson. Not this time, then," she said softly. "But I'll wait for you. One day you'll call me. And I'll be listening: I'll come!" She threw down her stick. What was happening? Her cloak twisted and clung to her body; she was growing tall and smooth. She jerked, twice, fell sideways and lay on the ground, kicking—no, flapping—an immense eel in gleaming loops as thick as Peer's leg. It raised its head with glinting narrow eyes and snapped its traplike jaws before slithering down the bank and into the pond. There was a low splash, and the black water closed in rocking ripples.

Peer wasted no time. He shot off the plank and raced back down the path, branches catching at his sleeves and whipping his face. His feet drummed on the wooden bridge. He hurled himself into the barn, dragged the door shut behind him with desperate hands, and threw himself into the straw, grabbing Loki and hugging him tightly. It seemed like hours before he could stop shivering.

"Loki! Oh, Loki!" was all he could say. Loki licked his face with an anxious tongue. After a while Peer began to laugh shakily.

"At least she didn't eat me," he said. "Oh, Loki, what shall I do? They're going to sell me under the hill. Under the hill!" As he calmed down, he began to think more clearly.

"There's no hurry," he told himself. "The wedding's not till midwinter. I don't need to run away tomorrow."

Had Granny Green-teeth lied? No, he was sure. Hilde's story showed that the Grimssons would do anything to get their hands on troll treasure. And they knew the entrance to Troll Fell. They had given up the idea of stealing—the trolls guarded the hill too well; it was impossible to trick them—and agreed to barter instead. To trade Peer, their own nephew, for troll gold! Peer suddenly found himself hot with anger. They had taken his money, sold his home, half-starved him, and treated him worse than their dog, and now they were going to sell him as well!

"We'll see about that!" he exclaimed to the dark barn. The oxen shifted in their stalls, munching. The hens, roosting in the beams, made disapproving noises and ruffled their feathers irritably. Peer no longer thought of them as his hens. They were selfish, faithless creatures who had transferred their loyalty to the uncles' black cockerel, and they now plainly despised him. He hugged Loki again.

"Featherbrains! Traitors!" he called. "I hope your eggs are addled!"

There was a squawk of shocked surprise and for a moment Peer thought the hens had understood his insult. Then he thought there was a weasel in the barn, for more hens began cackling, and Loki's hackles bristled under his hand. But it was the Nis, up to its tricks again, poking the hens and tipping them off their comfortable perches. Peer sighed exhaustedly; he felt he had had quite enough for one night. The Nis seemed in high spirits; Peer could hear it giggling to itself. Hen after hen fell clumsily from the rafters and ran clucking agitatedly about in the straw. One ran over him, digging its hard claws into his stomach.

"Oy!" called Peer. "Leave them alone. It's very late and I need to sleep."

The Nis pranced about in the beams, full of itself and kicking down dust and feathers and bits of cobweb. Peer wiped his eye.

"Stop it," he groaned.

The Nis crouched on a rafter just above him and looked

down. "News!" it said importantly.

"I don't care! . . . All right, what news?"

"News from Troll Fell!" said the Nis slyly.

"All right, I'm interested—go *on*!"

The Nis hopped about some more, unable to contain its delight. "The Gaffer's son will marry the King of the Dovrefell's daughter," it said.

"I know, you told me that before."

"But now there's more, Peer Ulfsson. Much more! I hear your uncles saying that *now*"—it took a deep breath—"the King of the Dovrefell's *son* will marry the Gaffer's *daughter*."

"Instead?" asked Peer in a daze, trying to work this out.

"No!" said the Nis impatiently. "As well!"

"Ah." Peer understood. "So it will be a double wedding?"

The Nis nodded ecstatically. "Even bigger wedding! Even bigger feast!"

Peer yawned. It had been a terribly long day. He appreciated that the Gaffer of Troll Fell had clearly pulled off a very important alliance for his son and daughter, but he didn't think it made much difference to his own plight. Still, one thing puzzled him. He asked, "But why should that bother my uncles, Nis? Why did they look so cross?"

The Nis had gone skipping off over the stalls and answered him from the other side of the barn.

"Now they has to find a girl as well as a boy."

"What!" Peer sat up wide awake. "What do you mean?"

"Trolls want a maid for the Prince as well as a page for the

Princess," explained the Nis casually. "Or the King of the Dovre will be offended."

Peer felt dizzy. "Then you knew all the time that Uncle Baldur wanted to sell me to the trolls!" he gasped. "And now— what are you saying? That the trolls want a girl as well as a boy, and Baldur and Grim have got to find one or not get paid?"

"Mm-hm!" replied the Nis lightly.

Hurt and frustrated, Peer almost wept. He knew the Nis was not very reliable, but he did think it should have told him about this before. In a firm voice, he said so. The Nis stopped scampering about.

"Doesn't you want to be a page?" it asked, amazed.

"No!"

"Why not?"

Peer struggled to reply. "I'm a human," he said at last. "I can't work for trolls."

"I'm a Nis," said the Nis huffily, "and I works for humans."

"Sorry," said Peer, a little ashamed. "But you can't *like* working for Uncle Baldur and Uncle Grim!"

"No, because of cold groute with no butter," the Nis agreed. "But for them that gives me hot, sweet groute with a big lump of butter, a bowl of cream, or a piece of honeycomb, then, Peer Ulfsson, I works willingly." It gave a mournful sigh as it finished naming these delicacies.

"It'd need more than a bowl of hot porridge to get me working for the trolls," muttered Peer. "Besides, there's nothing in it for me. My horrible uncles collect their gold and leave me as some sort of troll slave, stuck inside Troll Fell forever? Underground? In the dark?" He shuddered. "No thanks!"

"Under the hill is rich and splendid!" insisted the Nis.

"Yes, I'm sorry, Nis, but it doesn't appeal to me." Peer was overcome by an enormous yawn. He lay back in the prickly straw. It was getting lighter; the moonlight was blending into dawn. "I've *got* to get some sleep. I've been up all night, and I'll be expected to work all day. Thanks for telling me the news. Lucky I don't have a sister! I wonder what my uncles will do?" He yawned again, and vaguely heard the Nis replying:

"They has to find a girl, of course."

"Girls don't grow on trees," mumbled Peer. He was so sleepy that this seemed extremely funny, and he fell asleep chuckling, as the morning arrived and the Nis fell silent for the day.

The stringy black cockerel woke him. It was standing close by his ear and let rip with a deafening *Cock-a-doodle-doo!* that cracked in the middle and ended in a falsetto shriek. Peer sat up with a gasp, his heart hammering. The cockerel looked at him with a malicious gleam in its eye and stalked away on tiptoe, quivering its tailfeathers.

"I'll wring your neck," threatened Peer, opening the barn door. The cockerel strutted through it, followed by the hens, who turned their backs on Peer and jostled after their master, clucking eagerly. "I'll get the Nis to pull its tail," decided Peer spitefully. And all of a sudden he remembered everything he had found out.

I've got to tell Hilde, he thought. *Maybe I'm safe. If the trolls can't get a girl, perhaps they won't want a boy anymore. But I'll be careful. If there's the least chance of Uncle Baldur taking me to the Gaffer, I'll escape. Hilde would help—give me food if I need to run. But where, where? They'd surely find me at Hammerhaven, and that's the only place I know.*

He rubbed his face, desperately trying to think. The only hope seemed to be that Uncle Baldur and Uncle Grim didn't have a niece. They didn't have any female relations at all. Did they even know any girls?

Peer's eyes suddenly widened in horror.

Hilde was a girl!

They couldn't. They wouldn't.

Could they?

No! thought Peer. *But—all the same—I've got to warn her!*

CHAPTER 8

A Day Out

But Peer did not see Hilde again for a long time. Although he kept a good lookout, she never once came riding down to the village, and he did not have a chance to go walking up the valley to find her farm. Uncle Baldur and Uncle Grim kept him busy every minute, sweeping out the stalls, mending harnesses, filling flour sacks, digging the vegetable patch near the pigsty, spreading manure. Peer woke each morning sore and tired, went through the day hungry, and fell asleep at night half-dead with exhaustion. One week he helped bring down the sheep for shearing. Gripping the wiry, struggling creatures by one curly horn and clipping away at the shaggy fleeces, he wondered with aching muscles and breaking back how his uncles had ever done without him. They left nearly all the work for him, and not a word was said about trolls.

Perhaps they had decided that keeping him would be the better bargain.

The spring passed. White windflowers sprang up in the birch woods on the flanks of Troll Fell. Oats and rye grew taller in the small fields around the village, and the plowed field above the mill waved with green barley. June arrived, and the brief hot summer, with days that seemed nearly endless, awash with light and warmth, and nights when the sun dipped behind the hills only for a few short hours and the light never really left the sky.

One fine afternoon Hilde decided to take her little brother and sister down to the sea.

It was wash day. Gudrun and Hilde had collected nearly every piece of clothing in the house and carried them up the brook to where the water, icy cold from the upland glaciers, tumbled over a waterfall into a little pool. Here they had kilted up their skirts and bravely trodden the clothes down till their legs were blue and aching. On carrying the sodden and dripping load back to the farm, they discovered that Eirik, sitting outside the door in the sunshine, had nodded off. Left to themselves, Sigurd and Sigrid had taken it into their heads to try riding the cow, Bonny. They had untied her picket rope, scrambled on to her bony back, and allowed her to amble down the steep little valley where the wild garlic grew. She had gorged herself on the pungent leaves and flowers.

"The milk will taste of garlic for a week!" Gudrun scolded, dragging cow and children back to the house. "And I will make you drink it. It will serve you right."

"Let's make cheese with it," suggested Hilde. "It might be quite interesting! Sit down, Mother, I've got an idea."

"I need to rest," said Gudrun piteously, collapsing.

"So do I!" agreed Hilde, rubbing her cold fingers. "In fact I need a holiday. I'm going to take the little ones down to the fjord. They can paddle and look for shells. We'll take the pony."

"You can if you like," said Gudrun dubiously. "It doesn't sound much of a rest to me!"

"It will be a change, and get the children out of your way, Ma."

"That would be nice," Gudrun agreed. "I can sit in the sun and spin."

So Hilde caught the pony, sat her little brother and sister on his back, and put some bread and cheese into a bag for later. They set off down the valley.

The path from the farm followed the steep banks of the brook, which ran rapidly in a series of little waterfalls. The brown water flashed in the sunlight. As they walked downhill through the wood, the white trunks of the birch trees shone as if newly scoured, and the green leaves danced overhead. Sigrid sang one song, Hilde another; Sigurd clutched the mane and pounded the pony with his heels to make it trot.

The path left the woods and slanted down the fields toward

the wooden bridge. Hilde looked about eagerly. The mill was working, and the clattering sound made the pony fling up his head in alarm and walk with a bouncy stride as if he might run. Hilde grabbed his bridle.

"Good, they'll be busy inside," she told Sigurd. "See if you can see my friend Peer anywhere about."

As it happened, Peer saw her first. He was busy cleaning out the pigsty, a lean-to shed at the back of the mill on the other side of the millpond. The sty was ankle deep in stinking liquid manure. Stripped to the waist and barefoot, his ragged trousers rolled up, Peer shoveled out mud and smelly straw and rotten cabbage stalks, while Bristles the boar basked next to his sow beside the wall, their hairy sides heaving gently in the warm sunshine. Stinging flies buzzed round Peer's head. Halting his work to wipe the sweat from his eyes, he saw Hilde and the children coming out of the woods, and for a moment he almost ducked out of sight. Why did Hilde always have to see him this way, untidy and filthy? But there were things he needed to say, so he climbed out of the pigsty and hailed her.

"Hello!" called Hilde, waving. "We're going down to the sea."

"I need to talk to you," Peer called back. The mill was making so much noise, he didn't think his uncles would hear.

"Come with us!" shouted Hilde cheerfully.

What a marvelous idea! Peer fell for it immediately. Suddenly he didn't care what his uncles said or did: he just had to get away for a while. A sunny afternoon doing what he pleased would be worth almost anything that could happen afterward. He threw down the shovel. "What do you think, Loki? Shall we go?" Loki, who had been lying in gloomy boredom with his nose propped between his paws, jumped up wagging his tail.

"I'll meet you farther down," Peer called to Hilde, meaning to circle around and join the path nearer the village, out of sight of the mill.

"Swim across and get clean!" shouted Sigrid in her shrill little voice. Peer glanced at the millpond. It looked cool and tempting, but he shook his head with a laugh and a shudder. He turned, raising a hand and pointing to show Hilde which way he was going. He ran around the back of the barn, wading waist deep through a green bank of stinging nettles, and crept through the bushes beside the path till he was out of sight of the mill. Then he sat down to wait for Hilde and the pony, rubbing his tingling legs.

They soon came into sight. Peer fell in step beside Hilde, secretly pleased to notice that he was taller. She gave him a big grin. "Good for you!" she said. "I hope you won't get into trouble."

"Oh, I will," said Peer. His face hardened. "I just don't care this time."

Startled, Hilde glanced at him. He was burned brown as a berry from working in the sun with his shirt off. His hair had bleached nearly white. He was covered with splashes of mud, and worse than mud, and his trousers were nothing but rags.

He looked thinner, and older. Just then Loki came bounding up. His coat was rough and his ribs showed.

"Oh, Loki!" said Hilde, shocked.

Peer frowned. "He doesn't get enough to eat," he said angrily. "Grendel gets everything."

Hilde thought that Peer didn't get enough to eat either, but tactfully she changed the subject.

"Meet the mischief makers," she told him cheerfully. "My little brother, Sigurd, my little sister, Sigrid. Say hello to him, brats!"

"Hello," said Peer, smiling. The two little children looked very alike, with pale fair hair and big blue eyes. "Are you two twins, by any chance?"

They nodded. "We're five! But I came first," boasted Sigrid. "So Sigurd has to do what I say!"

"I do not!" Sigurd twisted around and punched his sister, she pulled his hair, and the next moment they fell off the pony and were wrestling in the road, while Loki leaped about barking. Hilde and Peer dragged them apart.

"What is it about twins?" asked Peer wryly.

"Goodness knows," panted Hilde. "Children, stop it! *Now!* Or we'll turn around and go home." She lifted them back onto the pony. "Behave, or Peer won't come with us."

"No, I'm coming," said Peer. "Where are we going exactly? Is there a harbor?"

"Not even a jetty," said Hilde. "It's a very small place, Trollsvik. There's a couple of fishermen I know, Arnë and

Bjorn. I want to see them because they'll help us cut the hay next month if Pa hasn't come back yet. I'll buy some fish. And we'll sit on rocks and talk while the children paddle."

"Me too," said Peer. "I want to swim."

He looked eagerly around as they came into the village. Though it wasn't far, he had never been allowed out of sight of the mill. Trollsvik seemed tiny compared to Hammerhaven, but there was plenty going on. He counted seven or eight houses, all with thin streams of white smoke rising from their grassy roofs. Goats bleated, tethered to prevent them eating the beans and peas in the little vegetable patches. A gang of dogs rushed over to sniff at Loki, who instantly made five new friends. A woman came out of the nearest house and threw a pail of water over her garden. Seeing Hilde, she called out, asking how her mother was and whether they'd heard from Ralf. The woman was very pretty, Peer thought, with long dark hair and green eyes. He stood shyly apart to let Hilde talk, but she dragged him forward.

"This is Bjorn's wife, Kersten. This is Peer Ulfsson, Kersten, who has come to live at the mill." Kersten smiled kindly at him, but Peer, embarrassed because he was so dirty, was glad when the conversation ended and she went back inside. Hilde tethered the pony, and together they walked the last few yards down to the shore.

The wide fjord was blue and sparkling. Baby waves lifted themselves an inch or two and turned over with a clear splash on the edge of a shingle beach, in which every pebble seemed a different color. There was so much light it hurt the eyes. A couple of fishing boats lay on the pebbles. Sigurd and Sigrid squealed with delight and went running ahead to pick up shells and red and green seaweed. Peer and Hilde breathed deep and stared at the bright water and the high mountains.

"I'm going in," said Peer happily.

"It'll be cold," Hilde warned him.

"Never mind, at least I'll be clean." He ran knee-deep into the water. "Whew! You're right, it's freezing! Here goes!" He threw himself forward with a whoop. Loki dashed to and fro, barking. He dared not go in himself, but he bit at the little waves in case they attacked his master. Getting a mouthful of salt water, he shook his head and coughed disgustedly. Hilde laughed.

"Poor Loki! Was it nasty?" She threw him a bit of bread, which he snapped up.

Peer came wading out, shivering. "I'm clean," he said with chattering teeth, "but I can't stay in any longer. Let's find a nice sunny boulder and sit down. I really need to tell you something."

"I brought a cloak to sit on," said Hilde. "Mother insists. Take it, it's an old one. Go on, you'd better!"

Peer wrapped it gratefully round his shoulders. It was old and darned, but clean and warm. Hilde led the way to a sheltered spot between two big stones, and they sat down. Loki trotted about by himself, exploring the smells of the beach.

The little children clambered into one of the boats and began playing Vikings.

"Peace at last!" said Hilde.

"Mm!" said Peer. The sun soaked into his bones and he would have felt sleepy, except that the swim had sharpened his hunger. His stomach growled noisily and he blushed. Hilde threw him the bag she had brought with the bread and cheese.

"Eat!" she commanded. "And tell me what's been going on."

So between mouthfuls Peer began his story. He explained how he had met the Nis. He described what a flighty little creature it was, and how he had promised to bring it some butter. He told how he had learned about the troll wedding.

"I've heard of the trolls of the Dovrefell," interrupted Hilde, who was listening intently. "Everyone has! That has to be a very important wedding for the old Gaffer of Troll Fell."

"Exactly," said Peer. With a shiver he told Hilde about his meeting with Granny Green-teeth, and how she had revealed his uncles' plans for selling Peer to the trolls as a wedding present to the Dovreking's son. He almost laughed at Hilde's expression.

"Peer," she said, horrified. "They couldn't!"

"Oh, yes, they could! And that's not all, I'm afraid. Later that night I heard from the Nis that now it's to be a double wedding. The old Gaffer's son and daughter," he explained carefully, "are marrying the Dovreking's daughter and son."

"Well?" asked Hilde, as he stopped.

"And it seems my uncles were very angry, because the Gaffer told them that the deal was off unless they could find a girl as well as a boy. You see, if he gives the Dovre prince a page, he wants a maid for the princess."

"So no gold for the Grimssons without a girl?" asked Hilde. She laughed in relief. "Then you're safe."

"I don't think so," said Peer quietly. Hilde stared at him.

"I think they're going to find a girl," he said. "I think you ought to be very careful, Hilde."

Hilde whistled. There was a moment's silence, except for the lapping of the waves and the cries of seabirds.

"So Troll Fell wants to impress the Dovrefell," she said.

"With two human wedding presents," nodded Peer.

"Well, it's unusual. I wonder what a troll page or maid has to do?"

"I don't want to find out. I'd hate to live underground, Hilde. I couldn't bear it."

"Of course you couldn't!" Hilde agreed warmly. "Neither could I!"

"Yes, but—" Peer bit off his words. No need for Hilde to know how much he dreaded being shut up in the dark. She flicked her plaits back over her shoulders, frowning.

"Peer, you have had extraordinary luck. Meeting a Nis— never in my whole life have I seen one. There's never been one in our house. And Granny Green-teeth taking a fancy to you—ooh, scary!"

"Taking a *fancy*?" Peer repeated slowly.

"You were lucky to get away from her!" Hilde told him seriously.

"Do you really think she—? Maybe she did. She said she'd *look after me*." He shuddered. "Either way, she wants me at the bottom of the millpond!"

"Nothing like that ever happens to me," grumbled Hilde. "All I ever get to see are trolls, and they're as common as mice. I wish we had a Nis in our house. Mother could feed it well and it might do the grinding! I'll get you some butter for yours, though. Will it help you? Can you trust it?"

"I doubt it," said Peer gloomily. "It's too keen about the wedding. It thinks I ought to be thrilled about meeting a troll princess with two tails."

"Does she really have two tails?" Hilde asked, goggling.

"No, actually I think that's her sister." He sighed. "Anyway I haven't seen the Nis much lately. The nights are so short, and I sleep like a log."

Hilde began to answer but was interrupted by excited shouts from Sigurd and Sigrid, who had climbed out of the boats to throw pebbles for Loki.

"Look! Look!" They pointed out into the fjord. Another small boat was dancing in toward them. Hilde jumped up.

"That's Bjorn," she said, shading her eyes with her hand. "Can you see his pet seal swimming along behind him?"

Squinting, Peer could just see a dark dot in the water behind the boat.

"It follows him each time he goes out, and they say it drives the herring to him. He looked after it when it was a pup," Hilde explained. "Found it injured on the beach and fed it fish till it was grown. Of course, some people say his wife Kersten was a seal woman, and this is really their own child, but my pa doesn't think that's true. Still, Bjorn and his brother Arnë know more stories about the sea than anyone else. I wonder where Arnë is? I can't see him."

They watched Bjorn pull strongly in to shore, ship his oars, and jump out into knee-deep water to drag his boat aground. The seal, clearly visible, frisked around him, now rubbing its sleek head past his legs, now flicking its tail. Bjorn reached into the boat and tossed it a fish, which it caught easily. With a hoarse bark, it disappeared.

Peer ran with Hilde to help pull the boat up the beach. Bjorn was a short, stocky fellow with a strong, friendly face, blue eyes, and long, untidy hair falling over his shoulders.

"Hello, Hilde my lass, who's your friend? Hello, sprats," he said to Sigurd and Sigrid.

"Hello, Bjorn. This is my friend Peer Ulfsson, who now lives at the mill."

Bjorn put out a callused hand and Peer shook it, liking him already. "The mill, eh?" was all he said, but his smile was sympathetic.

"Bjorn, where's Arnë?" asked Hilde.

"Now *there's* a story," said Bjorn, scratching his head. "You haven't heard? He's gone off south, and it's your doing, Hilde, you and your father between you. He's been kicking himself ever since you told him how Ralf sailed off on that blessed longship. He kept on and on about how he wished he'd gone too, if only he'd thought of it in time.

"So I said, 'If it means that much to you, go after them!'

"'How can I,' he says. 'They're a hundred miles away by now.'

"'Not necessarily,' says I. 'They've got stuff to trade. They'll be stopping along the coast. Go and follow them, and ten to one you'll catch them up.' He was doing no good to me, fretting about it all day long.

"'Do you really think so?' he says. So I said, 'Well if you don't catch up with that ship, you can always join another one. It's the sailing season.' And he went!"

"Goodness!" said Hilde. "How did he go? On foot?"

Bjorn laughed. "Arnë walk, when he could sail? He took his boat, of course. There's no faster way down the coast. And that was, oh, three or four weeks ago. He'll be back before winter. He knows how to look after himself."

He picked up a knife and wiped it on his sleeve. "You wanting some fish for your granddad? I know he dearly likes a bit of fish."

"Yes, please, Bjorn. And will you lend us a hand with the hay? Mother said to ask."

Bjorn looked thoughtful. "Now Arnë's gone I'm a bit short-handed. When?"

"In about three to four weeks?" Hilde suggested. "We really do need help, Bjorn. We haven't even sheared the sheep yet.

They're up on the Stonemeadow, and Mother won't let me go there in case of trouble with the Grimsson twins. Have you heard?"

Peer wriggled uncomfortably. He was afraid that Uncle Grim had already stolen some of Hilde's sheep.

"You should bring it up at the Thing," said Bjorn.

"The what?" asked Peer.

"The village meeting, where we agree on laws and settle quarrels," Bjorn explained.

"Umm," said Hilde doubtfully. "Eirik would have to do it, you see, since they don't let women speak!" She scowled, and Bjorn laughed and pretended to cower. "I think Ma would prefer to wait till Pa gets back."

"Well, I'll help you with the hay," Bjorn decided. He picked up a couple of fish. "How many?"

"Lots, please," said Hilde cheerfully. "We want plenty for drying and smoking. And Peer, this is a holiday for you and me. Let's light a fire on the beach and cook some now. Bjorn might tell us a story!"

Hilde was a good organizer. She sent Sigrid and Sigurd combing the beach for driftwood. They came back with handfuls of bleached twigs and tangled branches. When there was a good heap, Bjorn obligingly struck sparks for them from his iron knife and a big pebble. A piece of dry seaweed caught light, and the fire was soon blazing. They all sat on the stones, speared fish on sharp sticks, and held them near the flames. The smell was delicious. The fish were difficult to eat, and they all burned their fingers, but it was worth it. Peer carefully boned a fish for Loki, who gobbled his fill of the rich white meat and crisp flame-blackened skins, and lay licking his paws contentedly afterward.

"Tell us a story, Bjorn," begged Sigrid, and Hilde said, "Yes, Bjorn, go on!"

Bjorn lay on his back with his arms behind his head, soaking up the sunshine. "What sort of story?" he asked drowsily.

"Tell us about the merrows," said Sigurd.

So Bjorn told them about the merrows, or merfolk. He told a funny story about a fisherman who made friends with a merrow and went to visit his house under the sea. While he was there, he saw a lot of upturned pots. "What's under those?" he asked. "Oh, the spirits of drowned sailors," said the merrow. "I keep them there so they can't get away." The fisherman went away, but he couldn't stop thinking about the poor sailors' spirits trapped under the pots. He waited till he knew the merrow was out, swam down and turned over every pot. The spirits of the sailors went bubbling up through the water and escaped, but after that the merrow was never friends with the fisherman anymore.

"That's a great story!" said Hilde when he had finished. "Tell us another!"

"A scary one!" demanded Sigrid.

Bjorn grinned. And this time he told them about the

Draug, the ghostly fisherman who sails the seas in half a boat and can be heard wailing in the storm winds when someone is about to drown.

"Have *you* ever heard him?" breathed Sigurd. Bjorn looked at them sideways and shook his head, meaning that he would not say.

Hilde shivered. "I'm cold," she said, wrapping her arms around her legs. A cloud came over the sun and the warmth drained out of the world. "I wish you hadn't told that last story," she said to Bjorn, half laughing. "I shall think about it now and worry. I wish—" But she didn't finish the thought. "We'd better go. We'll see you in a few weeks, then! Thanks for the stories, Bjorn."

Bjorn grinned. He tousled the little ones' heads, patted Hilde on the shoulder and slapped Peer on the back. "Good luck, friend!" he said.

"Thanks, I'm going to need it," said Peer ruefully. He didn't like to think what Uncle Baldur and Uncle Grim would do to him when he got back.

CHAPTER 9

More Trouble at the Mill

Hilde kept uncharacteristically quiet as they trudged
back to the village, carrying the fish between them in a
sack. "What's the matter?" Peer asked at last.

"Oh, nothing." Hilde hesitated. "To tell you the truth," she
admitted, "I know it's silly, but as soon as I heard Bjorn's last
story, I started thinking about Pa. I'm not worried! I'm just—"

"Worried!" Peer finished. "But don't be, Hilde. I'm sure he's
all right."

"I know," Hilde agreed, still rather glumly. "But nothing's
really gone right since he left. And the trolls—well, besides
what you've told me, they're such a nuisance! They're around
the house every night, stealing things and spoiling things."

"A pity your father didn't know that before he left," offered
Peer.

"He did know," Hilde admitted. "I mean, it's got worse, but he did know."

"Ah," said Peer. There was an embarrassed pause, and Hilde imagined him thinking, *He knew, and he left all the same? What kind of a father is that?* She blushed miserably. Peer gave her a sideways look and suddenly squeezed her hand.

"You're just missing him," he muttered gruffly. "I know how it feels."

Hilde sniffed and smeared a hand across her eyes. "Goodness!" she said loudly. "Where are those horrid little twins?" She looked back. Loki was with them, playing tug-of-war with a slippery piece of seaweed. He growled ferociously, rolling his eyes, backing away from the children with paws braced and tail wagging. The seaweed slithered through their palms, and Loki bounded up the path, shaking it fiercely while they chased him.

"They're having fun!" said Hilde.

"And at least Loki and I got something to eat today," said Peer. "I don't suppose we'll get much supper tonight. Not that we ever do."

Hilde looked him in the eye. "Will you get into terrible trouble, Peer?"

"I don't know!" said Peer wearily. "I've never done this before."

Hilde bit her lip. "You don't have to tell me this, but do they beat you?"

Peer flushed. "They sometimes hit me," he said with difficulty. "It's more that—they really don't care about me, whether I'm hungry or happy or anything."

"I wish you could live with us, instead," muttered Hilde, staring at the ground. Peer glanced at her, then awkwardly patted her shoulder.

"Thanks," he said sadly, "but it wouldn't work. They'd only come and get me."

They marched on in silence. The sun had gone in and all the fun seemed to be over. In the village Hilde caught the pony and loaded him up with the sack of herrings. "Here's my next job, splitting all these for smoking," she said gloomily. "Come on, you little ones, the picnic's over, time to go home."

They plodded on up the track toward the mill, deep in their own thoughts. After a while Peer asked, "Has there been any trouble about the land yet?"

Hilde shook her head. "They haven't come banging on our door, if that's what you mean. Yet. But Bjorn's right, it really ought to be discussed at the Thing, and if Pa doesn't come home in time to put our side of the story, then I suppose we might lose it."

"Why do they want it so much?" Peer wondered. "They already know where to find the trolls."

"It's such an old argument," Hilde sighed. "I mean, their father started it. To be fair, maybe they really do believe that's their land up there."

"Oh, don't try to be fair," Peer joked bitterly. "Of course they don't think it's theirs! They want it because it's yours! Anything to make a profit. Look how they sold up my father's things! They'd dive into a dung heap to rescue a penny."

"There's trouble brewing," said Hilde darkly. "I can feel it in my bones. Trouble brewing all around. My mother is going to be so worried when she hears! Peer, what can we do? We can't let them sell you to the trolls."

"Then keep away from the mill," Peer begged. "I'm no good to them by myself. But it's a long time before midwinter. Are there any other girls living nearby?"

"I'm the only one about your age," said Hilde. "Do you think they want a—a matched pair, like a team of horses?"

"I suppose they do," said Peer thoughtfully. "Well, I shall be very careful. When the time comes, maybe I can hide for a few days—till after midwinter."

"Hide with us," Hilde offered. "Ma won't mind."

"No. They'd think of that and come after me."

"Yes, but Pa will be home by then!" said Hilde in great excitement. "Of course! *He* won't let them take you anywhere. He'll be home! You'll be perfectly safe with us!"

Peer lifted his head and stared into her flushed, glowing face. "Really? Would your father really do that for me?" he asked shyly.

"I know he would!" Hilde assured him. "Loki too. Don't worry anymore, Peer."

Peer took a deep breath of relief. He felt suddenly lighter

and stronger. He could hardly believe that the problem had been solved so easily. Hilde beamed at him, and they talked cheerfully about it as they went up the path. But by now the little ones were straggling behind. "I'm tired," Sigrid complained. "My feet hurt."

"We want to ride," said Sigurd, kicking the ground.

"Not on top of a sack of herrings," said Hilde.

Peer still felt strong and capable. "I'll give you a ride!" he said, bending down, and Sigrid gleefully scrambled onto his back.

"Me too!" yelled Sigurd.

"In a minute! Take turns!" puffed Peer. The little girl was heavier than he had expected, but he gamely carried on and gave Sigurd and Sigrid rides nearly as far as the mill, while Hilde led the pony and Loki trotted along beside him.

He was carrying Sigrid when they came in sight of the mill. There was a loaded cart standing in the yard. "Oh, *no!*" Peer groaned. Work for the mill, and he'd gone missing! Uncle Baldur would be furious. And there was a figure, guarding the entrance to the yard like a dark stone tower, glaring down the road.

"Which one is it?" whispered Hilde. Peer gulped.

"It's Uncle Baldur—I think."

"You! You ungrateful boy!" yelled Uncle Baldur as soon as he laid eyes on Peer. His voice cracked, shooting into a scream. "Come here *AT ONCE!*"

Heart thudding, mouth dry, Peer uncurled Sigrid's warm

little hands from their stranglehold around his neck and lowered her gently to the ground.

"I'm in for it," he muttered to Hilde out of the corner of his mouth. "Better get out while you can."

"Come *here*!" screamed Uncle Baldur again. His face was purple with rage. "Just where do you think you have been, you lazy, idle, no-good little runt!"

Sigurd and Sigrid were staring in horror. "Who is that nasty man?" asked Sigrid in her high, sweet little voice.

"The miller," said Hilde crisply, and, "My uncle," said Peer distractedly. "Go *home*, Hilde—get going!"

He went warily forward. Behind him Sigrid was asking piercingly, "Why is the nasty man angry with Peer?"

"You expect me to keep you—you and your useless dog!" Uncle Baldur shrieked. "Corn arriving and work to do—and you run off to play. Just *wait* till I get my hands on you!" Peer was in range. Uncle Baldur lunged, and Peer instinctively dodged. This was a bad move. It made Uncle Baldur even madder. He grabbed again, got Peer by the left wrist, and twisted his arm up behind his back. Peer yelled.

"You're a wastrel"—Uncle Baldur shook him to and fro— "just like your no-good father! How dare you run off without my permission? Leaving your work!"

"My father was a far better man than you!" Peer gasped through tears of pain. White-hot fire shot up his arm as Uncle Baldur wrenched it. Through the drumming blood in his ears, Peer heard Loki barking, Hilde shouting, "Let go of him!" and above it all little Sigrid screaming, "I don't like that nasty man! I hate him!"

"Hilde!" he yelled breathlessly, struggling to see through a red flood of shame. Uncle Baldur had him doubled over now. Blows thudded on him. *Hilde is watching all this!* "Hilde, for goodness' sake, *get those kids away from here!*"

"I'll give you such a thrashing!" Uncle Baldur screeched, so close that Peer gagged on his hot, foul breath. "I'll dust your jacket for you—I'll feed your dog to Grendel—it'll save me his keep."

The noise attracted Uncle Grim, who came out to see what was happening. He stood watching for a moment and then said, "Let 'im go, Baldur! Let 'im go!"

Surprised, Uncle Baldur stopped shouting at Peer and looked at his brother. Grim merely jerked his head toward Hilde, who was hurriedly lifting the shrieking twins onto the pony, sack of herring and all. Then he turned around and walked away.

"Ha," said Uncle Baldur, heaving a deep breath. He let Peer go. Peer fell to the ground. Baldur's little piggy eyes twinkled, black and calculating. He scratched his beard.

"On the other hand," he said, puffing, "a boy has to have friends of his own age." He forced an indulgent chuckle. "So you played truant, eh? I like a lad of spirit—just how I was meself.

"Don't you be scared, my dear," he cooed to Hilde, who was

dragging the pony toward the bridge. He followed along behind her. "This nephew of mine is really the apple of my eye. He is! I used to play truant myself, once, and my dear old dad used to beat me for it. 'A boy should be beaten three times a day,' he used to say. And can you guess why?"

"No," Hilde said briefly, trying to calm the twins and stop the sack from slipping.

"Once for what you *know* he's done, once for what he's *going* to do, and once for what he's done that you ain't found out about yet!" said Uncle Baldur, holding up three thick fingers. He spluttered with laughter. "That covers everything! Oh, he was a rare wit, my old dad."

"Very funny," said Hilde. "Good-bye!" she said quickly to Peer.

"Boys will be boys," went on Uncle Baldur, following her around the end of the building. "Don't go yet! How about a bite to eat or a drink of buttermilk?" Sigurd and Sigrid looked wildly around at him and screamed. He stopped and watched as Hilde urged the pony across the bridge and uphill toward the wood.

"Come again to play with the boy!" he called after her. "Bring the kiddies. Don't be shy!" Sigrid and Sigurd were still sobbing. Long after they had gone out of sight between the trees, Uncle Baldur stood staring after them. At last he turned on his heel and strode back into the yard. Peer stood up shakily against the wall, waiting for him. Uncle Baldur came up to him and, crouching down, put his hairy face near to Peer's.

"I'm a fair man, you see," he said, showing his rotten teeth in a yellow smile. "You deserve a bit of fun. Bring your friends here anytime you like. Make sure you tell them so. Any time! Show them how the mill works. They'll like that!"

"Yes, Uncle," said Peer woodenly, determined to do no such thing. His uncle stared at him for a moment longer, opened his mouth again as if to say something more, and changed his mind. He swung away, aiming a kick at Loki, who jumped deftly out of the way.

Harvest time came. For a brief week or so everyone was out in the small fields, swinging scythes and sickles, building haystacks, binding the barley into sheaves, threshing and winnowing. But to Uncle Baldur's rage and disappointment, the mill was no busier. Most people kept their barley in sacks at home, grinding only as much as they needed from day to day.

Uncle Grim borrowed Peer from his brother and set him to do most of the harvesting. While Uncle Grim lay on his back under the shade of a hawthorn tree, snoozing, Peer toiled in the sun. He wiped his sweaty face on his arm, longing to jump into the stream that babbled temptingly at the bottom of the field. But he noticed his uncle sneakily watching him with one eye open, and bent wearily to his work.

As he lay in the straw that night, wrapped in the worn old cloak Hilde had given him, Peer planned for the future. The hard work was bearable, because now he had something to look forward to. At midwinter, perhaps before if Ralf Eiriksson came home sooner, he and Loki would escape up the valley—away from his uncles, away from Granny Green-teeth, away from Grendel.

Ralf would protect them. Secretly Peer hoped that Ralf would let him stay. Surely a boy could help on the farm? Peer wouldn't eat much. He could train Loki to herd sheep. As for his uncles—well, perhaps once their plan had failed, they would not care enough to try and recapture him.

And he never really felt safe in the mill. As Hilde had said, it was a spooky place. Once, one evening when he'd been alone, he'd heard a rap at the mill door, not very loud. Peer had been about to open it when he'd noticed Loki shivering and showing his teeth in a white snarl.

"What's wrong, Loki?" he'd asked, disturbed. Loki had backed away stiffly from the door, hackles up.

Peer remembered standing absolutely still, listening. Outside, not a foot stirred. But there had been a sound, a tiny sound. A light *tick, tick, tick* of dripping water.

His skin had prickled. He remembered Granny Green-teeth: "*Sometimes I come knocking on the mill door! That always frightens them!*"

Peer had crept quietly away from the door and huddled with Loki in a far corner until his uncles returned. And later he'd checked the step. There was a dark wet patch on it, although it had not been raining.

His uncles did not notice. Unless something was under their noses, they never did. Even though they put out food for the Nis, they never talked about it, and Peer was sure they had never seen it.

He wrapped his cloak over his head and fell asleep, but dark water came spilling into his dreams, and he believed he was swimming in the middle of the millpond. He struck out for the bank, but he couldn't seem to reach it. Below him, Granny Green-teeth came rising through the water. She wrapped long, skinny arms around his neck and pulled him down for a kiss. *Good boy,* she crooned, *come to me, come to your old granny. Nobody else cares!*

No, no! cried Peer. He struggled to get away, but tangled in her strong arms he sank deep and deeper.

He woke sweating and shivering, all wound up in the cloak. The barn was completely dark, as there was no moon. Loki pushed a cold nose into his hand. A mouse whisked over his foot, and a scuffling noise overhead suggested the Nis. Peer stood up. He needed to go outside.

It was raining gently. A sweet smell of new-mown hay puffed from the damp fields. No chance of hearing Granny Green-teeth if she was out prowling through the wet bushes. The rain sounded like a thousand pattering troll feet, running toward him from all directions. It came on harder, as if it had been just waiting for him to step outside. Peer could not afford to let his only cloak get soaking wet. He felt his way along the side of the barn to the privy, a small stone shed built against the wall, pushed open the creaky old door, and slipped inside.

Here it was warm and smelly. Some Grimsson ancestor had built it years before, dug a deep trench, and erected a row of three wooden seats. Rudely, Peer pictured Uncle Baldur and Uncle Grim sitting there side by side with their trousers around their ankles. But it was a dry place to go. He sat down on the first seat.

It was really too dark to see anything much. *Just as well*, thought Peer, *or I might start imagining things*. There was a black shadow over to his left that was just the shape of a person sitting there. Probably a stain on the wall. He stared at it harder. Actually it wasn't so like a person. No one could really have such a short body and lumpy head, with one ear much, much larger than the other. No one could really—

The shadow sitting on the third seat coughed quietly, and Peer's hair stood upright on his head. Tearing the door open he hopped out into the yard, trying to run and haul his trousers up at the same time. He had the nasty impression, though he could not have sworn to it, that a second misshapen head had popped up through the middle seat as he rushed out.

He went quickly behind the barn after all, among the wet nettles, and returned to Loki, zinging with nervous shock.

It was a relief to hear the Nis again after all that. Peer called out to it and in a trembling voice, asked what he had seen.

"Lubbers," replied the Nis with a contemptuous sniff.

"Lubbers?" Peer cleared his throat. "What are they? I thought they were trolls."

The Nis would not come down and talk to him. Peer was out of favor. It was chasing spiders, and as he lay back he heard it muttering to itself: "Butter! They all promises butter to poor Nithing, but promises melt easy in the mouth!"

Oh dear. Peer propped himself up on one elbow. "I'm sorry, Nis. I did ask my friend to get you some butter, but she hasn't been able to bring me any. Please, what's a lubber? Would they hurt me?"

"Hurt you? Only if they catches you. Lubbers is stupid, slow," said the Nis impatiently. "Lubbers is low. Look where they live!"

Peer shivered. "I hate this place," he said vehemently. "Are there any more nasty creepy things living here? Besides my dear uncles, of course?" The Nis refused to tell him anything more, but still went stealing about with sudden little flurries of activity and snatching movements, which kept Peer awake.

"What *are* you doing?" he asked irritably.

"Collecting spiders," said the Nis from just overhead.

"Would you stop it and let me sleep?"

"Very well!" said the Nis, highly offended. "Too high and mighty to work for troll princess is too high and mighty to talk to poor Nithing!" It flounced away, and silence fell.

"Nis?" called Peer. "Nithing?"

No reply.

Next day there was an unaccountable plague of spiders in the mill. Big, small and medium sized, they scuttled here and there across the floor, ran out from every crack and cranny and wove webs in every corner. Uncle Baldur set Peer to get rid of them. It took him all day.

CHAPTER 10

Bad News

The days grew shorter as the summer passed. The weather took a turn for the worse, and sheets of stinging rain drove in on strong gales from the sea. People went about their work with sacks over their heads. Troll Fell vanished behind thick white mists and low gray clouds.

Autumn arrived with crisp biting mornings when the breath smoked on the air. Skeins of wild geese flew over, heading south. The birch leaves turned a clear pale yellow and fluttered to the ground. Some mornings the hilltops were white and the dips in the fields were blue with frost.

The trolls grew bolder. Things went badly at Hilde's house. Dishes mysteriously broke, and things were mislaid. The animals strayed, rain came through the roof, the children quarreled, and old Eirik kept losing his temper and saying that peace and quiet were what a poet needed, and could he not have them in his own son's house? As autumn grew older, the trolls became very active indeed. The family often saw them now at twilight, hiding near the walls, sending looks of ill will on the house or scuttering short and squat from behind the cow shed. They often heard their shrill, wailing cries. The little ones, Sigurd and Sigrid, met one rounding a corner one evening and were frightened by its pattering feet and slate-gray skin and odd eyes like live pebbles.

And safe inside in the warm, smoky room, the family sat worrying about Ralf. Gudrun expected him home daily. Every evening she sat at her loom, weaving a piece of good woolen cloth to make new clothes for him: "His old ones will be worn out for sure!" Nobody spoke of it, but everyone knew he was late, late, late.

And one frosty morning someone knocked at the door. As Hilde jumped up, it was pushed open and Bjorn Egilsson ducked inside, followed by his brother, Arnë. They stood awkwardly while Gudrun exclaimed and fussed, finding them seats and offering them breakfast.

Arnë looked tired and weatherbeaten. His hair and eyes were startlingly light against his brown tanned skin. His clothes were water stained. Hilde smiled at him, trying to coax an answering smile from his blue eyes, but he looked down nervously. Alf, the old sheepdog, shambled stiffly over to greet him, swinging his tail. Arnë stroked his ears as if grateful to have something to do.

"So—Arnë, tell us your adventures!" Gudrun invited him, but Hilde could tell there was a slight edge to her voice, and her hand shook as she poured ale for the visitors.

Bjorn and Arnë looked at each other. "Go on," said Bjorn quietly.

Arnë cleared his throat. "Well—as you know, I wanted to join Ralf's longship but missed the sailing. It was a week or two before I followed in my own boat. I was hoping to catch her at some point farther south. . . ."

He stopped and looked down at the floor again. Gudrun clutched Hilde's arm.

"At first I got plenty of news of her from villages along the coast. I didn't stop anywhere long and I was sure I'd catch up with them. Then—"

He took another deep breath.

"One day I got no news of them at all. And no news the next day. 'All right,' I thought, 'they've struck out to sea at last and I've missed them.' I was disappointed, but I joined one of those big, potbellied cargo ships instead.

"You know how news spreads among sailors? Everyone seems to know what everyone else is doing this season. There are no secrets. But I never heard anything more about *Long Serpent*. It was as though she'd vanished. And then—well, I'm afraid there's been news of a wreck. Part of a dragon-prowed longship was washed up on rocks south of Hammerhaven. No survivors."

Hilde gasped. Gudrun's fingers dug into her, and Eirik suddenly looked older than they had ever seen him. The little ones were pale.

"Is Pa dead?" wailed Sigrid. Hilde knelt and hugged her.

"We don't know that," said Bjorn quickly. "We just thought you ought to hear it from Arnë before the story got garbled all around the dale."

"Thank you," said Gudrun with a great deal of dignity.

Arnë looked very distressed. "I wouldn't have brought such news for the world," he muttered.

"It may not be true," said Bjorn.

"We must wait for more news," said Gudrun, knowing full well that more news was unlikely ever to arrive. Bjorn and Arnë got to their feet.

"I hope I'm wrong about this," said Arnë, taking Gudrun's hand. "If there's anything we can do, anything at all—"

Gudrun nodded, stifling a sob. Bjorn and Arnë exchanged a glance, and departed.

The household plunged into misery. Gudrun had been afraid for weeks, ever since the strong winds of early autumn. Now her weaving hung on the loom gathering dust while she sat silent by the fire with her head in her hand. Tears dripping from his face, poor old Eirik went off into a corner to make a funeral song. He mumbled a few brave lines, but then broke down. Hilde marched about furiously, doing the housework that Gudrun neglected. She made the little ones help, and taught them games to keep them busy. Spinning, knitting, cleaning, cooking—through all the endless round, she felt hollow with helpless fear. Was Pa really drowned? Would he never come home? Worst of all, would they ever know for sure?

The hardest work was the best. When the house was as clean as she could get it, Hilde took a pitchfork to the cow shed and began mucking that out. But at last she leaned against the smooth wooden rail of Bonny's stall and buried her hot face in her arms.

Now I know how poor Peer felt when he lost his father, she thought. And suddenly she saw just how much things had changed. If Pa never came home, how could she help to rescue Peer from his uncles?

She thought about that day in early spring when they had first met. She remembered Baldur and Grim jeering that Ralf would never come home. They had gloated about the dangers of the sea, storms, rocks, and sea serpents. She had laughed at them. Well, they had been right. The Grimsson brothers had won!

Hilde threw up her chin with a rush of anger and determination. "I won't *let* them win!" she exclaimed aloud. Bonny the cow looked at her in mild alarm. "They shan't have our sheep, for a start. If Pa's not coming back"—she swallowed tears—"then I'll go up Troll Fell and bring them down myself!" And she marched straight back into the house to tell her mother so.

Gudrun gasped in horror. "Go up on Troll Fell by yourself? At this time of year, with the trolls about? And wolves, and bears? And what about the Grimssons? After everything you've told us about them, why, I expect they're up there half of the time, thick as thieves with the troll king himself! You're not going, Hilde, not for a minute. As if we haven't enough trouble!"

"Then what will we do?" asked Hilde in a low voice. "Just give up? Hand everything over to the Grimssons? And what about poor Peer Ulfsson?"

"I'm sorry for the boy, but he's not our problem," exclaimed Gudrun wildly.

"All right!" said Hilde, very white. "But those are our sheep up on the Stonemeadow, and Baldur and Grim have already had the wool off them this year—and it was Peer who told me so. Oh, Ma! If I don't bring them down to our sheepfold, we'll lose them altogether. Pa would have done it weeks ago—if he'd been here!" Sudden tears rolled down her cheeks.

Eirik stirred. He had dried his eyes and a grimmer expression came over his face.

"The girl is right," he said unexpectedly. "If she was a boy, you'd let her go, Gudrun."

"Well she's not a boy!" Gudrun snapped. "She's my eldest daughter—and Sigurd is too young—"

"Girl or boy," Eirik persisted, "she can see what needs doing. The sheep *do* have to come down before winter. Ralf would be proud of her. Hilde, my lass, you stand up on your own two feet. That's the way to make them all respect you!"

Gudrun said with incredulous anger, "Are you encouraging her, Father-in-law?"

Eirik hunched himself a little and then nodded defiantly. Hilde mopped her eyes and planted a big kiss on the top of his head.

"I'll be all right, Ma. I'll take Alf. He'll look after me!"

"How can he? He's too old!" Gudrun protested.

"He knows every inch of the hills. He knows the sheep. I can't get lost with Alf. Look at him!"

The old dog had heard his name and was looking up inquiringly. Eirik slapped his thigh. "Knows every trick! The old ones are the good ones!"

With bad grace Gudrun gave way. "Well, I suppose you can go, Hilde—since your *grandfather* approves! But *be careful*! Get back before dark!"

"I'll try, Ma, but it's dark so early now—" Already Hilde felt better, wrapping herself up in a sheepskin cloak and pulling on a pair of soft leather boots. She grabbed a stick. "For cracking trolls on the head!" she joked.

"Oh, dear—is that wise?" Gudrun wrung her hands.

"Why not? Things can hardly get worse." She whistled to Alf, whose eyes brightened as he led her purposefully to the door.

"It doesn't look good," said Gudrun, looking out anxiously. The sky was overcast, and a chill wind swept across the farm-yard. "It looks like snow."

"All the more reason to fetch the sheep," Hilde retorted. "Look out, Granddad, it's slippery." Gudrun caught Eirik to prevent him from falling on the ice that the trolls now delighted in laying every night, smooth as glass, in all the places around the farm where people most walked.

"Get inside and keep warm," said Hilde impatiently. "And don't worry, I'll be fine. Come on, Alf!" She strode away, the old sheepdog trotting beside her.

Hilde knew that long hours of tramping hills lay before her. The high open pastures of Troll Fell, such as the Stone-meadow, were not fenced. The tough, independent little sheep could roam where they pleased and were often widely scattered. She and Alf would have to gather them all and make sure not to take any that belonged to a neighbor. Most of the sheep were marked in some way. Her father's sheep were clipped in the right ear, and an old ewe with a bell around her neck led the flock. Hilde hoped that the other sheep would stay close to her.

As she climbed up the shoulder of Troll Fell, the wind hit her, burning her ears and forcing tears from her eyes. More ominously, the first gray flakes of snow came whizzing past. Hilde tucked her chin into the sheepskin and pinned the cloak tighter around her neck. More flakes blew past. Then a heavy flurry of snow whirled down from the northeast. It swept about her, erasing the hillside, leaving nothing visible but a few blurred yards of wet, bent grass already catching the snow.

"Great!" muttered Hilde aloud. Alf looked at her question-ingly. "On we go," she told him. "I'm not giving up yet!"

The sheep seemed to have disappeared. Hilde listened carefully for the sound of bleating or the clonking of the sheep bell, but she heard only the wind hissing, driving the snow into the grass. The light was failing. Hilde trudged higher and higher up the hill, stumbling over stones and rab-bit burrows. She began to wonder if Baldur and Grim had taken the sheep away; perhaps there were none left to find! Then it dawned on her that the sheep would shelter from the weather on the western side of the crags, out of this keen wind. At once she turned her back to the wind and began plodding in that direction. Alf seemed to approve. He trotted briskly ahead of her, the wind blowing his thick fur up and showing the pale skin at the roots.

A blue, unfriendly twilight descended over Troll Fell, and the snow grew deeper. Hilde decided not to search for much longer. Gray shapes were slinking and sliding about on the edge of sight, and she remembered the trolls. And then Alf barked, once. He wanted her attention. He stood with one front paw raised, looking intently into the swirling snow.

"Have you found them?" Hilde asked. "Good lad! Go on then—bring 'em down." Alf leaped forward and disappeared into the gloom.

Hilde waited where she was, whistling and stamping her feet. In a moment a couple of sheep came jogging into view. The snow was piling up on their backs, but Hilde knew they couldn't feel it under their thick fleeces. Two more arrived at their heels—black faced and scrawny, but to Hilde a beautiful sight.

There was another distant bark from Alf. Hilde whistled again. Soon Alf arrived, head low, weaving along behind another little group of startled, huffy-looking sheep. A dismal bell clonked—he had found the old ewe. Alf looked extremely pleased with himself and grinned at her, panting, tongue hanging out.

"Good lad! Good boy," Hilde praised him. She did a quick head count and decided that there should be some more. "Go on, Alf! Seek 'em out!" Alf whisked once around the sheep he had found, nudging them into a compact group, and dashed off again into the gloom.

Hilde waited, rubbing her hands together and blowing on them. She was smiling to herself, thinking how nice it was to see the old dog so proud of his work, when something small and solid hurled itself into her back and knocked her down. Her stick flew from her hands. She groveled on the wet ground, twisting and grappling. The unseen attacker let go and backed off. She scrambled up dizzily, looking for her stick. It had spun off into the soft snow. Before she could find it, the creature scuttled back in and gripped her around the thighs. She looked down into the enigmatic yellow eyes of a small troll, doing its best to heave her off her feet. Hilde yelled and kicked. The frightened sheep scattered in all directions, but the troll clung with clammy strength, arms wrapped tightly around Hilde's legs, eyes unblinking. Frantic, she hammered its head and yelled again, then stuck two fingers in her mouth and blew a piercing whistle.

Alf came streaking downhill in answer, snarling ferociously. He was going so fast that he overshot and his back legs slid from under him as he turned in a flurry of wet snow to attack. The troll let go abruptly and melted into the darkness. Alf pursued it for a few yards, hackles up, barking furiously, before returning to Hilde to check that all was well. He was panting hard and his sides were heaving.

"Hey," said Hilde gently. "You brave old boy, what a good dog! Take it easy now!" She pulled him against her legs and patted him and rubbed his chest and neck. His heart was thudding hard against his ribs, but his eyes were bright. It was Alf's glory to be useful, and this was his great day.

"I think we'd better go," said Hilde. "Let's just round up the ones we've got, eh? They can't have gone far. Bring them in!" Alf soon collected the sheep again, and he and Hilde began to herd them along, Hilde keeping a sharp lookout. She was not quite sure of the way. They were probably near the top of the Stonemeadow, somewhere near the western edge, where the ground broke up into dangerous clefts, rocks, and cliffs. In the darkness and snow it would be easy to fall over the edge of one or simply get lost. The best thing was to go slowly and let Alf and the sheep pick their own path.

But following the animals was not easy. Alf seemed to know where he was going, but the sheep wandered. Alf kept busy trotting to and fro behind them to keep them moving, nipping this way and that to round up stragglers. Sometimes the sheep put on a burst of speed, their woolly backs jostling and bobbing ahead, and Hilde had to jog to keep up. It was now too dark to see where she put her feet, and she was afraid of twisting her ankle.

Suddenly an extra-strong gust of wind parted the whirling snow ahead of her and she saw, not too far ahead, a light, dim and smeary, such as might come from a traveler's lantern. Hilde's heart lifted. She was nearer the road than she had thought! She shouted, and heard an answering shout, blurred by the wind. Maybe Arnë or Bjorn had come looking for her. "Over here!" came the shout. "Over here!"

"Coming!" bellowed Hilde through cupped hands, wishing she had a lantern to signal back. The wind flung snow in her face like handfuls of gray soot. Alf barked, and the sound was whipped away.

"Come on!" Hilde told him. "This way!" She ran forward. Again the light gleamed through the snow, farther away than she had expected. Her feet stumbled on rising ground. "Where are you?"

"Where are you?" the voice blew back to her. Who was that? Bjorn or Arnë? Or maybe neither of them . . .

"I can't see you," Hilde called. She struggled on, her legs tiring. Each gasp filled her mouth with snowflakes. She coughed and panted on.

Another glimmer of light, farther away and weaker. Hilde

panicked. They were leaving her. She would be lost. She ran forward, with Alf bounding at her heels, leaving the sheep behind. The ground sloped away quite steeply. She slowed, afraid to go too fast. "Where are you?" she shouted again.

"Over here! Over here!" came the answering shout, nearer now. *The snow is confusing me*, thought Hilde, and reassured, she stepped out. But Alf sprang up and grabbed her sleeve with his teeth. Hilde slipped and sat down hard.

"What on earth—!" she began, rubbing her bruised bottom. "Alf, give over—let go!" Alf was tugging at her sheepskin cloak, growling. "What's wrong?"

An awful uneasiness overcame her; her skin crawled. The faraway light was returning, impossibly fast. No human being could run so smoothly over such rough ground. The light hurtled toward her, growing brighter and brighter, and halted suddenly in the air overhead. Hilde threw herself flat. With a soft *puff!* the light went out. There was a wild laugh. Something rushed past them in the darkness, and Hilde heard the loud laughter— *"Ho! Ho! Ho!"*—receding up the slope behind her.

Hilde sat shivering, afraid to move. She had nearly pitched over a cliff. She had just glimpsed the edge a few feet in front of her and didn't know how far it extended on either side. To go back would only lead her farther up to the top of Troll Fell. The creature, whatever it was—some kind of troll or mountain spirit—had led her completely astray. She sat tight, wondering what to do. But then Alf stood up beside her and shook himself, as if he was telling her the danger was over and he was ready to go on. Hilde got up too. Her knees wobbled with cold and shock, but she patted Alf's rough side with numb fingers and laughed.

"Good old Alf! They haven't done for us yet," she cried into the wind. "They don't know you! You can find the way back. Let's find those sheep!"

As she turned to follow the old dog, something odd happened. The dark night and the racing snow lit up as if a door had opened. And indeed it had. A few hundred yards up the slope, yellow light poured from a rift in the crag. As she watched in amazement, she saw a dark silhouette approach the lighted gap and disappear inside. Spindly limbs and large head—was this the troll-thing that had misled her?

And was it going home?

The wind whipped wet hair across her eyes and icy bullets of hail flew into her face. Hilde sheltered her eyes with her hands and looked again. The light was failing. A huge stone slab swung ponderously into place. The hillside rumbled at the shock, and all was dark. The troll door had closed.

Hilde touched Alf's neck. "Come!" she murmured, and they hurried down the hill, Alf leading her well away from the cliffs before finding the spot where they had left the sheep. After that it was a straightforward plod downhill. Hilde let Alf have his own way entirely. They reached the bottom of the Stonemeadow with no further adventures and found the road. Here the snow lay only a few inches deep, and Alf drove the little flock briskly along till they reached the track up to the farm. Then the sheep seemed to remember sheepfolds, shelter, and hay, and trotted willingly uphill again, bleating.

Gudrun had the door of the farmhouse open in a flash.

"Get in here this minute!" she ordered. Her face was white, and she began to hug Hilde but then held her off. "Get these wet things off straightaway—you're frozen!"

"The sheep!" Hilde protested.

"Oh, you clever girl, you found them! I'll put the sheep away. There's hot soup in the pot."

"Alf shall have some," declared Hilde. The old dog walked wearily into the house and collapsed by the fireside. He gave a perfunctory lick or two to his bedraggled fur and laid his head down.

"Dry him and give him some soup," Hilde called to Sigurd and Sigrid, rubbing her hair vigorously. "He was marvelous. I wouldn't be here if it wasn't for him. Ma, just wait till you hear our adventures! We found the door into Troll Fell!"

CHAPTER 11

The Dogfight

Down at the mill, Peer knew nothing about Hilde's adventures. But he soon heard the bad news that Ralf was missing. He heard it from Uncle Baldur's own lips.

He was sitting by the hearth one dark afternoon, cleaning his uncles' boots. Several pairs lay scattered around him, and he was painstakingly scraping them clean and greasing them to keep them supple and waterproof. The best pairs were thick, double-stitched deerskin lined with fur. Peer handled them enviously. His own shoes were so worn and split that he had wrapped string around them to stop them falling apart, and stuffed hay inside to try and keep his feet warm. They were always wet. His toes were red with painful chilblains.

He sat on a stool, as close to the fire as he could. He'd been out for hours, shoveling snow and carrying feed to the animals. There were a lot of them now. Uncle Grim had taken Grendel one morning and brought down some sheep that he claimed were all his, though Peer, looking suspiciously, spotted a variety of different marks. The sheep were penned behind a wattle fence in a corner of the yard, where their breath hung above their draggled woolly backs as they coughed. The cows and oxen spent each day munching quietly in their dark stalls. The hens never set foot beyond the barn door, now that the snow had arrived. They spent their days cackling and picking about in the warm straw where Loki lay curled up with his nose buried in his tail, giving them scornful glances from under his eyebrows.

As for the pigs, Uncle Grim's pride and joy—Peer hated his daily visits to pour a steaming slurry of warm mash into their trough. No matter how crisp and cold the day, how white the new-fallen snow, the pigpen was always a trampled mess of slimy black mud and rotten straw. Bristles and his sow would come screaming out of their hut, shoving to be first at the trough. Peer had to leap out of the way so as not to be trodden on or knocked over, or worse, sliced with Bristles' sharp little stained white tusks. And he hated the way they gobbled and grunted. They really did remind him of both his uncles.

The mill had stood silent for a week. The millpond was freezing. When the brook froze too, and it soon would, the mill would lose its power. Already the weir was fringed with icicles and the waterwheel glazed with dark ice. No power.

There was nothing that Uncle Baldur could do about it. While the ice lasted, he was no longer a miller. Just a farmer.

Peer glanced over his shoulder. Uncle Grim was asleep, rolled up in a rug on his bunk. He snored loudly and his little red mouth hung open in its vast tangle of black beard. Uncle Baldur was out. After ordering Peer to clean all the boots, he had left, telling Grim that he would stroll into the village to stretch his legs. Peer guessed his real intention was to share some ale with one of his few cronies.

Bored and lonely, Peer yawned, and smeared more grease onto the toe of the fifth boot. He hadn't seen Hilde for weeks. He supposed she was deliberately avoiding the mill; a good thing, for Uncle Baldur kept asking about her: "Where's your girlfriend?" and "When will you see her again?" Peer smiled scornfully. His uncle had even gone so far as to say, with a sentimental smirk, "Tell her to bring the little ones and brighten up the lives of two old bachelors." *Yercchh!* Peer rubbed the boot furiously.

Even so, he rather wished that Hilde would pass by. He missed her. Since the spider episode, the Nis was completely ignoring him, although he often heard it skipping about at night. There was no one to talk to. When he remembered last winter's fun, snowball fights and skating with the other boys in Hammerhaven, it seemed like another life. He tried not to think about it.

The door crashed open and Uncle Baldur stamped in, beating the snow from his mittens.

"He's dead!" he cried.

Uncle Grim jerked in mid-snore and opened his eyes. He struggled to sit up.

"Who's dead?" he snorted.

"Ralf Eirikson's dead, it's all around the village!" shrilled Uncle Baldur. "The ship's missing and they've all been drowned! Just what I said would happen, eh?"

He charged forward and pulled his brother to his feet; they flung their arms round each other and began a sort of stamping dance around the floor, thumping each other on the back, while Peer dropped the boot and sat in wide-eyed horror.

"Dead as a doornail," chortled Uncle Baldur. "Drowned!" He made horrible bubbling noises in his throat and pretended to throw up his arms as if sinking. Uncle Grim wheezed with laughter and Grendel leaped around them shattering the air with his heavy barks.

"Is this sure?" asked Uncle Grim, sobering suddenly.

"Certain sure," Baldur nodded. "Arnë Egilsson's been saying so. I went specially to ask him as soon as I heard. Seems the ship's been missing for weeks, and timbers washed up farther down the coast. She was due back long ago. They've sunk, that's obvious."

"Sunk, eh? And why?"

Uncle Baldur shrugged. "Who cares why? Shoddy workmanship, probably." He threw a spiteful glance at Peer, who sat with burning face and ears. "We know whose *father* helped to build it, don't we? It probably broke up in the first gale.

"Arnë didn't like telling me, but he couldn't deny the facts. And that brother of his, Bjorn, he married a seal woman. *He* knows what goes on at sea, if anyone does, and even he couldn't deny it. No, it's true all right."

Grim smacked his brother on the shoulder. "Good news, eh?" he grinned.

"The best!" Uncle Baldur agreed. "The land's ours now. No one will argue about that if Ralf's dead."

"What about the old man?" asked Grim.

"Old Eirik? That old dodderer?" Baldur laughed sneeringly. "If he tries to make a fuss about it we'll just say his memory's gone."

He paced up and down in excitement, slapping his great thighs. "We'll be rich, brother! We'll own the best half of Troll Fell! And after midwinter we'll be richer still. I'll put the new wheel in next spring. We can buy up the village and live like kings!" He shook his fist in the air.

"*Then* they'll know who's the big man round here! I'll *make* them bring their corn to me. We'll get the goods for the Gaffer now, all right. With Ralf out of the way, who's to stop us? We can do what we like!"

Uncle Grim nodded toward Peer. "The boy's listening," he growled.

"Who cares?" caroled Uncle Baldur. "He don't know what I'm talking about. Do you, boy?" He grabbed Peer by the back of the neck and shook him. "Do you?" he demanded.

"No," Peer lied. He felt sick. His father's lovely ship! Poor,

poor Hilde! Then with a stab of fear he realized what this meant for himself. No safety up at the farm. No shelter from Baldur and Grim.

Uncle Baldur whacked his ear and dropped him.

"This calls for a drop of ale," he declared, rubbing his hands together.

Uncle Grim shook his head. "Mead," he suggested.

"You're right," said Uncle Baldur, licking his lips. "Something strong."

He went rummaging in a dark corner and returned with a stone bottle, which he placed on the bench between him and his brother. Pulling out the stopper, he poured two generous measures into horn cups. He picked one up.

"Health!" He broke into a fit of coughing.

"Wealth!" returned Uncle Grim. They tipped back their heads and gulped it down. Uncle Baldur poured some more. Soon the two brothers were leaning on one another, giggling, choking, banging their cups down and singing noisily, while Peer mechanically finished cleaning the boots and lined them up by the door.

Then he sank to the floor and rested his head on his knees. *Midwinter,* he thought feverishly. *How can I escape before midwinter?* Midwinter! He had been talking and thinking and planning about it for months. Now he saw with a sudden, horrible shock that he had no idea when midwinter would be!

He thought back, counting on his fingers. How long since the first snow? Weeks? It seemed a long time. And the days were so short now: it was dark outside already. Midwinter must be close.

How stupid, how stupid of me, he thought anxiously. *I know, I'll ask the Nis. It's bound to know, it's so excited about the troll wedding and all that food. But then what?*

He gnawed his fingers. Uncle Baldur and Uncle Grim sounded so sure of themselves. What would they do? *"We'll get the goods for the Gaffer,"* Uncle Baldur had said. *"Who's to stop us with Ralf out of the way?"* Would they raid Hilde's farm? Kidnap her?

What can I do?

Someone banged on the door. Peer looked at his uncles. They were singing and shouting so loudly that neither they nor Grendel had heard. Peer shrugged and dragged himself up to open it.

With his hand on the latch he paused. What if Granny Green-teeth had come visiting, before the ice locked her in for the winter? Well, let her come! He jerked the door open but was relieved to see two ordinary men, muffled up against the cold. A cutting wind whirled into the house and snow powdered the floor as they stepped quickly inside and shook their clothes.

Uncle Baldur noticed the draft before he noticed the visitors.

"Shut that DOOR!" he yelled, breaking off his song. Then he saw the two men and staggered to his feet. "Hey," he prodded Grim, "look who's here! It's Arnë and Bjorn. The good-news bringers!" He waved his cup.

"Give 'em a drink," Grim hiccuped.

But Bjorn's good-natured face was stern. "Hey, Peer," he said quietly, dropping a friendly hand on Peer's shoulder. "Grim, Baldur," he went on, "we've not come to drink with you. We've come to say one thing. Leave Ralf Eirikson's family alone!"

Uncle Baldur sprawled back on the bench, sticking his legs out. His greasy red face gleamed in the firelight, and he laughed unpleasantly. He took another swig of mead and smeared his hand across his mouth.

"I don't know what you mean," he wheezed, winking at Grim.

"Yes, you do," said Arnë angrily. "We're talking about Ralf's land on Troll Fell. You're after it now he's dead. Like a couple of crows!"

"But you won't get it," said Bjorn. "Arnë and I'll support Eirik and his grandchildren when it comes before the Thing."

Peer felt like cheering. He glowed with admiration for the two young men. They looked like heroes as they stood there together, their faces tight with anger. Baldur and Grim exchanged dark glances.

"Why?" asked Baldur, with a suspicious scowl. "What's in it for you?"

"*Why?*" exploded Bjorn. "Because Ralf was a friend of mine. Because the land was his. Because you're a couple of cheating pigs who'd rob a widow and her family!"

"Don't bother trying to understand!" Arnë added.

Uncle Baldur went purple and surged to his feet. Grendel rose too, and the hair on his spine stood up in a bristling hedge as he lowered his head, growling.

"Out! Get out!" shouted Uncle Baldur. "Before I set the dog on you!"

"Oh, we'll go," said Bjorn coldly. "I wouldn't stay in your stinking mill for all the gold under Troll Fell!" He turned on his heel and strode for the door, but Uncle Baldur grabbed his arm. His face was blotchy and his breath whistled.

"Gold?" he croaked. "What do you mean? What do you know?"

Bjorn stared at him in distaste. "Get off me," he said, jerking his arm free.

"Who told you about the troll gold?" Uncle Baldur spat into his face.

"Oh, *that's* your game, is it?" said Bjorn. He whistled and nodded. "Well, don't you worry, Grimsson. The only thing I know about troll gold is this: It's unlucky, and I don't want anything to do with it. And if you'll take my advice, neither will you. Good-night!"

Peer scrambled hopefully to his feet and stepped forward. If he could only catch Bjorn's eye, if he could only go with him! But this time Bjorn did not notice Peer. He and Arnë slipped through the door and vanished into the night.

Uncle Baldur slammed the door and went back to the fire.

"He knows nothing," he said, sitting down heavily beside his brother. He tried to pour himself another drink, but the bottle was empty, and he swore.

"There's no fun for a man round here," he grumbled, tipping the bottle upside down and sucking the end. "Nothing but work, work—"

"Let's have a dogfight," suggested Grim suddenly. Peer sat up in alarm.

"What with?" asked Uncle Baldur scornfully. "That thing of the lad's? He wouldn't last a minute with Grendel."

"He's nippy," offered Grim. "Bet you he'd last five."

A grin spread over Baldur's face. "All right!" he said.

"NO!" shrieked Peer, leaping to his feet. "You can't! You can't, you bullies!" He hurled himself at Uncle Baldur, pounding him with his fists, kicking and biting. It was like attacking a mountain. His blows did no good at all. Uncle Baldur yanked him off the ground with one hand and chucked him across the room. Peer scrambled up, dazed but desperate, and rushed forward again.

"The boy's mad!" said Uncle Baldur. He grabbed Peer and twisted his wrist up behind his back in a painful arm lock. "Keep still or I'll break yer arm," he grunted. "Go and fetch the dog, Grim. The boy might set him loose."

"Let go of me," panted Peer, still struggling, as Uncle Grim nodded and went out into the yard. "Let me go!" He twisted and turned, but Uncle Baldur tightened the arm lock until Peer gasped with pain. Tears of fury and terror filled his eyes.

Loki trotted in at Uncle Grim's heels, looking wary and puzzled.

"They can't fight in here," said Uncle Baldur over Peer's head.

"No," Grim agreed, "we'll have it in the yard. Take a look at him. I give you ten to one he lasts a good five minutes before Grendel grips him. He's quick, you see."

"Done!" Baldur grinned. "Speed won't save him from Grendel. One good crunch and it'll all be over!"

Peer couldn't believe they were talking about his beloved dog.

"Loki won't fight," he said defiantly. "He can't fight, he doesn't know how!"

"Then I'll win my bet," said Uncle Baldur calmly.

"Grendel will kill him!" cried Peer.

"The dog's no use anyway," grunted Uncle Grim. "Can't work."

"I'll train him!" Peer begged. He knew it was no good. Uncle Baldur dragged him outside with Loki, while Uncle Grim brought Grendel along by the collar, holding up a flaring torch in the other hand to light the dogfight. The snow had stopped falling but was blowing about the yard, chased by a cruel little wind. It was an unbearably cold night.

Peer looked at the two dogs in despair. Grendel dwarfed little Loki. He was built like a wolf, but thicker and taller, with massive head and powerful jaws. His eyes, red with malice, were fixed on Loki in evil enjoyment. He growled busily, working himself up. The thick collar disappeared into the deep fur at his throat as he strained forward.

Loki was scared. His tail curled between his legs, and he trembled.

"Uncle Baldur! I know your plans," shouted Peer suddenly. "I know about the trolls' wedding, and your horrible bargain! If you kill Loki, I'll never go! You can't make me! And what's more, you'll never get Hilde. She knows it all, too! I told her! You'll never get Hilde without my help!" He stopped, wondering what he was saying. Uncle Baldur's grip had tightened, but he didn't move. Instead he laughed.

"Clever boy!" he sneered. "Cleverer than we'd thought, eh, Grim? Thinks he knows a lot. But it makes no difference. You've got no choice. You'll do as I say."

"I'll run away!" shouted Peer, beside himself.

"Run?" Uncle Baldur mocked. "You haven't got the guts. Where would you run? Who'd want you? Besides, there's no time, you little fool. Midwinter is here!"

Peer could not suppress a startled jerk.

"Didn't you know?" jeered Uncle Baldur. "The famous wedding is tomorrow night! And since you know so much, you know we're going to be rich. Loaded with gold!"

"You may be rich," Peer yelled, "but everyone will still hate you!"

There was a fractional silence. Then—

"Eat him, Grendel!" yelled Uncle Baldur, releasing Loki. At the same moment Uncle Grim let go of Grendel, who sprang snarling forward.

Loki took one look and ran for his life. But Grendel's long legs gained on him. At the edge of the sheepfold Loki doubled back, his front and back legs crossing each other in his efforts to escape, and his tail tucked in. Grendel overtook him and the two dogs merged in a rolling tangle near the barn wall, falling over and over in a spray of snow. "Gren–del! Gren–del!" shouted Baldur and Grim.

"Loki! Run!" screamed Peer, clawing at his hair. Grendel bayed and made savage worrying noises. Loki yipped wildly in terror.

Suddenly an avalanche of snow slumped off the barn roof on top of the two dogs, half burying them. There was a moment's surprised silence as they struggled to rise, shaking themselves free. Though his eyes were glued to Loki, Peer caught a flicker of movement scampering lightly along the eaves and was sure it was the Nis.

"Oh . . . thank you!" he breathed.

Loki got his wits back before Grendel did, and without a second's hesitation he jumped out of the drift and raced across the yard toward the road. "Head him off!" shouted Uncle Baldur. Grim tried to bar Loki's way, waving the blazing torch. But Loki, with a speed born of terror, whizzed between his legs and was out of the yard and over the wooden bridge before anyone could stop him. Grim staggered, slipped, and went down, cursing. Charging after Loki like a bull, Grendel trampled across his master. Peer and Uncle Baldur ran past and followed the two dogs over the icy bridge. Peer's freezing fingers clung to the handrail as he crossed in desperate haste. Where, oh where, was Loki?

Then he heard a noise that raised the hair on his neck. A deep shivering howl of triumph, that quivered up and up until it seemed to reach the frosty stars. It lingered in the cold air and held him motionless till it died away. Uncle Baldur, too, was frozen in his steps. Grim came limping up behind them, the blazing branch held in one hand, the other hand pressed to his hip.

"He's got the little beggar," he said in satisfaction.

Tears of horror rose in Peer's eyes. "No!" he cried wildly, running forward. Terrified of what he might find, he stumbled along the kicked-up tracks leading up the path to the millpond. His two uncles followed. Baldur was grumbling.

"No fun at all—didn't get to see anything. Call that a fight? Got any more good ideas, Grim?"

"Shut up," snarled Grim. "At least he got the little rat. And good riddance, I say."

Peer blundered out of the bushes at the edge of the millpond and stopped dead.

A few yards away Grendel stood with his back to Peer, hackles raised and head lowered threateningly. At the very brink of the millpond, Loki faced him at bay. Loki's head was up and he looked this way and that with quick, desperate movements.

Peer could see why Grendel had howled in triumph. Loki was trapped. There was nowhere for him to run. He was standing at the end of a narrow tongue of land between the millpond and the second sluice. On one side the millpond reflected the starlight with a thin layer of milky ice. On the other was the sluice, and a steep drop to the rapidly freezing stream as it looped away to join the millrace below the bridge.

Grendel looked around as Grim and Baldur lumbered up. His breath steamed in hot clouds around his open jaws. The flames from Grim's torch lit the snow to rosy warmth and glistened on every yellow tooth in Grendel's head. He was clearly waiting for his masters to watch him bring the fight to its end. Even across the yards of snow, Peer could see Loki trembling. He turned away, sick at heart.

"Good lad, Grendel," puffed Uncle Baldur. "Go get 'im!"

Savagely Grendel rushed forward. Peer clapped his hands over his eyes, but lowered them at a shout from Baldur. Loki had turned and leaped out onto the ice. Amazingly, it held him. He slithered across it, paws scrabbling.

"Oh, Loki . . . go on, go on," panted Peer.

Beside him Uncle Grim gave a bellow of alarm. "Grendel! Stop!"

It was too late. Mad with rage, Grendel launched himself after Loki. There was a splintering crash. Far too heavy for the fragile ice, he went straight through it and was left struggling in the black water.

Grim ran to the edge of the bank. He plunged the branch he held into the water. The flames sizzled out. "Here, Grendel!

Grip hold!" he shouted. But Grendel took no notice. He tried to clamber out on the other side, snarling murderously and raking at the ice with his claws. It broke into crazy pieces. He could smash his way across!

Loki had reached the far bank by now. He tried to scramble up, but it was steep and slippery. He got halfway, clinging desperately with his front paws, kicking himself up with his back legs, but the loose snow collapsed under him and he tumbled down onto the ice, which still held. It must be stronger there, where the water was shallower; but then it could hold Grendel too! Back on his feet, Loki flung himself again at the bank.

Grim straightened. He turned to Baldur. "Pay up!" he said.

"He'll catch him yet," said Uncle Baldur, watching Grendel crashing his way through the brittle ice.

"The bet was, before five minutes!" Grim reminded him.

Again Loki lost his feet. His twisting body fell back onto the ice. Grendel was halfway there by now, his great weight breaking a jagged passage. Peer could not stand it. Without even thinking, he filled his lungs and ran forward. *"Granny!"* he yelled, so loudly his voice cracked. *"Granny Green-teeth!"*

The echo jumped to and fro between the mill and the trees. Baldur and Grim glanced at him in angry surprise. Then Baldur bit off an exclamation and pointed.

Something had happened to Grendel out there in the middle of the pond. He was no longer forging his way across but writhed splashing in the water, biting at something that seemed to have risen beside him. It was hard to see in the bitter starlight. Peer strained his eyes. Could those be skinny white arms twining about Grendel's neck, pulling him under? And that strange lump that broke the surface for a moment among the floating ice—was it a head? A dark stain rose and spread like oil across the water; the chunks of broken ice danced and clashed; there was another thrashing struggle just below the surface, a choked-off bark—and Grendel was gone.

"*Granny Green-teeth!*" Peer whispered, hugging himself and shuddering.

There was a loud wail from Uncle Grim. "Grendel!"

"She's got him," said Uncle Baldur, shrugging, but his mouth was set.

"I was *fond* of that dog!" moaned Uncle Grim, wiping a tear from his eye.

On his third try Loki reached the top of the bank and hurtled away into the woods, out of sight.

"He'll never win another dogfight," said Baldur callously.

Uncle Grim forgot his sorrow. "You still owe me, Baldur," he said sternly.

"I'll pay you when we're rich," said Baldur. "And we'd better get on with that!" He stared at Peer, and Peer quailed, fully expecting to be blamed for Grendel's awful fate. But it seemed that Uncle Baldur had taken his shout as a warning, and wasn't thinking of that.

"Tomorrow is midwinter's night," he said softly, still staring at Peer. "Don't forget, Grim, we're going to a wedding! I think it's time we went to get the presents!"

Peer tried to dash for it, but Uncle Baldur caught him by the arm. "You're not going anywhere, my lad," he said. "What shall we do with him, Grim? We don't want to take him along with us, do we?"

Grim shook his head. "Lock him up," he growled.

"Good idea. But where?"

"Shut him in the privy," suggested Uncle Grim. "There's no window, and we can block up the door."

They grabbed Peer and hustled him down the path to the mill. Peer tried to fight, but he was utterly exhausted, shaking with cold and shock, and in the end he just hung limply and let them drag him along. Uncle Baldur hauled open the privy door and thrust him inside. "You'll not die of cold," he said, joking roughly. "Where there's dirt, there's warmth." He shoved the door shut and Peer heard his two uncles piling logs against it. With a last effort he beat his fists against the door, screaming, "Let me out! Where are you going?"

"To pay a little visit to Ralf's farm, of course," came Baldur's muffled voice. Peer caught a stifled sob from Grim and a hiccup of "Poor Grendel!" Then their feet clumped away, leaving Peer to gasp for his breath in the cold and stinking darkness.

CHAPTER 12
Stolen in the Storm

There's a storm brewing," Eirik said to Gudrun. "I can feel it in my bones."

Gudrun gave a vicious slap to the dough she was kneading. "And what if there is? I don't have to worry about storms anymore. Not since that accursed longship sank!"

Hilde, pulling on her thick, fur-lined boots, looked uneasily at her mother. Gudrun was very pale these days, and her temper had worn to a thread.

"I don't think it's snowing, Grandpa," she said peaceably. "It's just freezing hard." She stood up and pulled on an old jerkin that had belonged to Ralf. It was much too large for her: the sleeves came down over her hands and kept them warm, which was why she liked it. She belted it in with a piece of string, threw a cloak over it, and took the lantern down from its hook.

"I'll light this and go to feed the cows," she announced.

Eirik, rocking dreamily by the fire, looked up. "I'll help," he offered.

"Oh, I don't need any help, Grandpa!" said Hilde, dismayed.

"Don't be an old fool, Eirik," Gudrun said, adding in a more kindly voice, "You just sit still and have another nap."

Eirik's head came up. "When I was a young man," he said stiffly, "I could do three men's work in a day, and I had enough left over to thrash anyone who gave me a fight and dance all night in the Long Hall when there was a feast on!"

"Drink yourself under the table, more like," sniffed Gudrun. She poked the dough crossly. It took the imprint of her finger meekly and slowly began to ease out the dent.

"And I wasn't asleep," added Eirik sulkily. "I was composing."

Gudrun's expression showed that she thought the two were identical. She rolled her eyes and looked at Hilde.

"Well, it's all right," said Hilde hastily. "Sigurd and Sigrid can come out with me and Eirik can keep an eye on them. Let them have some fresh air."

She strode over to the sleeping benches, where Sigurd and Sigrid were playing a game that involved tunneling under the blankets, and dragged them out shrieking and resisting. She told them fiercely to keep quiet or else, pushed their boots onto their feet, and pulled on their woolly hats.

"We don't want to go out," wailed Sigrid.

"You'll do what you're told!" hissed Hilde.

"Can we have a snowball fight?" asked Sigurd.

"Certainly, if you don't go out of Grandfather's sight," said Hilde briskly.

"I don't want to," began Sigrid, but stopped when Hilde scowled at her.

"All set, Grandpa?" she asked. Eirik nodded. While Hilde had been getting the little ones ready, Gudrun had been wrapping Eirik up to the point where, if he fell on the ice, he would hardly even bruise himself. He was almost spherical with wrappings.

Alf lay curled up at the fireside. He raised his head and pricked his ears at the sight of all this activity, but Hilde told him, "Stay!" She did not need the old sheepdog just for tending the animals, and it was very cold outside. She wanted to look after him. He flicked his tail politely and laid his head back down.

Hilde filled her pockets with stones—she kept a small pile by the door, handy for throwing at trolls—picked up the lantern and an armful of hay, and bundled the little ones ahead of her out the door. They immediately screamed with delight and slid off across the icy yard. Gudrun appeared in the doorway, supporting Eirik, who shook her off irritably and stepped after Hilde. He staggered and she dropped the hay to help him.

"Pick it up, pick it up, girl," he shouted angrily. "Dropping good fodder all over the yard! I can manage."

"Sigurd, Sigrid," screamed Hilde, "come back here and pick up this hay!"

"Now, Father-in-law, do take care!" shrilled Gudrun.

"Women, women," shouted Eirik, really losing his temper. "Cluck, cluck, never leave you alone. I wish my son was here. He'd know I'm not in the grave yet!" He slipped on a particularly glossy patch of ice and sat down hard.

Hilde rushed to pick him up. Sigurd and Sigrid threw hay about, quarreling. Gudrun leaned half out of the doorway, clinging to the doorpost and calling instructions. Eirik sat puffing with shock.

"It's your fault, girl," he said to Hilde. "You distracted me."

Someone gave an apologetic cough. "Can we help?" Hilde looked up to see Arnë and Bjorn climbing over the gate. The household stood around in embarrassed silence while the two young men pulled Eirik to his feet and dusted the snow off him tactfully. Eirik dabbed at himself shakily, muttering things.

"Ah—it was the ice," explained Hilde awkwardly. "It was so slippery that he—he slipped."

"Ah, yes, it's slippery stuff, ice," said Arnë with a grin. He became serious again. "Are you all right now, Eirik? We've brought some news for you."

"What—again?" snapped Gudrun from the doorway before she could stop herself. Then she looked sorry and stood back into the room, holding the door open and saying,

"Come inside, then. You'll all freeze standing out there. For goodness' sake, hurry! I'm losing all the warmth."

They trooped into the house, Arnë and Bjorn at the rear. Once inside, they stood nervously, stepping sideways hastily as Gudrun came past them after shutting the door.

"Sit!" she told them sharply. "You're in the way. Hilde, where's your manners? Fetch Arnë and Bjorn some ale."

"In some houses," Eirik grumbled under his breath, "it's the man who calls for ale!"

Looking sheepish, Bjorn opened his mouth to speak, but Gudrun stopped him.

"Not a word! Not a word of your news do I wish to hear till we've shown you some hospitality. Goodness knows this house has had enough trouble since Ralf left, but we still know how to welcome our neighbors. That is"—she stopped in her tracks and stared at him, worried—"it isn't *bad* news, is it?"

Bjorn shook his head and Gudrun was reassured. Hilde passed the ale round and it was drunk in an atmosphere of polite discomfort.

"It's nothing much," said Arnë when Gudrun finally allowed him to speak, "only we spoke to the Grimsson boys today. We came on from the mill, in fact. Baldur Grimsson has heard about Ralf. As you know they were never—um— friends, so he was—celebrating, I'm afraid."

"Boasting how he was going to take Ralf's land," Bjorn explained.

"We wanted to wipe the smile off his fat face. We told him we're on your side, Gudrun. I'm sure most people are."

"We told him to leave you alone," added Bjorn.

"Did you see Peer? Was he all right?" Hilde asked quickly.

Bjorn looked thoughtful. "Yes, he was there. I hope he's all right.... There was a little bit of noise going on when we left, and I forgot to speak to him."

"Bjorn lost his temper," Arnë explained.

Gudrun's eyes were moist. She mopped them quickly with her apron. "You're such good friends!" she exclaimed, stretching out her hands to them. The young men flushed.

"So we'll keep an eye on the Grimssons for you!" Arnë went on hastily. "If Eirik has no objection, that is." Gudrun and Hilde, slightly startled, turned to Eirik.

"What?" said Eirik. "No, er—of course not. Keep an eye on them for all you're worth, young fellow!"

"Good," said Arnë. "If they start any trouble, let us know." He stood up.

"I'll come out with you," cried Hilde and slipped out ahead of them as Bjorn and Arnë said good-bye to Gudrun. She crossed into the yard and surprised three small trolls stealing the scattered hay.

"Drop it!" she yelled, scrabbling in her pocket for stones. They bolted under the gate, dropping armfuls as they went. Hilde knelt to gather it up. As she stuffed it under her arm and started for the cow shed, she met Arnë and Bjorn coming away.

"Are you all right? We heard you shout," Bjorn asked.

"Quite all right, Bjorn, thank you. I was frightening away a few trolls."

Arnë gave her an admiring look. "So you know how to deal with them?"

"I'm a pretty good shot," Hilde boasted.

"But where are you going with the hay? Feeding the cow?"

"Yes, I'm going to do the chores."

"Can I help?" asked Arnë. Bjorn grinned and nudged him.

"No, no!" said Hilde quickly, blushing. "You should get home. Grandfather's bones tell him a storm is coming." As she spoke, she realized that it had begun to snow again. "And it looks as if he's right!" she added.

Arnë and Bjorn said good-night and hurried off, while Hilde dived into the dark cow shed, shutting the door firmly. Smiling to herself, she threw her armful of hay into the manger and hung the lantern on a hook. The light was feeble. Close by, a black shadow heaved itself to its feet and mooed gently.

Hilde worked rapidly, cleaning the two stalls and throwing down fresh straw. When she had made Bonny and the calf comfortable, she left the shelter of the cow shed and tramped across the wild white yard. Banging three times on the farmhouse door, she waited shivering while Gudrun took down the heavy wooden bars on the inside. Then she jumped in, gasping and laughing and brushing snow off herself.

"Brrr! Shut the door, mother! Whatever are you waiting

for?" she asked, seeing Gudrun hold the door ajar.

"For Sigurd and Sigrid, of course. Aren't they with you?"

"No!" said Hilde, alarmed. "Weren't they with you?"

Gudrun slammed the door. "I thought they went out after you the second time. They went out just before Bjorn and Arnë."

"They never joined me. I've been mucking out."

They looked at each other silently.

"Listen," said Gudrun in a low voice. She pointed at Eirik, snoring by the fire. "Don't wake him yet. Take the lantern and go around the steading—call them. They may be building a snow fort or something. If not—ah!" She moved her hands despairingly. "What then?"

"What *next*?" said Hilde grimly. "Don't worry, Mother. I'll find them." She grabbed the lantern and plunged back out into the darkness.

The cold wind flung her cloak out behind her. The lantern shone on snow whirling on the ground, picked up and flung about by the wind. It was hard to walk straight.

"Sigurd?" she shouted. "Sigurd!" adding under her breath, "Miserable little scamp!"

"Sigrid, where are you? Come in at once. Come on, supper's ready!

"Sigurd! Come here *now*!

"Children! I'll smack you if you don't come!"

No answer. A night bird shrieked—what bird would be out in such a night?

"*Huuu—huuuu!*" She shivered in recognition: the trolls were out. The wind flicked a handful of snow into her face. She wiped her eyes and followed the cow shed wall around to the sheepfold. Snow was drifting against the fence on the windward side. She waded into it and leaned over the rail, swinging the lantern. The sheep lay huddled together in the shelter of the fence, half-melted snow on their backs. They chewed steadily; one stood up, hoping for food.

"You've been fed," Hilde told it. "Sigrid! Sigurd!"

No answer.

She had a new idea and held the lantern close to the ground, searching for tracks. But the snow was filling them up rapidly. Her own tracks were obvious, going to and from the cow shed, and there were a lot of larger half-covered prints, which must belong to Bjorn and Arnë. The small, light tracks of the two little children seemed to have disappeared as completely as they had themselves.

"Oh, where *are* you?" she wailed, tears pricking her eyes. The wind gusted and her cloak flapped. There was no reply.

Suddenly she saw two small gleams, close together and low down. Staring, she noticed stealthy movements. Trolls were creeping up to the very edge of her lantern's pool of light, and their eyes reflected flashes of green and red. Hilde stamped her foot and shouted. They scattered, but a moment later a snowball curved through the air and splashed against her ear. Another followed, and then a hail of snowballs flew at her, some weighted with stones. Covering her eyes, she stumbled back to the house.

Gudrun opened the door quickly.

"Have you found them?"

"No, not a sign. Ma, the trolls are out there. It's so dark, I can't see anything. They've been snowballing me. Ma, can the trolls have stolen them?" She clutched Gudrun's arm and they stared at each other, white faced.

"We must tell Eirik," said Gudrun. She ran to him and shook his shoulder. "Eirik, wake up! Wake up, Sigurd and Sigrid are missing!"

Eirik opened his eyes with a start and listened, bewildered, while Hilde and Gudrun gabbled.

"They're missing. . . ."

"It was after Bjorn left!"

"No, it was before!"

"They went out with you the first time."

"I know, but—"

"Did they ever come back in?"

"I don't remember. Did they, Grandfather?"

Eirik slapped his knee in irritation. "What are you talking about?" he asked.

Hilde repeated the story in desperation. "They're *lost*! In the *snow*! And the *trolls* are out! Oh, I'm so sorry I ever smacked Sigurd! And I made them go out! Oh, if only they come back, I'll never be mean to them again! Sweet little Sigrid with her little fair plaits!" She began to cry.

"Have you looked for them?" asked Eirik.

Gudrun's control broke. "Of *course* she's looked for them!

Why can't you *listen*? Oh, whatever shall we do? My poor little twins, lured away to die in the snow. Oh, I told Ralf there'd be trouble with the trolls, I *told* him, but did he ever listen to me? Oh, Sigurd, Sigrid, what shall we do?" She threw her apron over her head and sat down crying hysterically. Hilde hugged her, but Eirik struggled upright in his chair.

"Hush, Gudrun, hush," he began tentatively. This having no effect, he cleared his throat and then thundered, "Woman!"

It worked. Gudrun raised a startled face from her apron. She dabbed at her eyes and gave a final sniff and hiccup.

"Will you be quiet?" demanded Eirik. He got to his feet in great excitement. "It's not the trolls. It's not the trolls, I say. It's the Grimssons who've stolen our children away!"

"The Grimssons?" asked Gudrun wonderingly.

"Of course it is!" Eirik raised his stick and whacked it down. "What did you tell us about them, Hilde? Didn't they want a pair of children? And isn't tonight midwinter's eve?"

"They've taken *Sigrid*?" screamed Hilde. "They've taken *Sigurd* and *Sigrid*?"

There was pandemonium.

"I'll kill them!" yelled Hilde, shaking her fists. Alf leaped to his feet, barking loudly.

Eirik was still explaining. ". . . crept up under cover of the dark and snow—probably followed Arnë and Bjorn—lay in wait for the children—"

"All that fuss when you fell over," gasped Hilde, remembering. "Perhaps they grabbed them then! There did seem a lot of big footprints, but I never thought— Oh, I can't bear it! They'll be so frightened." She turned around. "Mother, where are you going?"

Gudrun, white lipped, was wrapping herself up. "To look for them, of course. Hilde, you stay here and look after Granddad."

"By Odin," shouted Eirik furiously, grabbing for his boots, "you take me for a fool, you do! Hilde, you will stay here. Gudrun, you may come with me. We shall go to Arnë Egilsson's and raise the village. Ha!" He stamped his foot down into a boot and broke into an old battle chant.

Hilde looked at her mother helplessly. Gudrun shrugged. Her pale face relaxed and her set mouth softened into a very faint smile.

"He's exactly like his son," she remarked proudly.

CHAPTER 13

The Nis to the Rescue

Peer leaned against the privy wall, taking deep, slow breaths to fight down the panic. He was so cold that in spite of Uncle Baldur's last words to him, he rather thought he might die before morning. That would spoil their plans, he thought bitterly.

He crouched down, shivering, wrapping his arms around his knees to try and preserve some warmth. The uneven dirt floor was usually wet, but now the puddles had frozen hard. It was too dark to see. He closed his eyes. If he did that, he could pretend there was a light. He could pretend the door was open—that he could walk out.

The only comfort was that Loki had got away. Peer couldn't think what would happen to him or where he would go, but at least Grendel had not killed him. It was Grendel who was dead!

"Never thought I'd be grateful to Granny Green-teeth," he muttered through chattering teeth.

Everything else was a disaster. Baldur and Grim were on their way up to Hilde's farm. They would capture her. He imagined the two big men kicking the door open and simply dragging her out. How could her mother and her old grandfather stop them? He groaned aloud. Trapped here—his heart banged painfully—trapped here, there was no way he could warn Hilde or do anything to help. With Hilde in their power, they would return to the mill for him, Peer, and drag the pair of them off up Troll Fell. Hilde and he would become slaves of the trolls, and the Grimssons would collect their golden reward.

As for Loki, he would probably die in the woods, lost and cold and starving. He was a pet, with no chance of surviving in the wild! Peer groaned again in anguish.

There was a slithering sound somewhere over in the corner. Peer went very still. New fear tingled through him. He had completely forgotten about the other inhabitants of this privy.

The slithering sound came again, accompanied by a sort of creaking noise. Peer imagined something hoisting itself through one of the holes in the wooden seat. Now there was a sound of snuffly breathing. Trying to control his own breathing, he sat motionless.

A voice spoke suddenly. "'Oo's there?" it squeaked.

Peer dared not answer. There were some more creaking and slithering noises. A second voice spoke from the pit below, hollow and muffled. "What's up?"

"There's someone 'ere!" squeaked the first voice.

"Light coming up," boomed the second voice. In utter amazement Peer saw the three holes in the long wooden seat light up, throwing three round patches of light onto the rough roof. Black shadows moved dizzily down the walls as an arm came up through the middle hole, carrying a bluish flame.

The creature in the corner reached out and took it; the flame transferred easily from the first hand to the second and seemed not to belong to any oil lamp or taper. It was just a flame, flickering away by itself.

The second creature's head now appeared through the hole, twisting this way and that. It spotted Peer and there was a squeal.

"Ooh! Look at that!"

"It's a boy," declared the first one in deep disgust.

Peer had never seen such strange-looking beings. Their heads reminded him of turnips. They were lumpy and blotchy and bewhiskered. The one in the corner had an ear that stuck out like a cabbage leaf on one side of its head, while the other ear was small and knobby. The one peering out of the hole seemed to have no ears at all. And the nose on it! And the mouth! Like a thin line with no lips!

The one in the corner sneezed juicily, and the flame bent and danced.

"Don't blow it out!" snapped the other.

"Can't help having a cold," said the first one defensively, smearing its hand across its face. Its great nose wobbled.

"Are you—lubbers?" quavered Peer.

The first one jumped and the flame swerved and nearly went out. "It talks!"

"Of course it talks," growled the second lubber. "All boys talk, you fool. Give me that!" It clambered awkwardly through the hole and snatched the flame back. Then it crossed its legs and sat on the edge of the seat, looking at Peer.

"Whatcher doing here, then?" it asked chattily, but its bald turnip head and slit-like features did not reassure him.

Peer cleared his throat. "I don't want to be here," he began cautiously.

"*No one* wants to be here," interrupted the first lubber. "*We* don't want to be here. Do we?" it asked its friend.

"No, I mean—my uncles locked me in," Peer explained.

The lubber seemed astonished.

"You mean you can't get out?" it asked.

"No," Peer faltered, aware of making a mistake. The lubber in the corner nudged its friend.

"He can't get out!" it said.

"Yeah," said the lubber with the light. "I heard."

There was a moment's silence while they both stared at Peer, and then as if by unspoken agreement they both shuffled a bit closer to him along the bench.

"So," said the lubber with the light. "Right cozy little party, this."

There didn't seem to be any reply to that. During the next minute's silence both the lubbers came a little bit closer again.

Peer shifted anxiously. Quietly he pushed the door, testing it. It would not move. The Grimssons must have stacked half the woodpile against it.

"That's interesting, your light," he said quickly. "How do you do it? I mean, what does it burn?"

"Gas," said the first lubber. But Peer had never heard of gas.

"Plenty of gas down there," said the second lubber, pointing into the hole behind it.

"Where there's muck, there's gas," they chimed together.

"It's the only benefit of living in a place like this," said the first lubber.

"Watch this," said the lubber with the light. It opened its mouth, wider and wider, till it looked as if its throat had been cut. It placed the flame inside its mouth and shut it. For a moment its cheeks glowed like a lantern, purple and red. It gulped, and the flame went out.

In the ensuing darkness Peer felt both the lubbers scuffling much, much nearer.

"Then I snap my fingers," said the lubber's voice, almost in his ear, "and back comes the light. Neat, or what?"

The bluish, bobbing flame appeared not far from Peer's nose.

"It's his party trick," said the other lubber. They were now one on either side of Peer and he did not know which way to look.

"It's very clever," he said desperately.

"It *is* clever," agreed the lubber. "It's very, very clever, but you know what? It always—makes me—*hungry!*"

Its mouth yawned open next to Peer's shoulder. He leaped aside, cannoning into the other lubber. The feel of it made his flesh crawl; it was clammy and cold.

"Grab him," shouted the lubber with the light, "the first square meal in ages, I'm sick of beetles and slugs—"

It would be like being eaten by frogs. Mad with loathing, Peer raised his arms to ward the hideous creatures off—and felt something hard being slipped into his hand from above. His fingers knew what it was; they closed over the hilt instinctively.

"Look out!" shrieked the second lubber. "He's got a knife!"

The two lubbers rushed for the holes. There was a scramble, two splashes, and the light went out. Peer was alone in the dark, though a mumbling, grumbling argument seemed to be going on in the pit below.

A small, pearly light dawned near the roof. Peer looked up.

"Thank you, Nis!" he said in heartfelt gratitude.

"That's all right, Peer Ulfsson," said the Nis. It giggled. "Lubbers is fools, no match for Nithing!"

"No, I'm sure they're not," said Peer. His legs gave way and he sat down.

"Get up! Get up!" hissed the Nis.

"What for?" groaned Peer.

"What for?" The Nis clicked its tongue in disbelief. "For to escape, of course! Hurry! Hurry!"

Peer didn't move. "Nis, I'm sorry, but I can't get through little holes like you do. And the door's barred with dozens of tree trunks, by the feel of it. I'm trapped!"

The Nis nearly spat, it was so irritated.

"The door is barred, I can't get out," it mimicked. "What is the knife for? To cut your way out through the thatch, of course!"

"Of course!" cried Peer, jumping to his feet. He climbed up onto the wooden seat (hoping no lubber would snatch at his ankles) and began stabbing away at the tightly packed bundles of reeds that made the low roof. The Nis sat swinging its legs and muttering to itself. It was sitting at the edge of a narrow tunnel running through the thatch; a rat hole perhaps. As Peer chopped away, he discovered to his delight that the roof was almost rotten, and riddled with holes, birds' nests, and passages. He shoved his way through, cursing as the thick snow covering the roof fell down his neck and onto his shoulders, and half slithered, half fell down into the yard, where a bundle of hysterical doggy joy leaped upon him and pushed him flat.

"Loki!" spluttered Peer, trying to sit up. "Loki, you're safe! All right now, stop it, that's enough! Stop it!"

He pushed Loki off and got up, gulping down fresh air in freezing lungfuls. It was snowing again. The Nis went scampering past him like a little whirlwind and opened the mill door. Peer and Loki ran inside and the Nis closed the door behind them.

It was blessedly warm. For a few minutes all Peer could do was lean shuddering over the long hearth, warming himself above the embers. The fire was dying; his uncles must have been away for at least an hour. Peer was afraid they would soon be back, but he had to get warm first. The red-and-violet embers gave hardly any light, but they were still hot. He turned himself around to get warm all over and saw the Nis perching on the back of Uncle Grim's big chair. It looked at him, eyes gleaming in the dim light.

"I don't know how to thank you," Peer said. "You've saved my life, and you saved Loki earlier, didn't you? You pushed down all that snow off the roof."

The Nis scratched itself uncomfortably and skipped down onto the floor, where it sat cross-legged near the fire, spreading out its long spindly fingers.

"Why did you do it?" Peer asked. "I thought you were so keen on this wedding."

The Nis looked at him sideways. "They hasn't invited me," it said dolefully.

"Oh . . ."

"Nobody remembers poor me," said the Nis. Its head drooped and its lower lip wobbled. "Such a big wedding . . . the hill to be raised on red pillars. So much food . . . but they forgets the poor Nis."

Peer was sorry to see the Nis so crestfallen. He tried to cheer it up. "Never mind, Nis, perhaps they're only inviting trolls!"

But the Nis shook his head. "Stromkarls, nixies, merrows even, all are going!"

Peer could see it was no use. "I bet the lubbers aren't going!" he said heartily. But this was a mistake.

"So he thinks the Nis and the lubbers can stay home together, does he?" the Nis snapped, very put out. It cracked its knuckles angrily and sat, twitching.

"Sorry, I'm sorry," cried Peer hastily. "I didn't mean that. Of course the two cases are quite different. I'm sure in your case it's been a—a dreadful oversight!"

The Nis was appeased. It pursed its lips and slowly nodded.

"They'll probably apologize!" Peer invented. "But, Nis," he went on, "Loki and I have to escape before my uncles get back. They went to get Hilde, so they can take the two of us up to Troll Fell and give us to the trolls."

Peer jumped up. "But it's not going to happen!" he said fiercely. "If I'm not here, they won't have the pair they need. And I'm leaving! I've had enough of living with Uncle Baldur and Uncle Grim!"

"Leaving for where?" inquired the Nis.

"Hammerhaven," said Peer. "I know some people there." He took a deep breath. Brand and Ingrid would look after him for a while, he was sure. The only problem (and a big one) would be getting there alive, in the freezing depths of mid-winter.

"Right!" he muttered. "I'm having what's mine, to start with!" He strode over to the locked bin where the money was and rattled the lid. He glanced at the Nis.

"I need to break into this. Any ideas?"

The Nis darted him a mischievous look. It reached out a long arm and hooked its wooden bowl out of the ashes. Tonight it was completely empty. Baldur and Grim had forgotten to fill it. The Nis showed him, dropped the bowl, and sat down again. "I has had enough too, Peer Ulfsson," it said importantly. "See me!" It scampered up the ladder to the loft and disappeared from view over the edge. It began puffing and groaning.

Bewildered, Peer climbed the ladder to see the fragile little Nis heaving away at the upper millstone, trying to lift it from its spindle. Its eyes popped and its thin arms stretched to snapping point as it tugged—uselessly. It had about as much chance of succeeding as a piece of thistledown.

"What *on earth* are you doing?" cried Peer. Then he saw. If they could roll the millstone over the edge, it would fall on the chest below. But it must weigh half a ton. They never could lift it, not even with a lever.

The Nis doubled up limply over the edge of the millstone and lay panting with its tongue hanging out. Peer looked about. Was there anything else they could use?

He clenched his fist in triumph. There was! Standing upright against the wall, dark with dust and cobwebs, was the old worn millstone that had been replaced in Baldur's father's time. No need to lift it: it was already on its rim, with just a couple of wooden chocks driven in on the underside to stop it rolling.

"Nis!" he called excitedly. The Nis looked, and the sparkle came back into its eyes. It skipped across and probed with long spidery fingers under the old millstone, pulling out the chocks. Peer grabbed the top of the stone and felt it stir. It rolled ponderously forward. Between them, Peer and the Nis trundled it to the edge of the loft, keeping their toes well back. At the very brink they paused and looked at each other. The Nis giggled. Peer grinned, and pushed. The millstone fell.

There was an earsplitting crash, and pieces of wood flew like daggers. Loki yelped and fled under the table. Peer opened his eyes—he had screwed them up at the crash—and peeped over to see the damage. The old millstone had cracked in two. The wooden bin was firewood. He jumped down, reached gingerly into the wreckage, and pulled out a soft leather bag. It jingled.

The Nis was skipping about behind him, looking smug. "I is strong, very strong, Peer Ulfsson, to move a millstone like that!" it crowed.

"You must be!" Peer agreed, laughing, and added, "That was a wonderful idea! Very, very clever!"

The Nis nearly purred.

Opening the bag, Peer checked the money. It was all there, his father's hard-earned wages; thin copper pennies and worn silver pieces that slipped gently through his fingers. At the bottom of the bag was something else. He knew it before he saw it: his father's old silver ring. He shut his eyes and pushed it onto his own finger. *Father*, he thought softly. *Are you there? Can you hear me? I'm doing what you did, Father. I'm going to run away.*

He waited for a moment, as if there could be an answer, before opening his eyes.

Next he pulled on one of Uncle Baldur's old tunics. It was smelly but warm, and came down to his knees. He looked around and grabbed the best of the blankets from Grim's bed.

"Shake out the fleas!" chirped the Nis. Peer grinned, gave the blanket a flip, and wrapped it around his shoulders like a cloak. Next he chose the smallest pair of boots. They were still huge, so he stuffed the toes with straw and laced them up tightly.

"We need some food," he said, boldly taking an entire loaf from the bread crock. He tore off a bit to munch and gave some to Loki. The Nis watched with bright eyes.

"Want some?" asked Peer through a mouthful. The Nis stretched out a hand and took a piece. It sprang into the rafters and sat nibbling like a squirrel.

"I'm off," said Peer, looking up. "Good-bye, Nis, I'll never forget you, but I have to go now before they get back. Come on, Loki!"

He took one last look around at the dark shadows, the glowing bed of the fire, the shattered millstone, and broken bin.

"I'm on my own, now," he declared. "And I'm never coming back!"

The snow was falling thickly in the yard. Peer trudged through it, pleased to find his feet warm and dry. All that rubbing in of grease was going to be useful to him now! Loki trotted alongside, his tail half raised.

They crossed the bridge carefully and set off uphill. Peer decided to leave the road and cut up over the muffled fields. He did not want to meet his uncles on their way home. Somewhere behind the snow-laden clouds the moon had risen. Even through the falling snow the white fields glimmered faintly. He could pick his way.

In spite of the cold and the dangerous journey ahead, he felt he had come to life.

"I'm free!" he said, savoring the word. His heart beat with excitement. It was a pity he would not see the Nis again, though. Or Hilde. He desperately hoped Hilde would be all right.

But leaving seemed to be the only thing he could do for Hilde now. And plenty of people would look out for her. Arnë and Bjorn, for example. It was a sharp memory, how they had walked out of the mill without a word to him. Of course, Hilde and her family belonged here; they were neighbors. But Peer? He was nobody's business.

We're just strays, Loki and me, he thought defiantly. *I'd better look out for myself. No one else will.*

By now he had reached the top of the big field above the

mill, the same one that Ralf had ridden over at a mad gallop, escaping from the trolls all those years ago. Peer stopped for a breather, leaning against the tall stone called the Finger. The snow was falling steadily, but the wind had dropped.

A white fox came trotting downhill from the Stone-meadow. Loki saw it and whined, pricking his ears. Peer caught his collar. The fox paused with one paw lifted and looked sharply at the boy and the dog.

"Hallo!" said Peer, amused. "Going down to the farms to see what you can find?"

The fox did not startle but continued to stare at him.

"There's a black cockerel at the mill," went on Peer. "You can have him and welcome!" The fox gave him a quizzical look. It shook its ears and sneezed. Then suddenly it took fright and sprang away with flattened ears, disappearing into the white world within seconds.

Peer laughed. But beside him, Loki was growling. A moment later Peer realized why.

Only a few yards away, two huge shapes emerged from the grayness, plodding uphill through the snow. He heard the grumble of two familiar and hated voices. His heart nearly stopped.

Uncle Baldur and Uncle Grim!

CHAPTER 14
Peer Alone

Peer dragged Loki around behind the big stone. He crouched, holding his breath. His mind was spinning. Were they after him? How could they know he was running away? What was happening?

His next thought was—had they got Hilde? Were they taking her to the Troll King after all?

Pressing his cheek to the cold stone, he looked cautiously around the edge. And one thing was sure: His uncles had no idea he was there. Their hoods were pulled well down and they had already trudged past his hiding place without looking left or right. He sighed with relief. They hadn't got Hilde either. But each of them carried a large bundle over his shoulder.

"Now what are they up to?" muttered Peer. It didn't matter. He had only to wait until they were well out of sight and then go on his own way. But he was curious. What *were* those bundles? He strained his eyes; was it just the poor light, or were they moving?

With a jolt of horror he suddenly understood what he was seeing. Two small children, bundled up in sacking and swathed in ropes, being carried heads down over his uncles' shoulders. They were mostly lying limp, but an occasional kick accounted for the jerking movement he had seen.

"Sigurd and Sigrid!" Peer breathed the words. A girl and a boy. Twins. A matching pair!

Once again his plans lay in wreckage. He stood in the snow, in full view if his uncles turned around, his mind racing. What was he to do?

Forget about it, go on to Hammerhaven, pretend it had nothing to do with him?

Or follow his uncles, risk being caught and dragged back to a life of drudgery? He groaned. What could he possibly do, all by himself? How could he rescue the twins from two huge, powerful men, or from a whole hill full of trolls?

If only he had been slower leaving the mill, or if he had gone by the road, he would never have seen his uncles—never known what they were doing. He gazed after their disappearing backs. It was nearly too late. In a moment they would vanish into the dim night and falling snow. *What can you do? Forget you saw it,* a little voice murmured in his ear. *No one will ever know.*

Slowly Peer turned away. It was useless. No one could blame him. "Come on, Loki," he muttered in despair. "Let's go."

But into his head slipped a memory, the memory of Sigrid's high little voice back in the summer, screaming at Uncle Baldur: "I don't like the nasty man! I hate him!" And he remembered carrying her on his back and the feel of her small hands clutching his neck. Sigrid and Sigurd were only little, but they were his friends.

Peer stood, as still as the big stone. He felt he was *turning* to stone. He saw now just what he should do. At the very least he should follow, and tell everyone where his uncles had taken the children. He should tell the whole village what they had done.

If he didn't, he would blame himself forever.

"Loki!" he said with a furious sob. "Let's go! *This* way!" And as the startled Loki bounded back after him, Peer began running, stumbling, laboring uphill on the track of his two wicked uncles.

The way was steep. As he feared, the men were out of sight, but their trail was easy to follow in the deep snow. Peer ran, as if in a bad dream. His cumbersome boots dragged half off at each stride. He could get up no speed. Loki gamboled along at his heels, thinking this was a game. Peer was terrified he would bark in excitement and give them away. Panting, he dropped into a slow plod, then forced himself to run again. Gradually the ground became less steep. He crested a rise and paused to rest a moment, head drooping. His breath came in painful, wheezing gasps.

He was afraid of getting too close to his uncles. Shading his eyes, he stared ahead and just made out their shadowy shapes disappearing down a little valley. Peer gave himself another minute and set off after them.

The valley turned out to be no more than a dimple on the hillside, but it was full of drifted snow. Both of Peer's boots came off as he plowed through it. Sweating and cursing, he burrowed around in the drifts to find them again. There was no time to empty out the packed-in snow; he just shoved his numb feet back in and plunged forward. All the time as he ran, a little voice at the back of his head kept whimpering, *Why am I so unlucky? Why did this have to happen?* Overhearing himself, he shook his head in furious disgust. The voice fell silent. He floundered stubbornly on.

The tracks turned steeply uphill again. This time Peer was reduced to a plod. Like a terribly old man, he struggled just to lift each foot and place it ahead of the other. Plod. Rest. Breathe. Plod. Rest. Breathe. The slope seemed endless.

It had stopped snowing. The moon sailed out overhead, and the flanks of Troll Fell revealed themselves, black rocks and white slopes, cold and desolate.

In front of him the snow was unmarked. It looked soft and smooth, delicate as the surface of a new mushroom. There were no footmarks.

He had lost the trail.

It was like having a bucket of water thrown over him. Peer gasped and shook his head, and came awake. He swung around. Loki cowered behind him, obviously cold, his tail curved under his belly.

"We've got to go back," said Peer. He pushed past Loki and started off downhill. Loki picked his way after his master as if wondering what all this was about. Had Peer gone mad?

"It's my fault, Loki," Peer muttered. "I wasn't watching the trail. They must have branched off, and I never noticed . . . Ah! Here it is!"

Deep dragging marks showed where his uncles had turned aside toward the foot of a cliff, twenty feet or so of glistening wet stone capped with an overhang of snow. At the base the tracks turned right and continued to a place where the cliff was lower. Peer scrambled up over a rockfall of boulders half smothered in snow, slipping and bruising himself on buried stones.

Now the moon was out, it should be easy to see. But hypnotic patterns seemed to dance in the air over the featureless white slopes, playing tricks with his eyes. He began to shiver, and the clammy sweat froze under his clothes.

At the top of the cliff the ground leveled out temporarily. There was a wide ledge. Peer doubled over, gasping for breath. Straightening up, he looked along the trail he was following. Clear in the moonlight, a few hundred yards ahead, two dark figures strode up the slope toward a narrow ravine. If they turned around, Peer would be plainly visible. But they didn't turn. He watched for a moment, not sure what to do.

Looking around, he saw he was not far from the top of Troll Fell. The land curved away in all directions and he could sense the bulk of the mountain below him. Other lonely peaks reared up white in the dark sky to the north. An inhuman silence reigned.

Peer shuddered. And Loki whined and pawed at his legs.

"That's right, Loki," said Peer, suddenly very thankful for company. "*Good* dog. Come on!"

Crouching a little for fear of being seen, he hurried up the slope in his uncles' tracks. The snow was shallow here. The wind had combed it thin between the boulders and bitter rocks. Peer scurried upward, not knowing in the least what he was going to do, just determined to keep his uncles—and Sigurd and Sigrid—in sight to the end.

Baldur and Grim were heading directly into the ravine. A steep cliff leaned out at one side, slashed black with shadows.

A shrill yell rang out, bouncing and reverberating off the rocks. Peer cowered. Uncle Baldur had reached his goal. He was shouting to the gatekeeper of Troll Fell to let him in. Again he shouted, and again: "Open up! Open up!"

And the troll gate opened.

A vertical hairline of light appeared in the dark root of the cliff. Silently and swiftly it yawned wider as the stone door turned on unseen pivots. Spellbound, Peer crouched in the snow as golden light spilled down the mountain.

The dark shapes of Uncle Baldur and Uncle Grim, and the

dark bundles that were Sigrid and Sigurd, stood out black for a moment against the gold as they vanished inside. Smoothly, silently, the door swung shut. The broad rectangle of light shrank to a line, narrowed to a filament, and was gone. The shock passed through the ground as though Troll Fell shivered, and Peer's skin came out in goose bumps.

The troll gate was shut.

Peer ran forward. He scrambled over the pebbles at the base of the cliff and threw himself against the cold face, patting and fumbling, feeling for the door. Nothing. Not a crack anywhere in the solid stone. He dared not shout. He felt tired and sick, ashamed to have come so far and been so useless. There was nothing to show anyone, except the trail of footsteps, and the next snow shower would cover those.

His legs buckled and he flopped wearily down on the ground. His hand felt something in the snow beside him. He picked it up. It was Sigrid's woolly cap, gritty with melting snow crystals but still warm. He lowered his head to his knees.

A few yards away Loki sensed Peer's despair. Sitting bolt upright in the snow, he lifted his muzzle to the sky and let the misery within him float away in a long, musical, mournful howl.

It was an eerie sound, echoed and re-echoed by the cliffs, and it brought Peer back to his feet. "Quiet, Loki," he said. "Hush!" But Loki, surprised and impressed by the noise he had made, was doing it again.

Oooo . . . ooo . . . ooo . . . ! The sound trailed away. To Peer it seemed as though all the mountains were *looking* at them. It was awful. "Loki, stop it!"

The rebounding echoes came fainter and fainter, while Peer held Loki's muzzle to stop him from trying again. And then came an echo that was not an echo.

"Loki!" Peer froze. "Was that—a *bark*?"

He strained his ears. Unmistakably a second bark, from somewhere below them on the hill. Loki stiffened, pulled free of Peer's hand, and shot off down the slope. A minute later he came back into sight, leaping crazily around another dog—an older, bigger dog, a sheepdog by the look of it, that was trotting steadily uphill. Peer couldn't believe his eyes. A shepherd? On top of Troll Fell at this hour? He ran forward to see.

Somebody was there all right, puffing up the slope. Somebody too small to be a shepherd. It wasn't—it couldn't be—!

"Loki!" cried a clear, incredulous voice. "Peer! What on earth are you doing up here?"

"Hilde!" yelled Peer. He rushed to meet her and almost flung his arms around her, but restrained himself in time: he grabbed her hand instead and pumped it up and down. He had never been so glad to see anyone in his life. Words tumbled out of him.

"It's Uncle Baldur!—Uncle Grim!—I was escaping—I saw them carrying the twins. They took them inside, Hilde, I couldn't stop them! What shall we do?"

Hilde pulled off her cap and pushed the hair out of her eyes.

"We're going to get my little brother and sister back," she promised. "You saw them, did you? And you followed? Oh, good for you, Peer!"

Peer flushed, remembering how he had nearly gone on his way.

"How did you know where to come?" he asked, still hardly able to believe she was here.

"Alf and I discovered this place when we were gathering sheep at the beginning of winter," Hilde told him. "Alf. My dog." Alf turned his grizzled head and licked her mittened hand. "We saw the door in the cliff open. Tonight, when we realized the twins had been stolen"—her voice shook— "Mother and Grandfather went off down to the village to rouse everyone. I was supposed to stay behind in case—in case the twins came back—but I knew they wouldn't; I knew what was happening. I couldn't bear to wait. I decided to come here: Alf knows the way."

"The door's shut," said Peer. "They went in not long ago. I didn't know what to do. I still don't."

"Well, if the door's shut, let's go and knock on it," said Hilde. She pulled her cap back on.

"Oh. I found this," said Peer unhappily. He handed her Sigrid's cap. Hilde looked at it silently and tucked it in her pocket.

"But, Hilde," Peer went on, "they won't open the door for us, and even if they do, what can we say?"

"I think they will," said Hilde with strange confidence. "Look at this!"

She struggled with her cloak and produced from inside her clothes a small bundle wrapped in cloth. She unrolled it. Peer gasped. "Is that—?"

"That's the famous cup. Yes," said Hilde. "Ma hid it. Good thing she told me where! I had to dig it out of the grain bin."

Peer gazed at it in admiration. The gold gleamed pale in the moonlight, and the molding winked white fire as Hilde turned it this way and that.

"The patterns seem to move," he said, fascinated.

"I know," said Hilde, not as if she cared. "We'll see how badly the Gaffer of Troll Fell wants this back. Come on, let's go."

She folded the cloth back over the cup and pushed it back under her cloak. Peer looked around.

"It's getting lighter," he noticed. The sharp-edged moonlight was being quenched by the approach of dawn, and a light mist blurred the slopes.

"It's been a long night," he said, shivering.

Hilde jumped. "Then we've no time to lose! They won't open the troll gate after sunrise! Quickly!"

She led the way at a run, Peer following and the dogs trotting resignedly behind.

Reaching the bottom of the cliff, Hilde bent and picked up a big stone. She pounded on the rock face with it, shouting, "Open up! Open up! I'm Hilde, Ralf's daughter!"

"Open up! Open up!" Peer joined in, picking up his own

rock. They hammered on the cliff, shouting. It sounded like a quarry at work. The dogs began to bark.

"Wait a minute," panted Hilde. They stopped to listen. The echoes died away. It was growing lighter every moment.

"Open up," called Hilde distinctly. "Tell the Gaffer I've brought his cup. Remember? The cup Ralf Eiriksson took, years ago!"

"Years ago! Years ago!" The echo sprang to and fro. Nothing happened. Hilde grimaced at Peer. Her face looked wan in the cold predawn glow.

"It's not working!" she said, biting her lip. Peer said nothing. He caught her arm and pointed. A vertical black seam ran down the rock face: a split, widening to a gash. They smelled sparks. The soles of their feet tickled as the ground trembled. The stone door opened, a thick slab of rock higher than a man, swinging slowly inward. No golden light shone from it now. Behind it was nothing but a gaping darkness.

As Hilde stepped forward, Peer dragged her back. "Hilde! You can't go in there!"

"Yes I can!" Hilde jerked her arm free. "Let go!"

"You can't!" Peer panicked. "Look at it—all dark—you'll get lost—trapped!" He hung on to her. She twisted a foot behind his leg and tripped him. They fell together. Peer bashed his elbow on a rock. He grabbed a fistful of her hair and hung on to it. Locked together, sobbing and gasping, they struggled on the uneven ground.

"*Let—me—go!*" Hilde shrieked, her face inches from his.

She glared into his eyes. "*You* don't have to come! They're not *your* brother and sister! Go away! Go home!"

Peer let her go and lay back on the ground, eyes closed, chest heaving. Tears leaked from under his eyelids. Hilde scrambled to her feet, breathing hard.

"I'm sorry," she said, between gasps. "I'm sorry."

Peer looked up as she stood over him. Above her loomed the cliff and the tall black slot of the troll gate. Everything was turning around, reeling dizzily as if in a nightmare. He got up. "If you're going," he croaked painfully, "I'm coming with you."

"Oh, Peer!" said Hilde. She wiped her eyes on the back of her hand. "Come on then. Wait! Just a minute." She bent to the dogs. "Go home, Alf! Good boy, go home now! You'd better not come with us."

"Can he take Loki?" asked Peer, fighting to keep his voice steady.

"Of course," Hilde reassured him. "Alf? You go home now and take Loki. You hear me? Find Eirik. Go home."

"Off you go, Loki," said Peer, clenching his teeth.

Loki hesitated. Alf sniffed him, turned, and trotted a few paces downhill. He stopped and looked back at Hilde.

"Go home, Alf!" said Hilde loudly. The old dog barked, and slowly Loki began to follow him.

"Good-bye!" muttered Peer. As he watched the two dogs going down the hill, he felt lonelier than he ever had in his life. He turned to face the dark doorway.

"Come *on!*" Hilde beckoned. The moon was paling and the sky was pink.

Sucking in a huge gasp of the cold fresh air, filling his lungs as if it was the last breath he would ever take, Peer turned his back on the sunrise and followed Hilde into Troll Fell.

CHAPTER 15

Torches by the Fjord

With a great effort, Gudrun steadied Eirik as he slipped. Struggling down the hill in the deep snow, she had been amazed at how well he was managing. With arms linked, they had waded through the drifts, encouraging each other, Gudrun with breathless gasps of, "Well done, Eirik!" and "Slippery here—hold up!" and Eirik with snatches of savage battle stanzas.

Once into the wood, Gudrun could barely trace the path. The pine trees whistled and bent overhead, and snow came whirling down through the branches. It was very dark and wild. She clutched Eirik's elbow as his foot went into a hole under the snow.

"Come on," shouted Eirik, staggering up. "On to Trollsvik!"

"Eirik," panted Gudrun, pressing her hand to her side

where she had a stitch, "we have to go past the mill!"

"What does it matter?" Eirik dragged her along, and she was astonished at his strength. "Bring on the wolf's brood! Rouse the steel storm!"

"What if the millers are there?"

"They won't be," said Eirik, "and if they are, I'll show 'em a thing or two! And so will you, too, Gudrun my woman. Eh? Eh?"

"Let me get my hands on them!" Gudrun agreed, thrilling with anger, and she led the way at a faster pace. But when they came out of the woods above the mill, it looked deserted. The moon, hidden behind the snow clouds, made the fields and the buildings glimmer in a gray, ghostly fashion. Not a light showed; no smoke rose from the roof.

Eirik paused, wheezing, and Gudrun hugged his arm. "Father-in-law! Are you all right?"

Eirik shook his head like a dog. "I'm fine," he growled. "Fine!" And he plunged forward down the path.

The black buildings of the mill loomed closer. There was the wheel, toothed with icicles. Gudrun and Eirik clung to the rail as they shuffled cautiously over the icy bridge, but they crossed successfully and were passing the yard when they heard the excited, sharp bark of a fox, followed by an unearthly cackling and screeching.

Fox among the hens, thought Gudrun at once, but she certainly didn't care. Serve the Grimssons right if they lost their hens! And Eirik thought the same; he was nodding to her.

"Foxes! I'll give 'em foxes!" he roared. "I'll *feed* them to the foxes, in tiny pieces! On we go!"

But he was getting very tired, Gudrun could tell; he was pressing more and more heavily on her arm, and slipping and stumbling more often. Still, the path was smoother now. It wasn't so far to the village. Her scarf whipped over her face and she pushed it back. Oh, but her legs were tired, trembling and shaking. What was she doing down here, when Sigurd and Sigrid must be far up the mountain? Why hadn't she sent Hilde with Eirik, and gone after them herself? She began to cry, big tears spilling over her cheeks and blurring her sight. Her woolen skirts dragged, clotted with snow.

Eirik leaned toward her. "Snow's stopped," he shouted. "And dawn's on the way." It was true.

Wiping her tears, Gudrun could see under the clearing sky the first houses of the village and smell the heavy tang of wood smoke. Letting go of Eirik, she launched herself in a stumbling run at the nearest door, and beat on it. "Kersten! Bjorn!" She pushed it open.

There was no one inside. The fire burned cheerfully; the blankets on the sleeping bench were disturbed, as though the sleepers had flung them back and left suddenly. Eirik hobbled up behind her.

"There's no one here!" cried Gudrun.

Eirik leaned on the door, breathing hard. "Try next door," he got out between gasps.

Gudrun flew past him and along to the next house.

"Arnë! . . . Harald! . . . Where are you ?" she begged. House after house was empty, though cats yowled from corners and in one a baby cried, alone in its cradle. Gudrun came out looking bewildered.

"That's Einar's new baby," she said. "Where are they all? Is it some evil spell?"

Eirik, who had recovered his breath, pointed to the ground. Tracks from every house joined to form a trampled path leading out through the village on the way to the fjord. "Listen!" he said, holding up his hand. Gudrun listened. It seemed she could hear a far-off shouting.

"Is it an attack?" she gasped. "Is it war?"

"Onward to battle!" shouted Eirik. "Let's find out!"

Alf went back down the trail at a businesslike trot. Confidently he wove his way in and out of the boulders and over the rockfall, and where Alf's plumy tail led, Loki followed, nose down. Interesting smells lingered along the trail: the heavy sweaty smell of Baldur and Grim, the clean smell of the little children, the wild, peppery smell of trolls.

The snow glittered suddenly in the rising sun. Loki sneezed. The dogs' long shadows ran ahead of them as they trotted briskly down the fellside. Loki was light enough to run on the frozen crust of the snow without breaking through; Alf, heavier, floundered through the deeper places. At last they came in sight of the tall stone where Peer and Loki had rested the previous night, at the top of the big field above the mill. Alf halted, stared down at the snowy furrows, then flattened himself into a tense crouch.

Light-footed up the hill the white fox came dancing, dragging something black by the neck. It stopped close to the big stone to lay down the burden and get a fresh grip. Limp and bedraggled, the black cockerel lay dead on the snow.

Alf sprang in ambush, barking with hatred. The fox jumped high in the air and came down in the same spot, bristling its thick white fur. But when it saw Alf and Loki, it sat down impudently and began to scratch.

Alf circled it, glaring and growling, but Loki stepped nimbly forward and trotted up to the fox, which lowered its leg and watched his approach warily. Lightly they sniffed noses. Loki's tail moved in a tentative wag, and the fox's brush twitched in reply.

Then its sharp ears pricked and it jerked aside, staring downhill in the direction of the fjord. The two dogs swung around. There was nothing to see, but a breath of wind brought to their acute hearing a distant clamor. Far away on the shore, many voices were shouting or cheering.

The fox shook itself, grabbed the cockerel, and went slinking away up the hill. Loki turned his head to watch, but Alf ignored it. He stood rigidly, his muzzle lifted, snuffing at the wind, straining after the sounds floating up from the fjord. Suddenly he gave a hoarse bark and bounded forward. His tail waved busily. Loki dashed after him.

Side by side the two dogs ran over the field, crossed over

the slippery wooden bridge below the mill, and disappeared into the trees on the path down to the village.

In the village all was commotion. Torches flared by the fjord, pale in the dawn, for the shadow of Troll Fell lay cold across the valley. Beached on the shingle, dwarfing Bjorn and Arnë's boats, an elegant longship reared its proud neck. The fierce dragon head was covered in sacking, so as not to frighten the timid land spirits of the homeland.

The whole village had turned out. Eirik and Gudrun, clinging together, made their way down onto the shingle, where Gudrun shrieked, let go of Eirik, and ran madly over the pebbles and ankle deep into the water, to seize the arm of a tall, burly man who vaulted laughing out of the ship.

"Ralf! Ralf, my man, is it really you?" She pounded his chest with her fists, laughing and crying. "Is it really you?"

Ralf bent down and scooped her off her feet. "Yes, my girl." He gave her a bristly kiss. "It's really me!"

CHAPTER 16

In the Hall of the Mountain King

As soon as Peer and Hilde stepped past the entrance, the stone door began to grind on its pivots and slowly swung shut behind them, extinguishing the dawn. The door closed with a boom and a suck of air as if a giant mouth had breathed in.

It was dark.

Peer's breath shortened and his chest tightened. He lurched giddily. "Where are you?" he panted.

"Here!" Their groping hands blundered together, and they clutched each other. "Oh, Peer, I don't like it," Hilde whispered. "I thought there would be lights."

"So did I." Touching her steadied him. Her fingers were warm, rough, and comforting. She squeezed back, so hard it hurt.

"Why is it dark?"

"It's daybreak." Peer remembered something the Nis had once said. "That's night-time for trolls."

"You mean they're all asleep? But who let us in?"

Their whispering voices created scuttling echoes. "Shh!" said Peer, freezing. They listened tensely. Was anything there?

In the silence Peer heard only water dripping and his own harsh breath. He opened his eyes wide, shut them tight. It made no difference. The darkness molded to his face, clung and clogged in his throat like black glue. . . .

"This is silly!" Hilde's bold voice startled away his panic. "I'm not lurking in the dark. Hallo! Gatekeeper!" Her hand clenched on his. "We want to see the Gaffer. Bring us a light!"

They held their breath. Just behind them, someone laughed quietly: *"Ho ho!"* As they whirled around, there was a soft clap and an explosion of brilliant golden light. Peer's hands flew to his eyes. The tunnel blanched in the intense glare, and he saw every piece of grit on the floor, sharp-edged in black. Painfully, through watering lashes, he made out a spindly figure twirling a bright sphere, like a little sun, on one crooked forefinger. It stood with its back to the troll door, and its black shadow streamed up the stone. Glistening rock walls leaned together overhead.

"We want—to see—the Gaffer," Hilde repeated breathlessly.

A dark, hooked arm bowled the ball of light toward them. Peer and Hilde dodged. It rolled past them, quivering and glowing, illuminating the first few yards of a long tunnel.

They looked back toward the stone door, but their own bodies threw huge shadows, blotting out the creature guarding it. Phantom colors floated on the darkness, sickles of purple and blobs of green. Peer screwed up his eyes, trying to see. Something scraped along the floor: a long, thin foot, with claws back and front like a bird's. Impatiently it raked and scratched. High, high above it, up in the black roof, wide wet eyes blinked white.

Peer and Hilde backed away, step by quiet step. At a safe distance they turned and scurried farther down the tunnel, away from the entrance.

"Oh my goodness," panted Hilde. "To think we were standing right next to that thing, in the dark!"

"What now?" Peer shivered. Hilde squinted along the passage. "It meant us to follow the light. I think. Come on!" She tugged his hand. Peer came, throwing a nervous glance over his shoulder, but only darkness followed them.

At first the passage was just wide enough for them to walk abreast. The ball of light wobbled along in front, not quite touching the floor. Peer clumped doggedly after it in his wet boots. Troll Fell had swallowed him. Now he was stuck in its long stone gullet. He took deep, uneven breaths. The air was damp in his lungs, still and cold. The floor rose and fell, and there were unexpected puddles.

"Ugh!" complained Hilde. "The roof dripped on my head!" A cold splash landed on Peer's neck too. Once a waterdrop plummeted, fizzling, straight through the ball of light.

From time to time the passage twisted around corners, or divided into side passages that corkscrewed up or dived into darkness. Sometimes the roof dipped, and they had to bend or duck under projecting ledges. Soon they felt hopelessly confused. The floor rose. The walls bulged, nipping the passage to a tight cleft. "One at a time here," muttered Hilde. She twisted her hand out of Peer's and slid sideways between fat stone bellies. For a moment her body blocked the light. Peer gasped as her shadow hit him. He stood blind and breathless.

"I'm through. Come on!" Hilde's voice came back with the light. Heart thudding, Peer squeezed after her. The stone felt wet and smooth, slick as a cow's tongue, and he slid through more easily than he expected. As he reached the far side, he heard a strange sound, a sort of hissing roar. There was a strong upward draft. Hilde clutched him, shouting, "Look at that!"

A rough cataract of yellow water shot from a hole in the ceiling and hurtled into a pit. The light danced around behind it, so the shadows of the rocks rose and fell. The only way to get past was along a narrow ramp by the left-hand wall. Peer craned his neck to look down into the pit below. The water careered into darkness that looked absolutely solid.

"We can't!" Hilde's cold hands gripped him.

"We must!" said Peer fiercely. "We can't stay here!"

Hilde hesitated. "We'll slip! What if the light's tricked us?"

Peer pushed in front. "All right! I'll go first." He had to keep moving. When he stood still, he felt the whole demanding weight of Troll Fell bearing down on his shoulders. "Look! Keep near the wall, like this, and—ah!"

His foot slipped on the wet stone lip. In panic, he snatched at the rocks. One hand curled over a sharp rim and he hung by an arm, kicking, poised over the drop. The water drummed on his back. He heard Hilde scream; then her hand bit into his flailing wrist and hauled. The rock edge ground into his midriff. He dragged his knee up and over, and clawed himself farther up the slippery shelf. With Hilde following, he crawled out of the spray to where the ledge widened at the far side and lay gasping on his face.

There was no time to rest. Darkness leaped at them, and the passage seemed to shrink. The ball of light had begun to flicker out, bluish and fitful. In fright they scrambled up. It turned a couple of brisk half-spins, brightened, and whirled off down the tunnel. Bruised and bedraggled, Hilde and Peer limped after it and suddenly noticed that they were climbing. They stumbled up a flight of shallow steps. At the top the light sprang up and hung overhead, rotating lazily.

Deep in the rock of the left-hand wall was a wide, dark crevice like many that they had already hurried past. But this one had been shaped into a rough archway. Set back into it was a solid wooden door.

Peer looked at Hilde, who gave an anxious nod. He raised his hand, hesitating, took a deep breath, and knocked on the door as loudly as he could, hurting his knuckles. In a moment the door opened a crack and a small troll looked out. It had short, pricked ears and held a smoking pine branch in one fist. When it saw Peer and Hilde, it hissed, exposing needle-sharp teeth, and began to shut the door again, but Peer stuck his foot in the way.

"We want to see the Gaffer," he said firmly, though his teeth clattered.

"The gatekeeper sent us," added Hilde, pointing to the floating light, which was drifting to and fro against the stony ceiling.

The little troll hissed again, and jerked angrily at the door. Peer got his fingers around the edge and dragged it back. Feverishly, Hilde unwrapped the golden cup.

"Look here!" she called, holding it up for the troll to see. "This is for the Gaffer! A present! We want to see him!"

The troll's eyes grew round and black with excitement. It let go of the door and sprang forward, tail lashing. "Give! Give!" it squeaked.

"Not likely!" Hilde held the goblet high in the air. "The Gaffer will be angry," she warned. "We want to see him now!"

The little troll's claws shot out and its ears folded flat like an angry cat's, but it stood back sulkily and opened the door wide. Jostling, shoulder to shoulder, Peer and Hilde stepped in.

They were in a large chamber, gloriously warm and smelling of pine needles. Peer straightened his bent back and rubbed his clammy hands. A brazier stood in the middle of the room, filled with pine logs that flared and sizzled noisily, bubbling with resin. The troll pitched the burning branch back into the flames.

On the other side of the brazier was a stone bed. Its four crooked pillars seemed to have dripped from the ceiling and grown from the floor. Above it hung folded curtains, drapes and scallops of curdled stone, gleaming like soap. The bed was piled with sheepskins. Somebody lay there, snoring loudly. Hilde and Peer tiptoed forward, hearts hammering.

The old Gaffer of Troll Fell seemed to be asleep.

He lay on his back, the sheepskins heaped over him in a hillock. His bulbous nose sprouted with whiskers. His mouth hung open a little, and two long, brown, curving teeth stuck up out of his lower jaw. His eyes were closed, but in the center of his forehead another eye glared open, red rimmed and weeping, glancing this way and that. It spotted Peer and Hilde immediately and rolled around to fix on them.

"Strangers!" croaked a voice, and a black crow hopped down from the pillow, rattling its feathers.

"Strangers!" squawked the little troll that had let them in.

"I see the strangers," the Gaffer mumbled in his sleep. He yawned, showing a lot of red tongue and ragged teeth, stretched, and sat up, opening his eyes. As he did so, the eye in the middle of his forehead fluttered slowly shut, a red wrinkle fringed with a few scanty bristles.

Hilde and Peer grabbed hands and backed away.

"*Hutututu!* What's this, what's this?" growled the Gaffer.

Hilde's mouth was dry, but she spoke up bravely. "I'm

Hilde," she gulped. "Ralf Eiriksson's daughter. My—my little brother and sister are here somewhere. The miller of Trollsvik stole them."

"We came to get them," added Peer, determined to help. The Gaffer began to scowl.

"I brought this in exchange!" Hilde added. She held up the golden goblet so that he could see it, and the little troll scurried forward and leaped at her arm, mewling like a kitten. The Gaffer bounded off the bed and kicked it in the bottom. It rolled across the floor shrieking.

"This cup is yours. It was lost years ago," Hilde raised her voice. "Let me have my brother and sister and in return—"

"Lost!" The Gaffer interrupted her. "Stolen, you mean! Stolen by your father, a thief himself! How dare you bargain with me?"

"A thief!" screamed the crow.

"What?" Hilde cried, flushing. "You trolls tried to poison him! How dare you call him a thief?"

"Hilde!" warned Peer.

"It wasn't poison!" shouted the Gaffer of Troll Fell. "And he never even drank it!"

"Well, it burned all the hair off his pony's tail," yelled Hilde. "That sounds pretty poisonous to me!"

"Aark! Aark!" screamed the crow, flapping its wings.

"Hilde, calm down!" Peer called, dismayed at how things were going. But Hilde had sprung forward. She grabbed a sheepskin from the Gaffer's bed and shook it at him.

"See that?" she said, panting. "See that mark? That's ours. That came from one of our sheep—and so did that!" She seized another fleece, and another. "So—who's a thief now?" She threw them down and stood glaring at him.

For a horrible moment Peer expected the Gaffer to call on his trolls and have both of them torn to pieces then and there. To his surprise, and immense relief, the huge old troll began to laugh. He screwed up all three eyes and rocked backward and forward on the edge of his bed, choking and spluttering.

"Well, what's a little borrowing between neighbors?" he coughed, slapping his knees. "Give me that!" He snatched the cup from Hilde's limp hand and turned it this way and that in his black claws, admiring it.

"Nice timing," he grinned at her. "We want this for the wedding. It's the Bride Cup of Troll Fell, always used at weddings. Traditional! Belonged to my grandmother."

"Well, then?" demanded Hilde.

"Not so fast, not so fast," grunted the Gaffer. "*Skotte!*"

The little troll in the corner gave a shrill squeak of alarm.

"Get everyone up," said the Gaffer. "If I'm awake, no one else sleeps. There's plenty to do. I want the Hall ready before midnight. Wake up the princess. I want to see her." The little troll doubled itself up in a bow and scuttled out. The Troll King yawned again and his middle eye twitched. He reached out for his cloak, which was made of cat skins, mostly tabby. There was a slit in the back. He thrashed about, trying to get his tail through the hole.

"Help me!" he growled. Seeing Hilde shudder, Peer gingerly bent down and hooked the tail out. It was thick and bony, like a cow's, with a tuft of hair at the tip.

"Follow me," the Gaffer commanded, hitching up his cloak. The crow dived after him as he threw open the door and stomped out, switching his tail. The ball of light, which had been idly drifting to and fro against the rocky ceiling, brightened rapidly and bounded ahead of him as he led the way farther down the passage.

Peer and Hilde followed, glancing about nervously. As they walked, they began to hear noises ahead: bangs, crashes, and whoops. They turned a corner, the passage ended in some steps, and they found themselves looking into the splendid Hall under Troll Fell.

It was a huge cavern. The roof soared up into darkness, patrolled by many floating lights, golden and blue. Their own ball of light tumbled past them, rising, and whirled aloft to join the others.

Opposite them a waterfall found its way in white threads down between rocks. At the base of the waterfall was a stone chair. The water divided around it and flowed away in a dark channel under an archway at the side of the Hall.

The Hall was filling with trolls and other creatures, all rushing about. Some tumbled from dark chimneys in the roof and dropped to the floor like bouncing balls. Others scrambled out from underneath boulders. Gangs rushed in with long tables and benches, dragging them here and there, dropping them with a crash, trying to get them in the best order. Over by the channel a group of dripping water spirits, or nixies, scoured a pile of golden plates with fine white sand, trying to get them as bright as possible. Others with brooms swept the floor, raising clouds of dust. (With a wistful pang, Peer thought of the Nis.) And everyone was shouting at once:

"Fetch another high seat for the King of the Dovre!"

"A special table for his son and daughter!"

"How many tubs of water for the merrows?"

"We need to have just as many for the nixies!"

"Couldn't they sit on wet stones? ..."

As the Gaffer arrived, a sudden silence fell, and every face turned toward him. And such faces! Hilde, searching the crowd eagerly for a sign of Sigurd or Sigrid, found her eyes confused by the jumble. Trolls with pig's snouts, trolls with owl's eyes, trolls with bird's beaks. There did not seem to be a human face among them, unless you counted the nixies, whose faces, though beautiful, were narrow and sly with curious, slanting eyes.

Then she saw them. Not the children, but the tall burly, black-haired figures of the Grimsson twins. They were slouching side by side on some rocks at the bottom of the waterfall, looking as surly and bad-tempered as ever. Beside her, Peer winced.

"Don't worry, Peer," she whispered helplessly.

"I'm not worrying!" Peer growled.

"Can you see the children?"

Before Peer could reply, the Gaffer set off down the shallow steps, and they had to follow him. It seemed a long way over the uneven stone floor to the throne at the other side. The trolls fell back for them, hissing and murmuring.

Cold with fright, Peer threw his head back and stared at his two uncles. They hadn't yet seen him, and he wasn't looking forward to the moment when they did. Baldur glanced casually across. He jogged his brother's elbow and got to his feet— and then he spotted Peer. His jaw dropped. So did Grim's. Their faces registered blank astonishment changing to pop-eyed fury. Scared though he was, Peer had to giggle.

The Gaffer walked straight past the Grimsson brothers, ignoring them completely, and climbed onto his throne. He swept his tail out of the way and settled himself comfortably. But as Hilde and Peer drew level, the two men came out of their trance. With a fierce exclamation, Baldur shot out a thick arm. He grabbed Peer by the back of the neck and shook him like a puppet.

"Let him go!" Hilde shrieked, trying to pull him free. Grim kicked her feet from under her and she fell heavily. As if the violence was a signal, the trolls rushed from behind and flung themselves on her, burying her under a pile of arms, legs, and whisking tails. She rolled on the ground, hitting out blindly. Something bit her arm; she scraped her knuckles on a scaly hide; claws scrabbled and scratched. Screams, snarls, shouts, and howls filled the hall. *It's the end!* thought Hilde desperately, and wished it weren't going to be quite so painful. Then—

"STOP THIS AT ONCE!" roared the Gaffer, stamping in fury. He flung the crow from his shoulder and it dived over the struggling crowd, stabbing here and there with a beak like blue steel.

Baldur and Grim dropped Peer, cursing, beating the crow away from their eyes. The pile of trolls on top of Hilde rolled off and crept away, ducking and cringing. The crow circled and returned to the Gaffer's shoulder. It lifted its huge black wings and folded them, nibbling the feathers into place. "Aaark!" it cried in harsh triumph. Hilde sat up, her arms and face scratched and bleeding, and threw the hair out of her eyes.

"Cool down!" ordered the Gaffer, as silence fell.

There was a hiss of rage from the assembled trolls. "Bite them! Tear them to pieces!"

"I said QUIET!" shouted the Gaffer. He folded his arms and glared at the crowds. The crow rocked on his shoulder. "Get on with your work," he bellowed. "*Huuuu!* If we're not ready by midnight for the King of the Dovre, there won't *be* any wedding! And if that happens, I'll look at you all with my other eye and shrivel you into earthworms!"

Everyone immediately began to bustle about.

Hilde looked up to see Baldur bristling.

"You vixen!" he spat. He turned to the Gaffer. "Don't listen to her lies! We've done what you asked. We got you those children—just what you wanted!"

"S'right!" said Grim, punching a heavy fist into the palm of his other hand.

"Keep your promise! Give us our gold—as much as we can carry!"

"I'll *do* as I *please*," growled the Gaffer, and the two brothers fell unwillingly silent, clenching their fists.

There was a discordant blast of horns from a corner of the hall, and the little troll came hurrying in. It bowed several times, out of breath. "The princess!" it gasped. "And the prince!" it added.

Into the Hall came the Gaffer's eldest daughter. She was in a bad temper, for the occasion was so great. She had never been married before! She was pretty, for a troll: her mother had been a nixie. Her eyes were large, slanted like birch leaves, and she had only one tail.

"The spiders haven't finished my wedding dress!" she complained bitterly. "And my hair is a bird's nest. And look at all the dust! You should have raised the hill already and aired the place. Then North Wind could have swept in here. Whatever will they think of us? We shall never be ready in time!"

"Now, now, my dear," said the Gaffer fondly.

The troll princess stamped her foot. "I don't want the Dovreking to think I'm a bad housewife!"

"He won't think that as long as there's enough beer," chuckled the Gaffer. "Besides, my dear, look what I have for you! The Bride Cup you so foolishly lost, long ago!"

The troll princess looked at it carelessly. "That thing? You've got it back? So now you'll stop fussing. You're so hidebound, Father."

"It's an heirloom, my dear!"

Up came the troll prince, wearing a sulky expression on his piggish face. He took after his father, though he had only two eyes.

"These children you've got for us are terrible!" he burst out. "They won't fetch or carry or dance or sing. They won't do anything but scream and cry!"

"I can't possibly give the boy to my husband," agreed the troll princess.

"I can't possibly give the girl to my bride!"

They stamped their feet together and glared at their father, who in turn scowled at the Grimsson brothers.

"*Just what I wanted*, eh?" he growled threateningly. The eyelid in the middle of his forehead flickered, a red blink. The two huge men shifted their feet uneasily.

"How can they *sing* when they're unhappy? Where are they?" Hilde cried in distress, imagining the two little children locked up in some dark cave. But Peer pulled her arm and pointed. There, creeping nervously into the Hall, holding hands tightly, were Sigurd and Sigrid. Their dirty, tear-streaked faces brightened as they saw Hilde and Peer, and they raced across the floor to Hilde as she rushed to meet them. She grabbed one in each arm and hugged them hard against her.

"This'll teach you to go running off!" she choked. "I *told* you to stay near Grandpa!"

Sigrid sobbed. Peer tousled her hair, feeling a brotherly lump in his throat. "Don't, Hilde!" he whispered. "It's not their fault."

"I know," sniffed Hilde. "Don't cry, Siggy! It's all right now. We'll take you home."

"Will you, though?" asked the Gaffer drily.

Hilde turned and stared at him. "But I brought you the cup!" she exclaimed.

"And your son and your daughter don't want the children!" added Peer.

"It's what *I* want that counts!" The Gaffer grinned ferociously. "And it boils down to this! *I* want two of you for the Dovreking's son and daughter. Two humans, right? That's the bargain. So two of you may go—but two of you must stay!"

There was an awful silence. Hilde's mouth fell open.

"I'm feeling generous," added the Gaffer genially, "so I'll let you choose."

"You don't mean this!" said Hilde in disbelief.

"Oh yes I do!"

"But—" Hilde began. She stopped, gasping. "How *can* we choose?"

"Take your time!" the Gaffer advised with glee. "Think hard! Don't decide in a hurry!"

Sigurd and Sigrid tugged at their sister.

"Can't we go home?" Sigrid wept. Her mouth turned down at the corners. "I want to go home!"

"So do I!" cried Sigurd. They buried their faces in Hilde's clothes. She looked down at them hopelessly and bit her lip.

"Then I—I suppose I had better stay here," she whispered.

The Gaffer shifted his fat body and looked at Peer.

Peer felt sick. He looked around. He opened his mouth and closed it again, unable to say the words that would condemn him to a life of slavery under Troll Fell. Why, oh why, had he ever followed his uncles when he could have left them and gone safely to Hammerhaven, with Loki?

He looked at Hilde, and Hilde looked away. Peer thought it was scorn. He gritted his teeth. Why did she have to be so brave—showing him up? *It's easy for her—the twins are her family!*

Easy! He stole another glance at Hilde. Her head was bowed, her shoulders rigid, her fists clenched. *I'm lying,* Peer thought, ashamed. *How could it be easy?*

He stared dizzily round the Hall, his eyes passing over the scurrying trolls, the white strands of the waterfall, the moving lights in the dark roof. It was horribly strange and meaningless. Even though the cave was so large, his throat tightened. Under how much earth and rock was he buried? *I've got to get out!* he thought, choking. *Out, where the sun shines and the wind blows!* Again he looked at Hilde, who still would not look at him. And at last his eyes came to rest on his uncles; the stupid, brutal, calculating faces of Baldur and Grim.

A cold thought penetrated. What sort of life would it be, to go back to the mill with those two? Even if he escaped again, how could he live, knowing that he had abandoned Hilde?

I'd be as bad as they are! he thought in slow horror.

It was the same choice he had made on the mountain. But this time it was much harder. He closed his eyes, pressing his fingers over his eyelids. *I can't keep running away, Father,* he said silently into the darkness. *It doesn't work. It's time to stand up to them.*

He opened his eyes, his heart thumping so hard, it nearly burst his chest.

"I'll stay here too," he said in a loud voice, surprising even himself.

Hilde shot him a look of amazed and shining gratitude. Peer avoided her eye. If she thanked him, he might break down. He turned brusquely on the Gaffer. "I'll stay," he repeated, bleakly but firmly. "So look—don't give my uncles any treasure! They haven't earned it. You're not keeping Sigurd and Sigrid, and *we* came of our own free will!"

"Why, you little—!" screeched Uncle Baldur. "Don't listen to him, your majesty! Besides, that boy's my own nephew. You'll have to pay for him!"

The Gaffer howled with laughter, opening his mouth so wide he showed every jagged tooth. "Good boy! Excellent!" he chuckled. Baldur and Grim looked at each other, their brows blackening.

"Our treasure—our reward!" began Baldur.

"Nothing!" snapped the Gaffer. His mouth shut like a trap. The two brothers looked completely confounded. Peer was savagely delighted.

"When can the children go home?" Hilde demanded.

"Not till after the wedding," said the Gaffer. "We're too busy till then."

"And keep them quiet," ordered the troll princess. "Or I'll bite them!" She cast a critical at Hilde and Peer. "Come here, you two. Let me look at you." Her brother beckoned to Peer. Hilde squeezed Sigurd and Sigrid, whispering, "Hush now! It's all right. Wait here!"

"Humph!" said the troll princess. "They're bigger and stronger. I suppose that's better. Oh! Look at her boots! Why, they're better than mine!"

Hilde looked down. It was true she was wearing a good pair, made by her father and embroidered around the tops in red and blue thread.

The princess hoisted her skirts and showed a foot shod in a clumsy wooden clog.

"Let her have 'em," Peer advised from the corner of his mouth.

"Take them," said Hilde quietly. She pulled them off and gave them to the princess, who kicked off her clogs. Hilde slipped her own feet into them with a slight shudder.

The princess tugged the boots on. She was very pleased, and stuck out her feet. "Now I shall be finer than the

Dovreking's daughter! They pinch, it's true—but that's the price of elegance!"

"Now, there's plenty to do," the Gaffer shouted. "Has the beer come in yet?"

"Not yet. The bog wife has been brewing for us all week. I ordered twelve barrels. When the steam rises from her vats, the humans say, 'Oh, there's mist on the marshes!'" laughed his son.

"Twelve barrels of strong black beer? Excellent, my boy!" The Gaffer licked his lips with a long red tongue and turned to his daughter. "Take the girl away, my dear. She can help you to dress. As for you, boy, roll barrels or move tables. Make yourself useful!"

Peer looked at Hilde with a jolt of fright. They were being separated! They would be alone! Hilde understood, but she could only squeeze his hand and whisper, "I'll take the children with me. Good luck! I'll see you later."

And so Peer was set to work. It was like a fevered dream. The tables were now in place, so he joined a group of trolls sweeping the dance floor. It was made of polished black stone from an old volcano. As soon as it was shining like a sheet of black ice, he was called away to help to stack barrels. The bog wife's beer had just arrived. Meanwhile the nixies were laying the tables with a gold plate at every place. There were no knives: the guests would eat with their fingers.

Or paws, or claws, thought Peer, looking at the strange creatures working beside him. No two trolls were alike. He stopped one that went trotting past him with huge eyes and a long beak like a curlew's, and asked it what to do next.

"Come to the kitchens," piped the troll. "Help the cooks!" It seized his arm and rushed him over to a dark crack in the floor. Hot air rose from it, and the strangest smells. As Peer teetered on the edge, the troll pushed him. With a cry he shot down into the darkness, whipping down a natural slide, and was spat out into a lower cavern filled with a red mist of steam and smoke and cooking fires. He landed on all fours. The troll popped out beside him. Peer got up painfully, rubbing bruised knees. He choked on the fumes.

"Whatever are they cooking?" he coughed. The troll piped something hard to hear—had it really said, "Frog soup, eel pie, spittle cakes—bone bread"?

So these were the kitchens. Hot fires blazed everywhere, and frenzied trolls rushed about with ladles, wooden spoons, colanders, and platters. A rhythmic thumping came from one corner, where a couple of trolls were working a huge pestle and mortar, pounding a pile of bones into smaller and smaller fragments. Nearby was a hand quern for grinding them into flour and a series of wooden troughs where several small trolls danced up and down on the dough. Batches of the gritty bread were being lifted out of the ovens.

Great steaming pots hung over the fires. Peer glanced into one. It held a bubbling, glutinous mess that looked like frog spawn. He gulped and backed off.

By one fire a greasy little troll was crouching, turning a spit on which a whole pig was roasting. Or was it a—?

"Dog!" squeaked the troll. That wasn't—*Grendel, by any chance?* Peer wondered. It looked big enough. He looked away quickly, feeling ill, and wondered how he and Hilde would live. Never, never could they eat troll food.

We'll escape, he swore to himself. *They can't guard us forever. We'll pretend to be happy. When they trust us, we'll escape. Perhaps we can follow the stream—it must find its way out somewhere!*

A particularly pungent smell caught him in the throat and he coughed till he retched. Now the Hall above seemed an airy refuge. How could he get back up? Surely the food couldn't go that way? Through streaming eyes he spotted a flight of steps. His troll had forgotten him, and he darted across and ran up a twisting spiral. Emerging into the cool Hall, he blinked. It must all have taken longer than he'd thought, for the tables were prepared and guests were arriving and being shown to their seats. It was confusing to look at so many different creatures, but he did notice the merrows, sitting in their tubs of water. The women were beautiful, with long, mournful faces, but the men had swarthy green skin that looked rough and scaly. Everywhere, gold gleamed and silver shone. Jewels winked on the crowns of the Gaffer of Troll Fell and of his son and daughter, who stood in front of the throne, welcoming the arrivals. Peer noticed that the crow was now perching on the rim of the Gaffer's crown, where it looked like a strange black crest.

Where was Hilde? Over there, sitting forlornly on the rocks by the waterfall, with Sigurd beside her and Sigrid on her lap. He waved his hand. She spotted him and gave him a wan smile. And there were Baldur and Grim, seated at a table, heads together, deep in some grumbling conversation. They wouldn't go without their gold. Peer smiled grimly: they would have to wait a very long time! A group of pig-snouted musicians tuned up—or maybe they were playing! One blew a twisted ram's horn; another sawed notes from a one-string fiddle; a third rattled a stick up and down a sheep's jawbone. It was a terrible noise.

There was a shout. "The King of the Dovrefell! He's arriving, he's here!"

"Raise up the hill!" shouted the Gaffer of Troll Fell. "Time for some fun!"

CHAPTER 17

Raising the Hill

With a rumbling and rattling of all the dishes on the tables, the roof began to rise. All around the Hall a gap appeared, a widening strip of night sky, fringed with trailing roots and ragged earth. Clods rained down from the edges, and a draft of cold air rushed into the Hall, smelling of snow, fresh earth, and freedom. Hoisted up on four strong red pillars, the hill stood open to the midwinter night, spilling light to all sides. Dazzlingly bright, Troll Fell shone like a beacon.

As the musicians struck up a lively march, sadly out of tune, the King of the Dovrefell and his party swept down into the Hall on the night wind. They landed in a chattering group, collecting themselves and adjusting their clothes. Peer pushed forward, trying to see. The King of the Dovre was taller than the Gaffer of Troll Fell, very cool and dignified. He threw back the hood of his white bearskin cloak and strode forward, with his son behind him and his daughter clutching his arm. Peer couldn't see her face. He remembered that this was the princess whose elder sister had two tails. Hadn't the Nis said she was beautiful? She lifted her veil, and a murmur of admiration ran around the hall. The Troll Fell princess was looking as cross as two sticks. Peer edged around curiously.

The Dovre princess had three tails. Two were draped nonchalantly over her elbows; the other sprouted from the middle of her forehead and was knotted up elegantly to keep it out of her eyes. The Troll Fell prince greeted her eagerly, looking smitten already. Peer closed his eyes and shook his head.

The Gaffer and the Dovreking clasped hands. "Welcome!" boomed the Gaffer. He slapped the Dovreking on the back. "A drink to warm you after your journey! And we'll let the young people get to know each other, hey?" He laughed loudly.

The two princesses were bristling at one another like cats.

"What a funny little place you have here," observed the Dovre princess loudly. "Very rustic. I see you have a sod roof. At home in the Dovrefell, our Hall is so high that the roof is carved from ice."

The Troll Fell princess smiled coldly. "That must be very chilly. Here we enjoy simple comfort and despise ostentation."

"I imagine you have to," replied the Dovre princess.

"Will you dance?" asked the Troll Fell prince hurriedly. But his bride said she was tired and would rather sit down.

The Dovre prince bowed to the Troll Fell princess and remarked that her dress was charming (*The spiders must have finished it in time!* thought Peer), but after that he fell silent and found very little to say. They sat stiffly together and the Troll Fell princess yawned.

"Now then! Brighten up!" shouted the Gaffer. He and the Dovreking were laughing and drinking and seemed to be getting along famously. "You're not allowed to quarrel till *after* you're married, you know! You boys, don't be shy. Give your brides a hug and a kiss to break the ice!"

"Vulgar old fellow!" muttered the Dovre princess.

"Let's exchange presents," boomed the King of the Dovrefell in a deep voice. "That'll cheer them all up! We brought a few small things from the Dovrefell."

He snapped his fingers. Two stout trolls stepped forward with a heavy sack. They untied the mouth and poured a stream of jewels onto the floor. Diamonds, rubies, amethysts, and emeralds rattled out of the sack like peas and lay on the floor in a shimmering drift. Many bounced and rolled under the tables. Baldur and Grim crashed heads as they both lunged to pick up a skipping diamond. They climbed off their chairs and groveled, crawling about stuffing more gems into their pockets.

"Very pretty!" said the Gaffer. From its perch on his head the crow peered down at the glowing heap and croaked derisively. The Gaffer beckoned to various servants, who went scuttling off and came staggering back with piles of gold:

necklaces, rings, bracelets, chains, and crowns. It looked like a dragon's hoard.

"Part of a dragon's hoard," said the Gaffer, waving his hand casually. Peer glanced at his uncles. They were stretching their necks, and their mouths were wet with excitement.

The Dovreking frowned, and snapped his fingers again. This time his trolls laid out piles of beautifully woven and embroidered clothes, each one of which would have taken a human seamstress a year to make. But these were not made by mortals. There were scarves snipped from the trailing ends of the Northern Lights, embroidered by fireflies. There were petticoats trimmed with the most delicate frost. There were seven-league boots lined with ermine. The Troll Fell princess got a cloak of moonshine that pleased her so much she threw her arms around the Dovreking and gave him a kiss.

"Aha!" said the Dovreking, pinching her cheek.

But the Gaffer grinned triumphantly.

"Now for a little extra—a special present," he gloated. "You won't have brought anything like *this* from the Dovrefell!"

Two little trolls dashed forward and caught Peer by the arms. They dusted him down quickly and hung a clammy cloak over his shoulders. Two more were doing the same for Hilde. Peer's heart leaped uncomfortably. He caught Hilde's eye, wishing he could tell her his idea about escaping along the stream. She mouthed at him, "Here we come!"

Together they stepped forward. *Better make a good job of it!* thought Peer gloomily, and he bowed low. Hilde was curtseying to the three-tailed princess, who screamed in mock terror and clutched her bridegroom's arm.

"Oooh! What is it? What is it for?"

"A little rarity," the Gaffer boasted. "Something you don't see every day. Your highness's new maidservant!"

"Humans!"

"Yes, of course!" broke in the Troll Fell princess. "We wanted something different." She pushed the pile of jewels with a contemptuous toe. "We see so much of this kind of thing. We decided to be original!"

The two free tails of the Dovre princess swished angrily; the one knotted up above her face could only twitch.

"What a strange idea," she said. "She's very plain. All that unhealthy daylight, I suppose. Turn around, girl. I thought so! This ugly creature has no tail at all!"

"We don't have tails!" said Peer, angry for Hilde, who was blushing miserably.

"Take her away at once and fix one on!"

"Oh, no! Please!" cried Hilde. "We think tails are ugly— only on humans, I mean!" she hastily added.

"Oh, what an insult!" screamed the Dovre princess. But the Gaffer stepped forward and bowed as gallantly as he could. "Now, now," he rumbled. "No cause for concern. We all appreciate your beauty, my dear. I myself have three eyes"—he coughed modestly—"but three tails are rare indeed."

His daughter scowled. The Dovre princess simpered.

"No," the Gaffer went on, "we've simply neglected one

small ceremony. After that, these humans will see things as *we* do. Here, you two!" He snapped his fingers and led them aside.

"Ceremony?" Peer asked apprehensively as they followed.

The Gaffer turned. "You haven't yet tasted our food or drink! A morsel of bread, a sip of our beer, and you'll see things our way for ever and ever!"

"For ever and ever?" Peer repeated blankly.

"Excuse me—but we'll think the Dovre princess is beautiful?" asked Hilde.

"You will indeed," agreed the Gaffer.

"Then we won't notice that tail growing out of her face?"

"You'll glory in it!"

"And the food?" Peer was too shaken to be polite. "We'll enjoy eating frog soup and rat stew?"

"And the music," put in Hilde quickly. "At the moment it sounds like—like a cat on the roof and a cow in pain. It's giving me a headache."

"I'm getting annoyed!" said the Gaffer ominously. He squared up to them. "Now, look! This is all a matter of opinion! See my son! Isn't he handsome?"

Hilde looked. The Troll Fell prince swaggered a little. He was wearing his bejeweled crown tilted over one hairy ear.

"We can't have servants who don't admire us!" the Gaffer went on. "Once you've drunk our brew, you'll think black is white! You'll think night is day, and wrong is right! And so they are. It's only another way of looking."

"But then," said Hilde, appalled, "we won't be *us*!" She looked around wildly. "We *are* what we think! We won't be human anymore. Inside, we'll be trolls!"

"AND WHAT'S THE MATTER WITH THAT?" roared the Gaffer.

There was a moment's silence. Peer and Hilde stared at the glittering crowds, and then at each other. Everything seemed very sharp and clear, and also a little distant. Peer tasted fear, sour in his mouth. Between the red pillars supporting the roof he could see the dark spaces of the night sky. Out there lay freedom, the snowy slopes, the stars. But he would never reach it.

We won't escape, he thought in horror. *We'll never follow the stream out of the hill. I thought we'd get out one day, even if we had to wait months or years. But now!*

He shuddered. He who eats a troll's food becomes a troll. And so, when he and Hilde had eaten a mouthful of bone bread, or drunk a drop of the bog wife's beer, they wouldn't even *want* to leave. They would live forever like earthworms under Troll Fell. They might still look the same, but on the inside they would have changed completely.

We might as well be dead.

One of the Gaffer's trolls came trotting up. Dimly Peer recognized it, the kitchen troll with the long beak. It bowed to the Gaffer, presenting a gold platter and a cup. The platter was heaped with fragments of crumbly whitish bread. The cup was Ralf's cup, the Bride Cup, the one they had brought with them, and it was half full of beer.

"Right!" said the Gaffer, briskly lashing his tail. "Who's going first?"

Hilde met Peer's eyes, despairing but steady.

"I'm so sorry I got you into this, Peer," she muttered.

"You didn't!" said Peer. "I wanted to come."

She reached out for the goblet, but Peer was quicker and snatched it up first. "Wait!" he said breathlessly.

He looked down into the cup. The dark liquid swirled, a bottomless whirlpool. He glanced up, to look at the world for the last time as himself. His throat closed. There was a drumming in his ears. Or was that the Gaffer, growling as threateningly as Grendel himself? He bent his head over the cup, lifting it reluctantly to his lips, spinning out the seconds . . .

The moment dragged past. There was no time left.

And Hilde shouted. "Peer! Stop!" He lowered the cup. Out in the dark, beyond the pillars, he saw lights. Lanterns! People were out there, real people struggling up through the snow! Someone else shouted; a dog barked. The trolls began to turn around, chattering uneasily. With a rattle of feathers the crow took off from the Gaffer's crown and swept out into the darkness and back again, croaking a harsh warning. More shouts, closer! A scuffle broke out, a clang of metal! Then uproar as a band of rough-looking men came shoving their way into the Hall. They were staring about in amazement, pointing here and there. Hey, that was Bjorn! And there was Arnë! But who was that big man in front, wearing a dented iron helmet over his long hair? He was looking about and shouting, "Hilde! Hilde!"

Peer felt Hilde reel against him. He turned and saw her shocked white face, mouth open, eyes like stars. "Peer! That's my *father*!" she whispered.

"Pa! *Pa!*" There were screams from Sigurd and Sigrid, who picked themselves up from the corner where they had been sitting like mice and tore across the floor to fling themselves at their father. Ralf hoisted Sigrid to his shoulder. Behind him, Gudrun appeared, bundled in furs, her thin face alive with gladness as she seized Sigurd.

The trolls backed away, and the Dovre princess screamed. Two dogs dashed through the crowd, barking madly. As neatly as if he were cutting through a flock of sheep, Alf threaded his way up to Hilde, followed by Loki, who threw himself on Peer, bowling him over. Both dogs were bursting with pride and excitement.

"The dogs knew!" Ralf bellowed, thrusting his way toward Hilde. "By thunder, they knew! They've dragged us all the way up from the fjord—ripped my clothes, see? We had to leave poor old Eirik behind—he'd have killed himself trying. *Good* dog! *Good* dog!" (This to Alf, who was fawning around him.) He reached Hilde and wrapped her in a bear hug. "The dogs showed us the way, but the gate was shut!" He squeezed her half to death. "We've been desperate—searching the slopes for hours. Thank God they opened the hill!"

The din was bewildering. Men shouted, children screamed,

dogs barked. The Dovre princess was fainting; the Dovreking had drawn himself up, looking outraged and alarmed. Trolls howled, squeaked, and grunted. The Gaffer of Troll Fell raised his arms and tried to speak. No one listened. His tail coiling in fury, he grabbed a horn from the nearest of the musicians and blew and blew and blew, a deafening blast. Peer thought his cheeks would split, but the horn cracked into two pieces. The Gaffer threw them away.

"QUIET!" he roared. And quiet fell.

"Get out of here, Ralf Eiriksson," yelled the old troll, swelling with rage. He glared at Ralf out of a red triangle of all three eyes, like an old spider. "Get out before it's too late. It's all settled. You can take your younger children home, but the elder girl stays. And her friend, too."

Ralf strode forward through the ring of trolls pressing around the villagers. He looked tall, strong, and dangerous. Peer, sitting on the ground with his arm around Loki's warm side, looked up in hope. If this was Hilde's father, surely he could save them? He spared a glance for his two uncles. They had pushed themselves back from their table and were staring at Ralf with horrified, bulging eyes, as if they had seen a ghost.

"Do you think I'd leave my children?" demanded Ralf. "How dare you trolls steal them!"

"Trolls didn't steal 'em," shouted the Gaffer. "Men did!" He pointed to Baldur and Grim. Ralf, who had not noticed them before, swung around in a fury.

"Men?" he asked contemptuously. The two brothers rose blustering to their feet, dropping handfuls of gems. "*Men?* Those aren't men. Those are beasts—animals!"

"No, they're men," snarled the Gaffer. "Your own sort! Don't get all high and mighty with me, Eiriksson. You humans think you're so much better than the rest of us. Dream on! We trolls are realists. That's the difference! Anyway, you can take away the children they stole. The other two are staying of their own free will."

"That's a lie," Ralf said. "Hilde?"

"We—we did promise," said Hilde faintly, "but it was only to rescue Sigurd and Sigrid. He says he needs two of us as—as servants. Wedding presents for them!" She nodded toward the princes and princesses. Ralf's eyes followed, and he spotted the Troll Fell princess with a frown of recognition.

"I know you," he said slowly. The Troll Fell princess gave him a sly, curling smile. Ralf clenched his fist. "By heaven, that's it!" he exclaimed. "You're the one who gave me the cup all that time ago. Aren't you? Well, here's a deal." He swung around on her father. "Give me the children and you can have your gold cup!"

In response, the Gaffer picked up the cup from where Peer had put it down on the table in front of him. He raised it to Ralf in a mocking toast, slurped the beer in one greedy gulp, and set it down with a bang. Ralf stared at the goblet, speechless.

"I already tried that, Pa, and it didn't work," said Hilde

miserably. Ralf rubbed a big hand desperately over his face.

"What's to prevent us grabbing the children and leaving now?" he inquired.

The Gaffer nodded toward the crowd of trolls.

"What's to prevent us tearing you all to pieces?" he asked with a grin. "Just relax, Ralf Eiriksson. I'm the master of Troll Fell, and what I say goes!"

Ralf looked around, poised tensely on the balls of his feet, as if ready to attack. Arnë, Bjorn, and the other men edged closer to him. Peer and Hilde looked around too. There were too many trolls to be counted, all waiting with teeth and claws and hooves and horns, their glittering eyes fixed on the village people. The odds were hopeless. Peer held his breath, steeling himself for a frightful battle. But then Ralf sighed deeply and his shoulders slumped in defeat. The Gaffer saw it and clapped his hands.

"But no fighting at a wedding!" he roared. "Beer all around! It's time to pledge the health of the two happy couples!" All the guests broke into cheers and laughter. With a rumbling sound the big barrels were rolled forward and broached. Little trolls sprang forward with cups, jugs, and pitchers and rushed to serve the tables. Up from the kitchens poured a stream of even more trolls bearing huge trays of smoking and steaming food.

Hilde ran to Ralf and disappeared into another huge hug. Peer felt a nudge at his elbow. A small troll was impatiently shoving a jug of beer at him and making signs that he was to pour it out for the top table. Peer took it uncertainly and held it for a moment.

"I suppose I'm still a page," he thought, sniffing the beer cautiously. It smelled all right, though it looked thick and black, like liquid mud. Perhaps there was a slight marshy whiff, but the bog wife obviously brewed well.

He glanced around. The royal party was coming back to life; the princes and princesses were seating themselves at their tables. The Gaffer laid an arm over the Dovreking's shoulders and led him to his place.

Uncle Baldur and Uncle Grim were happily sitting on their benches again, comparing fistfuls of jewels they had collected from the floor. Their bushy black beards wagged as they argued about their shares. Peer hoped that the Gaffer would notice they were stealing, but none of the trolls seemed to care. The Gaffer of Troll Fell was not going to fuss about losing a few jewels when he wanted to impress the Dovreking.

Peer looked for Hilde and saw her leaning against her father and mother, sniffing. Ralf patted her shoulder, saying soothingly, "Don't worry. Don't worry. We'll never go without you."

"Pa, what can you do?" Hilde asked desperately.

Ralf clenched his fist. "We can fight! We can form a shield wall—go down like heroes—"

"Don't be silly," said Gudrun bitterly. "You don't *have* any shields."

Peer looked back at his two uncles and absolutely hated them. There they were, they had caused all this misery, yet so far as he could see they didn't care a fig. In fact, Baldur was chuckling now and rubbing his hands. They would walk out of here with all those jewels and go back to the mill and carry on with their horrible lives. Ralf couldn't stop them, unless he killed them. And somehow Peer knew Ralf wouldn't kill them. Ralf wasn't the type.

If anyone's going to get them, Peer thought suddenly, *it'll have to be me.*

And the very next moment he saw the way to do it. Simple, obvious, and beautiful.

Could Baldur and Grim have overheard what the Gaffer had said about troll food and drink? Peer didn't think so. They had not been close enough. He walked quietly over to the high table and picked up the beautiful golden goblet. No one was watching him, and even if they were, he was only doing what a servant should. He gave it a quick polish on his sleeve and filled it with beer.

The bog wife's brew rushed foaming into the goblet, a rich bitter broth with a tang of moss and, again, that faint, half-attractive rotten whiff. Careful not to splash, Peer carried it smoothly over to his uncles and set it down between them.

They didn't even look up to see who he was. Arguing over a couple of big emeralds, Uncle Baldur seized the goblet in one massive hairy hand and set it to his lips. He tipped his head back and swallowed. The bog wife's beer glugged down his throat.

"Here—give me some!" His brother snatched the cup and swirled it. "There's only half left!" he snarled, gulping the beer down quickly and shoving the cup back toward Peer. "It's good! Here, boy—fill that up!" Peer did so gladly.

As Baldur once again raised the cup to his lips, it jarred and slopped. It had struck something hard. Peer held his breath and backed away. Something strange was growing through one side of Baldur's beard. And on the other side, too! Baldur dropped the cup and grabbed at his face. He felt something hard and curved and pointed. He stared at his brother. Grim, too, was feeling his face. Out from the hairy tangles of black beard protruded two curving white—

"Tusks!" Peer's yell of delight echoed through the Hall. "Look! Uncle Baldur and Uncle Grim have got tusks!"

Everyone turned. And from both trolls and men, there came a mighty roar of laughter, as Baldur and Grim stood rubbing their jowls in bewilderment, their treasure completely forgotten.

"Pigs! We always thought they looked like pigs," Hilde called to Peer, laughing between her tears.

The Troll Fell princess came slipping up to Ralf. "That would have happened to you, too, if you had drunk from it!" she murmured, pinching his arm. "What a pity you didn't stay with me. So big and strong!" Ralf brushed her off angrily, but as he did so his face suddenly altered. His eyes widened. He sprang forward.

"Hey, your majesty, or whatever you call yourself!"

The Gaffer turned.

"You wanted two?" Ralf asked. "Two human servants? A matching pair?"

"You know I do," scowled the old troll.

Ralf swung around and pointed straight at Baldur and Grim.

"Then there they are!" he roared. "THERE'S YOUR MATCHING PAIR!"

"Oh, yes!" shouted Hilde in delight. "Twins! And they've already drunk your beer! Oh, Peer, well done!" She beamed at him.

Peer grinned breathlessly back. They looked at the Gaffer, who looked at his guests. "I *wanted* a girl and a boy. But it's for the bride to say!" he remarked, staring at the Dovre princess, who shrugged ill-temperedly. She rose to her feet and took a look at Baldur and Grim, who still stood, swaying and fingering their faces. She flicked her napkin.

"Yes, yes, they'll do," she said pettishly. "Better than the others, in fact. They have such nice, trollish faces."

"Yes!"

Peer rushed at Hilde and hugged her, swinging her off her feet. Laughing and crying, she hugged him back. And suddenly Peer found himself surrounded by a crowd of friendly villagers, all trying at once to shake his hand and rumple his hair and bang him on the back. He came face-to-face with Gudrun. She flung her arms around him. "Oh, Peer! You blessed boy!" She kissed him on both cheeks. Beside him,

Loki was leaping, jealously trying to squeeze in and get his share. He nipped Peer's fingers.

And now Ralf and Bjorn and the others were shepherding them out. The trolls were falling back to make a path for them. Peer cast a backward look over his shoulder. Good-bye, the glittering splendor of the Hall under Troll Fell! Behind him the musicians were already striking up again. Couples ventured onto the dance floor. Wasn't that the Troll Fell prince, doing an astounding somersault to impress his bride? And there were Uncle Grim and Uncle Baldur, sitting down heavily, reaching for more of the beer that had turned them into trolls. Much good those jewels would do them now!

"Perhaps they always were trolls, on the inside," Peer murmured. "Perhaps it won't change them very much!"

A dark figure flitted through the throng. Could that be Granny Green-teeth? He tried to wave to her, but Hilde had his hand and was dragging him along.

"What's the matter with you, Peer? Come on!"

His foot sank into snow. A chill wind curled around him and his breath smoked. He had crossed the boundary and was outside, on the slopes of Troll Fell.

CHAPTER 18
How It All Ended

"B ut where had you been?" Hilde asked Ralf, the next day.

It was late morning, and the little farmhouse seemed very full. Peer and Hilde had only hazy memories of the journey back down Troll Fell the night before. They had been asleep on their feet. They didn't remember how, in the end, Arnë and Bjorn had picked them up and carried them. They didn't remember being put to bed. They only knew they had slept long and deeply, and had awoken to the savory smell of breakfast.

Gudrun was baking oatcakes on the griddle.

"A special breakfast for a special day," she said, smiling. She put a dab of butter on the first one and handed it to Peer over the heads of Sigrid and Sigurd. "For the guest of honor!"

It was smoking hot. The butter ran over his fingers. Peer juggled it from hand to hand before taking the first nibble. It was delicious, crumbly and buttery and salty, the best food he had ever tasted.

"Mmmm!" he exclaimed, wolfing it down. Loki materialized beside him, thumping his tail hopefully and glueing greedy eyes on the last piece.

"Go on!" said Peer, giving in. It vanished like lightning.

"Give Loki a whole oatcake, Ma," begged Hilde. "He deserves it. Alf, too."

"Waste good food on the dogs?" asked Gudrun. But she was only pretending to be indignant, for she patted Alf as she passed him, and said "Good boy!" to Loki.

"It's amazing how they found us last night," she said, shaking her head in wonder. "How could they tell we were down by the fjord? We shall never know."

Everyone looked at the dogs in silence. The dogs looked embarrassed, ducking their heads.

"So they *do* deserve an oatcake," said Hilde.

"They can have the one Sigurd dropped," said Gudrun. At that, Sigrid deliberately dropped hers, so that the dogs could have one each.

When Gudrun had finished scolding (and she didn't try very hard) and they were all sitting up with a couple of oatcakes each and a big jug of buttermilk on the table, Hilde asked, "But, Pa, where had you been?"

"Now, *there's* a story," said Ralf happily, "that will keep us busy for many a winter's night." He leaned back on his bench and looked around the room.

"We know you got down the coast, way below Hammerhaven," said Gudrun. "Arnë told us that. But afterward . . . and he told us there'd been a sinking—"

Her voice trembled and she stopped abruptly.

"Poor old girl," exclaimed Ralf, squeezing her hand. "How I wish Arnë had never told you that. He meant well, I know, and some poor sailor men must have drowned. But it wasn't us, you see. We were as right as rain."

"So what did happen?" asked Hilde impatiently.

"We sailed west," said Ralf. "West for the Shetlands and then northwest for the Faroes. Small islands with a few settlements. They live there by keeping sheep, like us, and catching whales! Aye, they drive the whales onto the beaches and kill them there. We helped! And seabirds! I've never seen so many.

"But our skipper, Thorolf—you saw him yesterday, he's staying with Bjorn now—he has a brother in Iceland, on Breidafjord. So from the Faroes we set off again, northwest for Iceland. And this would be late summer.

"Now here it gets exciting!" He winked at Hilde. "We never made Iceland! We were struck by a terrible gale and driven due west. Three days it blew. The steering rope snapped; we spent all our time bailing, soaked to the skin and our lips cracking with the salt. We hoped to make Greenland. But after the storm we had a north wind, and then fog. For days we were lost, helpless. I tell you, we all wished then we had never left home!"

"Go on!" gasped Gudrun.

"At last the sun came out," said Ralf, "the fog began to clear, and there we all were, hanging on to the ropes, staring out for a sight of where we might be—and we saw it. Land!"

"Greenland!" said Hilde knowingly.

"No!" Ralf shook his head. "Not Greenland. Greenland is all ice and mountains. We saw low hills covered in green shaggy forests."

He leaned forward impressively. "We had found the land at the other end of the world!"

The family sat with their eyes and mouths wide open.

"Did you land?" gasped Hilde.

"Aye, that we did! We were gasping for fresh water, and dry ground underfoot. But as we rowed into this lonely bay, we all wondered if the land was real or an enchantment. Would it vanish as we set foot on it and leave us struggling in the gray salty sea?

"Well, it was real." He looked around at their riveted expressions and said mischievously, "I'm still hungry, Gudrun! Any more of those oatcakes?"

"Oh!" Gudrun jumped up. "I'll make some—but go on, Ralf—keep talking!"

"This is the stuff of a fine saga!" said old Eirik in a voice quavering with excitement. His bowl of groute was going cold on his knee, and he had dropped his spoon.

"You've got to make a poem about this, Grandpa!" Hilde encouraged him. Eirik slapped his thigh. "I will indeed. What a story—*what* a story! To find a new land, with no people! Go on, my son."

"But there were people!" Ralf spoke through a mouthful of oatcake. "We didn't know that for a long time, though. First we had to mend the boat. Then we went hunting and fishing. What a wonderful place! The rivers full of trout and salmon. Beavers and deer in the woods. I tell you I half thought of coming back and bringing you all!

"We decided to call it Wood Land, and the days just slipped by. . . ."

He jumped to his feet. "But why spoil a good story by rushing it? This should last us for many nights. Not another word now!" His eyes twinkled at their disappointed faces.

"Just tell us one more thing," begged Hilde. "The people—what did they look like?"

"Brown faces!" declared Ralf dramatically. "Brown all over, like smoked oak. And black hair—black as jet. With feathers in it."

"Ohhh!" wailed Hilde. "I can't wait. You have to tell us more!"

"Tonight," Ralf promised. He stretched his arms. "Now I want to go and look all around the farm—check the sheep—visit the cow—look at the fences. I want to really feel I'm home again. I want to get down to some good, solid work."

Peer glanced up. Perhaps this was his chance.

"Ralf," he said shyly. "You don't happen to need a boy, do you?"

"Oh, yes, Pa!" said Hilde quickly. "Can't Peer live with us?"

Ralf looked quizzically at Peer. "A boy?" he said, turning the words over in his mouth as though seeing how they tasted. "A boy? No, I can't really say that I need a boy. I've got Hilde, you see, and the twins growing up, and it's a small place—no, I don't really need a boy."

"Oh, Ralf!" cried Gudrun reproachfully while Peer bit his lip. But Ralf was still talking. "So, I don't need a boy, as such," he went on. "But Peer Ulfsson, who went after the twins— Peer Ulfsson, who stood by Hilde and helped her—Peer Ulfsson, who offered to stay in Troll Fell to rescue Sigurd—I think we certainly need him!"

"Hooray!" Hilde cheered. Peer blushed scarlet. Ralf put his hands on Peer's shoulders and shook him gently.

"It's not for the work you can do, my lad," he said, "though I'm sure you'll be useful. It's not because we need you—it's because we want you."

Peer tried to speak. To his horror, he felt his eyes filling with tears. Gudrun stepped forward and put her arms around him, and he was glad to hide his head against her apron.

"You belong in this family now, and we're proud of you!" she said briskly. "Yes, and you, too!" She nodded to Loki, who gave a surprised sneeze. Peer managed a shaky laugh and went to make a fuss of Loki till he had control of himself again.

"That's a good little dog," Ralf approved. "Smart and loyal. We'll soon train him to be a fine sheepdog, won't we, Alf?" Alf gave his master an adoring look. He had practically glued himself to Ralf's side, and now, as Ralf reached down his old coat and headed for the door, Alf followed like an extra shadow. He had no intention of allowing his master to escape ever again!

Peer watched Ralf go out and then reached for a cloak himself. He was happier than he could have imagined, but he was not yet quite comfortable just sitting there and chatting. And there was something he wanted to do.

"Where are you going?" asked Hilde.

"Down to the mill," said Peer quietly.

"I suppose it belongs to you, now!" said Hilde in surprise. "Does it?"

"I don't know," said Peer, startled. "But there's animals there. Someone has to feed the sheep. . . ."

"Shall I come?"

Peer hesitated. He really wanted to go by himself, or his idea might not work. Still, it was only fair to tell them about it.

"You see," he stammered, "there's the Nis."

Hilde put her hand to her mouth. "The poor Nis! I'd forgotten about it. Nobody lives at the mill now, do they?"

"So I wondered," said Peer, "if it might like to come here. Would that be all right, Gudrun?"

"Gracious!" said Gudrun. "I suppose so. Is it well behaved?"

Peer thought. "Well, not very," he said, "but I think it would be if we treated it nicely. With Baldur and Grim it wasn't."

"That's no surprise," Gudrun sniffed. "Very well, Peer, you can try. But mind, you'll have to tell it to be good!"

Wrapped up warmly in a thick cloak, Peer set off by himself down the valley. It was midafternoon. It wasn't snowing, but the wind was keen and the skies were gray. He tramped down through the wood and came at last in sight of the mill.

It seemed an age since he had been there; so much had happened. But he could still see the broken ice on the mill-pond, frozen over again but still visible as the spot where Grendel had gone through. Was it really only two nights ago?

He shook his head and tramped on downhill to the foot-bridge and over it into the mill yard. The sheep in their pen began bleating hungrily as soon as they saw him. He pushed open the barn door to fetch the hay and stepped into a star-burst of black feathers.

There was a chorus of anxious clucks. Peer squinted up into the rafters and saw the huddled shapes of his chickens. He counted them. All nine were there, but not the black cockerel or his scrawny wives. There were feathers everywhere. And there was a strong smell of fox. The hens had clearly had a terrible experience.

"Hmmm!" said Peer. He scattered grain on the floor. "Come down and eat, you silly things!" Subdued, repentant, humble, the hens scrambled down from the rafters and began picking away gratefully.

"Ralf and I will come for you tomorrow, with a basket," Peer told them. "We'll take you somewhere safe." The hens cackled pathetically.

Peer fed the sheep and the oxen and tossed a few armfuls of hay to Bristles and the sow, although he could hardly bear to look at them for being reminded of his uncles. *Maybe Bjorn and Arnë would like to have them,* he thought.

Finally he pushed open the mill door and ventured inside. It was dark and cold. The fire had gone out. The wreckage of the millstone still lay where it had landed on the splintered wooden chest. There was no sound.

"Nis?" called Peer quietly. "Are you here?"

He looked around, hoping to see a small shadow flit from beam to beam or to catch the gleam of its eyes, but nothing moved.

"Nis?"

It was growing dark. The short day was done. Peer backed out of the cold and lonely mill, wondering with a sigh if the Nis had already gone. He stood for a moment leaning on the doorpost, looking into the yard. Did all this really belong to him now? It wasn't something he felt ready to think about yet. The pile of snow that the Nis had pushed off the barn roof still lay there in a long heap, and he remembered the dogfight with a shudder.

It was then that he heard a light sound, a scuffling noise, and before he could move, a white fox came skipping into the yard. It was playing games in the snow, chasing its tail, running in rings, dashing about. Peer watched, enchanted. So here was the culprit, probably back for a few more hens! He decided to make sure the barn door was firmly shut.

He blinked. There seemed to be a little whirlwind blowing about the yard—a thin, swirling column of snow playing with

the fox. He rubbed his eyes. Or was it a little wispy gray creature with big hands and feet, scampering wildly in the snow
beside the fox?

"Nis?" he called. There was a scurry of snow. Something ran
across the yard, kicking little spurts from its heels. The fox sat
down suddenly and turned its sharp face toward him, panting
as though it was laughing. Something jumped onto the mill
roof. A large chunk of snow flumped off the eaves on to his
head and shoulders and went down his neck.

"Stop it!" Peer yelped, laughing and wriggling his shoulders. A cross little voice muttered above his head:

"They all forgets the poor Nis!"

"Nis!" said Peer firmly and kindly, "I haven't forgotten you.
Listen. You don't have to stay in the cold mill. I'm living up at
Ralf Eiriksson's farm now. Please come too! We'd love to have
you in the house. There'll be hot groute with butter every day.
I promise!"

He heard no reply. But the wispy little wind whirled itself
onto the fox's back, and the white fox straightened out and
went streaking out of the yard and over the wooden bridge.

Peer followed its tracks in the snow all the way home, grinning to himself. The Nis was wasting no time!

Hilde greeted him at the farmhouse door. "Suppertime!"
she called. "And it's a funny thing, but the floor seems to have
swept itself in the last half hour, and the logs have stacked
themselves neatly, and it didn't seem to take half as long for
the kettle to boil. I think your Nis has come home!"

Gudrun peeped over her shoulder. "It's like magic!" she told him in an awed whisper. "At least—I suppose that's what it *is*, really. It's a marvelous help, Peer! I hope it stays here. What do you say it likes to eat?" And before she sat down, she poured out a full bowl of groute, carefully stirring in the butter, and set it on the warm hearthstone. As a final touch she spooned in some honey.

From then on the Nis was positively spoiled!

That evening, and for many more to come, they listened spellbound to one another's stories. Peer and Hilde had much to tell of the wonders they had seen under Troll Fell. Eirik spun the tale of how he and Gudrun had struggled down to the fjord, their despair at finding the village deserted, and their joy at discovering the longship. He made such a good job of it that Gudrun herself shook her head and declared, while they laughed at her, "What an adventure!"

But the best and the newest story of all was Ralf's. With his arm around Gudrun and the little ones on his knee, he told them more and more about the green forests at the other end of the world, of the dark-haired people who spoke a strange language, of the bright feathers in their hair, of their houses built deep in the woods. And he told of the long journey home.

"Will you ever go back?" asked Hilde curiously. Gudrun clutched Ralf's hand defensively, shaking her head. Ralf paused a long moment and sighed.

"East, west; home's best," he said at last. "But who knows? It's a wonderful land out there, Hilde. A wonderful land."